ALSO BY JENNY SILER

Easy Money

Iced

Shot

Shot

JENNY SILER

A NOVEL

A JOHN MACRAE BOOK

Henry Holt and Company | New York

Henry Holt and Company, LLC
Publishers since 1866
115 West 18th Street
New York, New York 10011

Henry Holt® is a registered trademark of
Henry Holt and Company, LLC.

Library of Congress Cataloging-in-Publication Data
Siler, Jenny.
    Shot : a novel / Jenny Siler.—1st ed.
        p.   cm.
ISBN: 0-8050-7203-9 (hb)
    1. Widows—Fiction.   2. Television
journalists—Fiction.   3. Murder for hire—Fiction.
I. Title.

PS3569.I42125 S56 2002
813'.54—dc21   2002024950

Henry Holt books are available for special
promotions and premiums. For details contact:
Director, Special Markets.

First Edition 2002

Designed by Paula Russell Szafranski

Printed in the United States of America

1   3   5   7   9   10   8   6   4   2

For my father, John Siler,
my grandmother Pat Siler,
and Platteville

Shot

Carl Greene drew the curtains back, pressed his forehead to the cold plate glass, and looked out across Elliott Bay toward West Seattle and the green smear of Bainbridge Island. The sun had just started its downward arc and the light was crisp and flawless. Late summer burned like a small pyre on the tip of each lazy swell. Sailboats tacked back and forth, white spinnakers snapping in the breeze. Manned by two tiny silhouettes, a sea kayak glided along the waterfront, paddles working in perfect tandem.

Carl wanted out. He wanted to fly home to Lucy. He wanted things as they had once been: the two of them in a simple ranch house in Arvada, the kitchen given over to oil paints and canvases, the whole place rich with the stink of turpentine. He wanted a weekend of skiing in the mountains, the snow fine and dry, his wife racing ahead of him on the last run of the afternoon, bright as a cardinal in her new red jacket. And later, in a cheap motel room in Avon, Lucy fresh out of the shower, her hair wet, her skin flushed.

Carl lifted his head from the window and looked at his watch. It was just after six-thirty. Rush hour had come and mostly gone. There were only stragglers in the streets below: a panhandler working the main door of the cineplex, a group of tourists moving in a slow pack along Fifth Avenue, toward the Old Navy or the Hard Rock Cafe. A bus labored up from the market and on toward Capitol Hill, its electric tethers jerking and jostling.

From Carl's room on one of the upper floors of the Hilton, all this seemed to happen without sound. A couple fought and made up on the corner of Sixth and Pike. An ambulance sped past the Gay Nineties bar and disappeared under the convention center. A breeze kicked up from the bay and whistled through the granite canyons of downtown. But all Carl heard was the hum of the ventilation system and an occasional faint *ding* and sigh from the hallway as the elevator doors opened and closed.

Yes, he thought, crossing to the bedside table. He and Lucy would go away for a few days. To the mountains, maybe, someplace where he could explain everything. He picked up the phone, dialed the garage, and asked for his rental car. A half hour on the ferry, then another hour or so of driving, and he'd be in Elwha Beach. Still early, he told himself; still time enough to do what he needed to do and make the last boat back. By morning he'd be on a plane heading home.

Carl stood near the ferry's open stern and watched the wake unfurl behind it, the foam sculpted into ornate ruffles. He preferred to stay at water level during these short trips, to wander the mostly deserted automobile deck or sit in his car and listen to one of the classical radio stations. Tonight, he made a slow curcuit, from stern to bow and back.

As late as it was, the boat was packed, the cars and trucks crammed together, bumpers kissing. Just a handful of passengers had stayed below. A woman in an elegant suit sat in a green Explorer, poring over papers. A man napped in the front seat of his Acura, head back, mouth open, eyes shut tight. Another woman nursed her baby.

You never knew, Carl thought as she glanced up at him through the window of her little Honda and smiled, what tragedy might have entered these lives, what misfortune was waiting to happen. Dead children, lost spouses, the lure of the bottle. All the innumerable possibilities for wreckage. The baby was tight against her chest, wrapped in a flannel blanket, and all Carl saw of the woman's breast was a crescent of pale and swollen skin, one thick blue vein.

The horn that signaled their impending arrival sounded, deep and resonant, and Carl made his way back to his car, fishing in his pocket for his key. He'd been scared the last few days, frightened by his own knowledge, by what it might mean for him, but he was getting accustomed to the idea of fear, habituated to the tightness in his throat.

The boat had slowed, and people were returning to their cars. This time of day the passengers were mostly commuters, the upper echelons of the middle class, men and women with enough disposable income to afford a piece of land along the water, something big enough for a garden and a few apple trees.

Carl pulled his key out and glanced around. A few yards in front of him a door popped open and a man got out of a tan SUV. He turned in Carl's direction and stretched, adjusting his waistband. He was not far from Carl's age, clean cut, in khaki slacks and a red polo shirt. He smiled briefly, courteously, one commuter to another. Nice day. Good to be going home.

Nodding in agreement, Carl put his hand on the door of the rental car, turned the key, and heard all the locks click open. Vail, he told himself, that's where they'd go. They'd stay in one of those quaint fake Tyrolean hotels in the village and have dinner on a terrace near the creek. He would explain everything, and somehow his accounting would change things for the better. They would go back to the room and he would watch Lucy undress, slowly, carefully.

He opened the door and slid into the driver's seat, settling in. The town of Winslow slipped into view and the ferry found its moorings, the engines laboring, the prow gently nudging the dock. Far ahead, a car started, then another, and the vehicles began to move forward.

Carl rolled across the gangplank, onto the blacktop apron, and past the line of cars waiting to make the crossing in the opposite direction. He headed north with most of the ferry traffic, toward Poulsbo and Port Gamble and the Hood Canal. By the time he passed over onto the Peninsula, late afternoon had given way to evening, and the deciduous forests were thick with shadows. Gnats hovered in black swarms along the road.

He cruised west through Blyn and Sequim and on past Port Angeles, the evening darkening to night around him, the traffic thinning until he was alone except for the occasional flicker of headlights coming toward him. North, through the trees, the Strait of Juan de Fuca ducked in and out of view. A light rain started, misty and gray, and Carl hit his wipers, heard the rhythmic whine and squeal of wet rubber against glass.

Just these few more miles, he told himself, thinking now that he shouldn't have come, thinking he could be on a flight to Denver or even driving home across the plains, dry lightning crackling in the distance, virga sheeting down over the heat-scorched fields, a curtain of rain stopping midway between sky and earth as if sheared off by a pair of giant scissors.

The road curved away into the woods, and through the trees and undergrowth Carl caught a glimpse of flames. A campfire, he thought, but as he rounded the next corner he could see that it was not a fire but a flare. Beyond it, bathed in the pinkish light of the sparks and flames, an SUV and a smaller car were sprawled out across the road, blocking the way. An accident, he thought, though from his viewpoint there didn't seem to be any damage. He braked to a stop and surveyed the scene from the car.

It was raining harder now. The flare sputtered and smoked. There was a figure inside the car and another in the SUV. Carl watched as the person in the SUV popped the door and climbed out.

"You need help?" Carl called, rolling his window down.

The man nodded, running his fingers through his rain-wet hair. There was something decidedly familiar about him, the red shirt, the pants, and as he came closer Carl realized it was the same man he'd seen on the ferry's car deck.

"Sorry about this," the man said genially, putting his hand on Carl's door, bending to lean slightly into the car.

"Can I give you a ride somewhere?" Carl asked.

The man looked back down the road, as if contemplating the darkness and the distance, the hum and patter of the rain. Then in one swift motion he pulled a beetle-black pistol from the back of his pants and brought the barrel just level with Carl's face. "I'd appreciate it," he said.

He yanked the door open; Carl felt his bowels constrict and then loosen. The man was so close that Carl could smell his deodorant. Old Spice? Carl wondered. Mennen? It seemed a strange thing to think about, but better than whatever was going to happen next, better than the rain beading on the barrel of the gun. Carl tipped his eyes and looked down at the man's pants. Dockers, he concluded, and his last thought was to be insulted by the casualness of the man's dress, the informality of death.

Chapter one

Kevin Burns pulled his ticket stub from the back pocket of his shorts. The game was heading into the fifth inning and he was starting to think maybe he was sitting in the wrong seat, or even that he might have come on the wrong day.

"This *is* row eleven, section nineteen?" he asked, turning to a group of elderly ladies seated to his left.

The woman closest to him nodded and smiled, then turned her attention back to the field. "Get the sons-of-bitches!" she yelled, evidently addressing the pitcher. She was wearing a Rockies sun visor and a T-shirt that said FUNKY GRANDMA.

Kevin checked his stub again. Section nineteen, row eleven, seat nine. The plaque on the empty chairback to his right read eight. He was definitely in the right place. Saturday afternoon. One o'clock. The Rockies versus the Padres. That's what his ticket said, and that's what Carl had said on the phone.

The pitcher seemed to have taken the grandmother's words to heart. He struck out the first two batters and got the third on an easy pop fly. Leaning back in his seat, Kevin looked out over the electric green of the field and watched the players change sides. It was a beautiful day, sunny and blue-skied. The Rockies were ahead by three runs, but Kevin was too preoccupied to enjoy the game. He kept turning to look back up the aisle, searching the crowd for Carl Greene.

Todd Helton strode to the plate, and the funky grandma stood up and did a little dance. "We love you, Todd!" she yelled, her hips gyrating in Kevin's face. Helton kicked at the home-plate dirt with his shoe and settled into his stance.

Kevin had just walked through the door of his apartment when Carl called. Kevin had been at the Starbucks down the street on his midmorning coffee break. It was a strategy he'd recently devised, an excuse to brush his teeth, put on his clothes, and get out of the house. After two weeks of watching home improvement shows and Spanish soap operas in the same Kung Pao chicken–stained robe, Kevin had finally decided that his life needed some structure.

It had been three weeks since he'd lost his job at MSNBC, and Kevin was starting to realize just how dim his future in broadcast journalism was. At first, he had tried to look at his new employment situation as a gift, a sabbatical of sorts. He could do some freelancing, he told himself, write the novel he'd always been thinking about. Though he had learned how to slipcover a sofa and install a wall safe, so far all he'd written was a bad first paragraph about a lonely ex-journalist in a cramped Manhattan apartment. But he'd been certain his new routine would change all that.

Kevin hadn't seen or heard from Carl Greene for almost six years, since the last trip he'd made back to Pryor, the winter his grandmother died. He was taken slightly aback by the unexpected voice on the phone, the flat non-accent of the Colorado plains.

"Carl," he said. "How you doing?" Then, knowing he sounded too eager but unable to stop himself, "How's Lucy?"

"She's okay," Carl told him. "We're both okay."

"Good," Kevin said, a twinge of time-worn sourness rising up in the back of his throat.

"We've been keeping track of you back here. Local boy makes good and all. That was a nice piece you did a couple of months ago, the Earl Sykes story."

"Thanks." Kevin rose to the flattery like a trout to a well-cast fly. The specificity of the praise was a particularly nice touch. Most people just told him they *admired his work*. "So," Kevin asked. "Is there something I can do for you?" He couldn't see Carl calling just to say hi. They'd never had the kind of friendship that suited itself to reminiscing.

"I was thinking more along the lines of something I can do for you," Carl said.

"Oh, yeah?" Kevin was skeptical.

Carl hesitated, and Kevin heard him take a deep breath. "I've got a story for you," he said.

"What kind of story?"

"An important one," Carl told him.

"You're going to have to give me more than that."

Carl cleared his throat. "I don't want to talk about it over the phone."

Kevin rolled his eyes. Who did Carl think he was, Deep Throat?

"Listen," Carl went on. "This is the kind of stuff that makes careers, or at least saves them."

Kevin winced, reminded of the unpleasant fact that his firing had made more news than most of his stories ever had. It hadn't really been his fault. He'd been down in Nogales trying to put together a story on the business of smuggling Mexican illegals across the border. Kevin had wanted to get someone to take him and a cameraman across on a night trip from the Mexican side, but even for the right price he couldn't find anyone willing to do it. He'd spent a good week in Nogales asking around without luck. In the end, the best he could come up with was a document forger named Leon who said he'd fake the whole thing for five hundred bucks.

He hadn't thought much of it at the time. After all, the story was there. If it hadn't been for a guy at some other network who'd grown up in southern Arizona, and who recognized Kevin's Mexican border landscape as Patagonia Lake State Park, no one would have been the wiser.

"And exactly why are you doing me this incredible favor?" Kevin asked.

Carl lowered his voice a notch. "Because I know you. Because I need someone I can trust."

There was fear in the other man's voice, just the faintest hint but enough to make Kevin take notice. "We could meet somewhere," he offered.

"Do you like baseball?" Carl asked.

"Sure."

"Let's say Coors Field. Saturday. One o'clock. We're playing the Padres. I have season tickets."

Kevin coughed. "You know I'm in New York, right?"

"A five-hour flight," Carl said flatly. "I can FedEx you a round-trip ticket by tomorrow afternoon. It won't cost you a dime to get here."

Christ, Kevin thought, he was serious. "Listen, Carl. I'm not flying out to Denver without at least a partial hint at what you've got to say."

"I'm not wasting your time," Carl insisted. "Trust me, there's a story here, a big one. An important one."

Kevin thought for a moment. "Saturday," he said finally, thinking he had nothing to lose by going.

"Saturday," Carl repeated. "One o'clock. Coors Field. I'll leave your ticket with will-call." The line went dead, and Kevin heard a rush of static in his ear.

He's just late, Kevin reassured himself now, trying to focus on the field, on Todd Helton's bat poised in midair, waiting for the pitch. But even with four more innings to go, Kevin had a bad feeling that Carl wasn't going to show. The pitcher released the ball and it came screaming in, straight as an arrow. As soon as Kevin heard the crack of Helton's bat he knew the hit was heading out of the park. "Run!" the grandmother screamed. "Run!" But Helton stood for a moment, his hands still on his bat, his knees still turned into the swing, his head moving with the ball, up and gone over the right-field wall.

Chapter two

Lucy Greene had stopped listening to the minister. He was reading from Paul's First Letter to the Corinthians, the passage that borrows from Hosea: "O death, where is thy sting? O grave, where is thy victory?" But Lucy had tuned his voice out and was concentrating on the stained-glass window above the altar. Several yellow jackets had flown up past the top of Christ's head and were hurling themselves against the semicircular representation of the sun, looking for a way out. Lucy could hear their bodies bumping drowsily against the glass.

A loud *Amen* rippled through the congregation, catching her off guard, and Lucy lowered her head, letting her eyes rest on her husband. She had never seen someone laid out like he was. Her father had been cremated, and when Eric died they'd had a private burial, just the two of them and the casket. Though she had not seen Carl after the accident, she knew his face had been badly damaged. Even the man at the mortuary had warned her they might not be able to make him look "natural."

It was Eleanor who'd insisted on one last look at her son. And now Lucy knew she had been right in not wanting to see Carl like this. His eyes were closed, but it didn't look like he was sleeping. When Carl slept his lips were always slightly apart and his hands sometimes moved, as if he were telling a story. The hollow of skin at the base of his neck jumped up and down with his pulse.

Eleanor had chosen the coffin, along with everything else: the stiff calla lilies and the hymns and the suit Carl was wearing. The casket was cherry, buffed and polished so that it gleamed under the church lights. There were sturdy handles on each side, and white satin where Carl was lying. The top was divided in two, like the Dutch door in the kitchen of the house Lucy grew up in, and the bottom was closed. Lucy knew they hadn't fixed the parts of Carl that couldn't be seen. The way she understood it, they wouldn't have been able to even if they had tried.

Though everyone commented on how good Carl looked, the truth was that in the end they *hadn't* been able to achieve the desired "natural" air. The pew where Lucy sat was only a few feet from Carl and she could see the pancake makeup they'd used, the loose grains of face powder and blush. She could see exactly where Carl's head had been broken. There was a hint of a gash across his forehead, a blue line, pale and dark at the same time like veins showing through skin.

They sang one last hymn; then Lucy felt Chick's hand on her arm, felt him pulling her to her feet. A group of men came forward and stood around the coffin: Carl's best friend, his old roommate from CU, two cousins, and an uncle. Someone closed the casket and the five men hoisted it up onto their shoulders.

It was a sunny afternoon, bright and cloudless. Coming out of the dark church behind the casket, Lucy was momentarily blinded and put her free hand up to shield her eyes. It was a familiar gesture, a familiar place, and she was struck by a brief sense of déjà vu. She had been married in this church, had emerged on a similar day. She could remember it clearly, Carl's arm where Chick's was now, her own hand tucked under it.

Lucy rode up to the cemetery with Chick in his old Ford Fairlane. He had just cleaned it, and the inside smelled like Armor-All and the lingering tang of cigarettes. The cemetery was on a small hill east of town, and they had to cross the state highway and the train tracks to get there. Lucy didn't get out of the car right away. She sat in the front seat and smoked one of Chick's cigarettes while the pallbearers carried Carl's casket from the hearse to his grave. Lucy was hot in her funeral suit. It was several years old and out of season, bought the winter her father had died. The backs of her legs were wet with sweat, her nylons slippery against the Fairlane's seat. Chick stood outside the driver's door, waiting for Lucy to climb out. His hands were in his pockets, and she could hear him jingling loose change.

The grave was cool and shady, the bottom and sides lined with several inches of cement. The ground was soft and the heels of Lucy's shoes sank into the turf. The minister said a few words, Eleanor threw some dirt on the casket, and it was all over. Lucy could feel mosquitoes on her scalp, clustered on the skin where she had parted her hair.

Things had happened so quickly that Carl's stone had not arrived yet. There was a temporary marker at the head of the grave, a thin pole and a small flag that read GREENE, CARL. Next to the open plot was another grave, a smaller mound well-covered by several years' growth of turf. The stone that marked it lay flat to the ground, and from where she stood Lucy could not read the inscription, but she knew what it said. If she had been a woman of faith, if she had believed in the resurrection of the body and life everlasting, she might have been comforted by the small plaque, by the proximity of father and son, Carl's body and the baby's lying side by side. But Lucy put little stock in the afterlife. The only thing she knew for certain was that she'd lost a son and now a husband.

She and Chick were the last ones to leave. On the way back to town Lucy made her brother pull off the road by Bud Nordgren's cornfields. She got out of the car and threw up into the irrigation ditch. Chick came over, put one hand softly on her shoulder, and held her hair back with the other.

"I'm sorry," he offered.

Lucy spit, then turned to look up at her brother. "I need a drink," she said.

Chick went to the car and came back with a small flask and a pack of cigarettes.

Lucy took a long sip and drew the back of her hand across her lips. "What am I going to do?" she asked. She slid her damp panty hose off and tossed them into the Nordgrens' field.

"It'll get better, Luce." Chick smiled weakly, glancing toward where the stockings had landed. They were sheer and black, a rumpled suggestion of his sister's legs, like a skin sloughed off.

Kevin stayed through the ninth inning and then walked back to his hotel, a bland convention monolith at the far end of the Sixteenth Street mall. Downtown Denver was no longer the place he remembered from the twice-yearly shopping visits he and his grandmother had made. They'd come at the end of every summer for school clothes and then again at Christmas time. Kevin could remember the slightly chemical odor of new polyester, the stiffness of never-washed dress shirts, the large-bosomed saleswomen at the department store. Sometimes there were hippies on the sidewalks, stringy-haired girls asking for change, bearded men in moccasins. Kevin's mother had gone off with these people; at least that's what his grandmother had told him. "Up and run off with a bunch of hippies," she used to say, matter-of-factly. And each time they'd gone to the city he'd watched them with a mix of longing and terror, hoping and not hoping that he'd see his mother's dimly remembered face among them.

Denver today was like any other thriving city in America. They'd bricked over Sixteenth Street, closing it to traffic. The mall was lined with Tuscan bakeries and espresso bars. There was a Wolfgang Puck's next door to a Banana Republic, next door to a Barnes & Noble, next door to a Gap, next door to a Sharper Image. No hippies and no homeless people, just a bland throng of overweight consumers in comfortable clothing.

Kevin didn't go up to his room right away. He sat in the hotel bar and drank a couple of pints of overpriced local beer and watched the Mets lose to San Francisco. The fact that Carl had missed their meeting sat badly with him. It had been Carl's idea, after all, and Kevin knew the last-minute plane ticket from New York hadn't been cheap. He waved the bartender over. "You got a phone book?"

"White or yellow pages?" the man asked.

"White," Kevin told him.

Ducking behind the bar, the man produced a thick Denver directory. Kevin opened the phone book and thumbed through it to the G's. The last he knew, Carl and Lucy had been living in Arvada, but there was no listing for either of them now.

"Is there a pay phone around?" Kevin asked the bartender.

The man pointed out the door to the hotel's lobby.

Nodding, Kevin pushed off his stool. Odds were good that the Greenes' number was unlisted, but Kevin wasn't going to give up without pursuing a few more options. He dialed Boulder directory assistance and was told there was no number for Carl or Lucy Greene. When he tried Pryor information, however, a computerized voice spit out a string of digits. Kevin jotted the number down and set the phone back in the cradle.

It was hard for Kevin to imagine anyone wanting to go back to Pryor, especially Lucy, who'd kept a stack of *National Geographic*s under her bed and pored over them at night the way Kevin pored over his dog-eared *Playboy*s.

Kevin waited for a moment, steadying himself. Then he picked the phone up and dialed Carl and Lucy Greene's number. He had a sudden aching memory of her from the first summer they'd spent digging beets at Roy Miller's farm. They'd been thirteen or fourteen, and the image he still carried was of Lucy in a pink bathing suit and cutoffs, her angular legs crusted with dirt, her shoulders and back dark as stained oak. When she'd knelt next to him she'd smelled of coconut suntan lotion and sweat.

It had been hard work, the summers he and Lucy and Carl and Chick had worked out at Miller's. Kevin could remember sitting in the back of Roy's truck on the drive home each evening, how good the air felt on his face, the way his back ached, the half-moons of dirt under his fingernails. Roy would drop him off first and he'd stand at the end of his grandmother's driveway and watch them drive away, watch Lucy propped on the truck's wheel well, her hair flying around her face.

Kevin crooked his neck and held the receiver against his shoulder. At the Greenes' house the phone rang and rang, but there was no answer.

Lucy had never seen so many casseroles in one place. There was enough food on her dining room table to keep her through a nuclear winter, each dish covered with plastic wrap and marked neatly with a piece of masking tape and someone's name. More than the quantity, it was the variety that surprised her. Of course the old standards were there, tuna noodle and turkey tetrazzini, the kind she remembered from her childhood, from the time after her mother left and before she became officially old enough to cook. Each day there had been a neighbor on their porch with a Pyrex dish and a plate full of cookies. Now there were newer, stranger dishes: shiitake mushrooms and quinoa, Moroccan lamb and couscous. All those old ladies with satellite TV and too much time on their hands, she thought.

Someone, Lucy figured it must have been Eleanor, had changed the air-conditioning setting. Though Lucy could see an oily film of hot air wavering over the fields out beyond the yard, inside it couldn't have been more than 65 degrees. Lucy crossed through the living room and turned the thermostat up.

She was surprised by the number of people who had come, by how many parts of Carl's life they represented, how many parts of her own life. There were teachers Lucy remembered from as far back as first grade. Carl's basketball coach. Her father's friends. Friends of the Greenes'. The girl she'd sat next to in her high-school Spanish class. Carl's old housemates from Boulder. Former classmates. And more than a few people Lucy hadn't known, people she assumed knew Carl from work.

Lucy's family had always been an oddity in Pryor, especially after their mother left. Their father, without a wife, had become somehow dangerous. But they had been part of the town, and people had looked out for them nonetheless. There had always been food, work, and hand-me-downs for Lucy and Chick.

Carl's family, though, was different, separate. Lucy could remember this from her childhood, the tidy perfection of their house. The only time she ever saw Dr. Greene in the yard was when he cut the junipers, and then he wore stiff cotton coveralls and gardening gloves. He didn't sit on the front porch drinking Coors like the other fathers did. No one would have left their children's outgrown winter coats on the Greenes' doorstep, as they did for Lucy and Chick. And somehow, in the years since she'd married Carl, Lucy had become separate as well.

Lucy propped herself in the door to the dining room and lit a cigarette. As far as she knew, no one had ever smoked in their house. They had been the only owners, and it was not something Carl would have allowed. She inhaled and felt the sweet succor of the act, the warm smoke in her lungs. She could hear her mother-in-law in the kitchen, a cupboard door opening and closing, the sound of running water and then the faucet being shut off.

Eleanor came into the dining room and started to pick one of the casseroles up.

"I can put those away," Lucy offered. "Will you take some?"

Eleanor shook her head and wiped her hands with a dish towel. Lucy didn't know what to say to her, had never known what to say.

"It'll be okay," she told her mother-in-law, not believing it herself.

"I've got it pretty much cleaned up in there," Eleanor said. She seemed shrunken, pale and tired. Her breath smelled of stale coffee. "I guess I'll be going," she murmured.

The phone rang in the kitchen and Lucy ignored it. Unable to hear Carl's voice each time the phone rang, she'd turned the answering machine off a few days earlier. Eleanor looked around nervously, as if they were about to be caught doing something bad. "Should I answer it?" she asked.

Lucy shook her head, and they both stood there in silence until the ringing stopped.

"I guess I'll be going," Eleanor repeated finally.

Following her mother-in-law into the foyer, Lucy opened the front door. The air was sticky, hot as a sauna, and she felt her skin go moist.

"Goodbye," Eleanor said awkwardly. She hooked her purse over her arm and headed down the steps and out the driveway to her car.

The door closed with a click, and for the first time Lucy was left with the silence of the house, the soft hum of cool air forced through the vents. The sound of the rest of her life, she thought—and was afraid.

Lucy woke in the early morning, her arms and legs knotted around a sweat-soaked sheet. The windows were open to let the night air in, and the room smelled of the dairy that lay to the east, of fertilizer and the brackish odor of water left to sit in the fields. Lucy reached over and ran her hand across Carl's side of the bed. She had heard something downstairs and wanted Carl to go check the house. At the very least she wanted him to tell her there was nothing to worry about. But she was alone in the bed.

Maybe he was awake, Lucy thought, her fingers finding the vacant space beside her. Maybe it was Carl she heard, but somehow she knew with absolute certainty that it could not be him in the dark house below her. Groggy, still half asleep, she struggled to think. Had he gone away? To a conference? To the Seattle office? Was he working late? The clock on his side of the bed read 4:13. Lucy blinked hard, willing her brain awake. Her tongue was heavy in her mouth, her eyes dry. Something moved in the house below, a sole squealing on hardwood, the metal of hinges grating against each other.

"Carl?" she murmured. Swinging her legs over the side of the bed, she found the switch on her bedside lamp.

She could see the room now, the curtains she had made when they moved in, white with tiny flowers. Carl's plaid robe hung from a hook on the back of the door. There was a half-finished bottle of gin on the nightstand, a freshly filled prescription for Seconal. For an instant they made no sense to her, as if someone had sneaked in while she was sleeping and put the two strange bottles there. Then the last few days came racing back to her, the weight of her grief. There had been an accident. She remembered now. There had been an accident and Carl was dead. Lucy felt her skin go cold, felt goose bumps rise along her arms. A tight lump rose up in her chest.

Somewhere in the distance, past the neighbors' onion field, a dog barked and another answered. Lucy held her breath, strained her ears. Below her a drawer opened, then slid closed. My husband is dead, she told herself, as if taking inventory of what she knew to be true, and there is someone in my house. Lucy switched the light off again and let her eyes readjust to the darkness. Normally she would have been afraid. She dreaded the nights Carl worked late, the darkening winter afternoons. She hated being alone in the big house with its honeycomb of rooms, its walk-in closets and heavy drapes. So many places for someone to hide. But tonight she felt strangely fearless, emboldened by her loss.

Lucy opened the top drawer of the little table on her side of the bed. Pushing aside Kleenex and hand cream, she felt for the 9-millimeter Carl had bought her when they were first married. It was a compact little gun, a Glock 26. Lucy was no stranger to firearms. She'd grown up hunting with her brother and father. When Carl brought the Glock home he'd insisted on giving her lessons, and she'd easily outshot him that first day at the range.

Lucy wrapped her fingers around the Glock and crept to the bedroom door. She was naked, and the breeze coming off the plains felt good on her skin. She tried to imagine what the intruder might want: money, valuables, her body. She thought briefly of what this person might do to her, the various ways in which she could be injured or violated or worse. And then she thought of Carl, of his body in the cool cement hollow of his grave, and she was no longer afraid.

A night-light illuminated the upstairs hallway and the closed doors of the two guest bedrooms, Lucy's office, and the spare bathroom. A curved banister led down to the front entryway. Bringing the Glock to her chest, Lucy peered down into the foyer. She took the first carpeted step, and the second. A chair scraped the floor in Carl's office.

"Who's there?" she called out, surprising herself. A single bead of sweat dropped between her shoulder blades. Silence answered her.

"Who is it?" she called again, her bare feet finding the cool tiles of the entryway. Resting her finger on the Glock's trigger, she moved forward.

Two tall windows flanked the front door, catching whatever illumination the prairie offered: the phosphorescent glow of a dairy, the pale light of a sickle moon, the bluish streetlamps of the subdivision. The door to Carl's office was open and Lucy could make out the first few feet of the room, but beyond there was nothing but a black maw. Lucy was suddenly self-conscious, acutely aware of her nakedness. Whoever was in the office had a good view of her, was watching her.

"I'm armed," she said into the darkness, keeping her elbows rigid, the Glock trained on the door. She was surprised by the authority her own voice carried.

There was a rustling from inside the room and a figure burst forth. Lucy fired blindly, bracing herself against the recoil. In the flash from the Glock's barrel she could see a dark torso and a face covered by a black ski mask. The person brushed past her, knocking her down, and barreled out the front door.

Lucy put her hand to her lip and felt blood. She had gone down hard, dropping the Glock in the fall. Groping for the gun, she stood up and headed for the open front door. She was angry and it felt good, felt better than the dull fog of grief that had engulfed her. She stepped out onto the front porch, her heart racing. There was no sign of the intruder. Across the road the fields were head-high with corn. A breeze kicked up and the green husks rustled against each other.

Resting her back against the door frame, Lucy let the gun dangle at her side. She felt untethered, freed of something, though she didn't yet know what.

Chapter three

Lucy didn't call anyone right away. The Pryor Police Department was a small operation, and she couldn't see the point in pulling its one geriatric officer out of bed at four in the morning. The way she saw it, the Glock had done its job. She didn't think the person would be back, and honestly she didn't much care one way or the other. She told herself it had been some kid up from Denver or a meth head from Greeley, looking for a nice stereo and maybe some jewelry to pawn.

Lucy went up to the bedroom, threw Carl's robe on, and stuck the gun in one of the pockets. She grabbed the Tanqueray and the Seconal and made her way down the stairs and toward the back of the house. The pool lights were on, reflecting aqueous shadows onto the ceiling of the kitchen. The pool itself was calm and luminous, a perfect aquamarine wound carved out of the darkness. Grabbing a glass from one of the kitchen cabinets, Lucy opened the door to the patio and stepped outside.

East, far past town, past the river and the highway and the train tracks, the blue of dawn had started to bleed into the black sky. There was a strong smell of diesel in the air, of industry warming up for the day to come. Flat and open as the land was, Lucy could hear things miles away: the purr of an engine out near Frederick, the predawn hustle of activity at the truck stop over by the interstate, a train heading north toward Cheyenne. She went out past the pool to her studio, unlocked the door, and slipped inside.

Kevin's flight back to New York was scheduled for just after noon on Sunday, but he'd already told himself he wasn't leaving without at least talking to Carl. If there was a story, the kind of story Carl had hinted at, Kevin couldn't afford not to find out what had happened. He had enough money in the bank to carry him for a while, but sooner or later it would run out. The freelance work hadn't exactly been pouring in, and, realistically, the novel didn't look like it could be counted on to pay the rent. He needed something that would make people forget about Nogales.

Besides, something Carl had said just wouldn't let him go. The word *important* richocheted around Kevin's mind all that night. It had been a long time since he'd looked at a story that way, and there was a luster to the promise of something weighty and worthwhile, to something besides the latest congressional mistress, the most recent movie-star divorce. That's what his TV work had come down to recently: whatever it took to keep people's fingers off their remote controls.

Kevin couldn't remember the last time he'd actually cared about a story. Even the Nogales piece had been a ratings grab, a nighttime adventure that had little to do with the real issues of illegal immigration: poverty, prejudice, and the price third world countries paid for globalization. Of course, the real issues never brought in viewers.

When he woke up Sunday morning, Carl was the first thing to enter Kevin's mind. He rolled out of bed, dressed, shaved, tried the Greenes' number one more time, and then called the garage for his rental car.

The day was perfect, the sky electric blue, dotted with a few high, downy clouds. Kevin took the interstate north toward Pryor through the ubiquitous sprawl of Denver. It was already hot, and he cranked the air conditioner up full blast. To the west the flinty faces of the Rocky Mountains, still snow-packed in August, rose abruptly from the plains. After living in Manhattan, this kind of opened-up driving felt good to Kevin. He eased his foot down on the gas, pushing the speedometer up past eighty.

His grandmother never used the interstate. Even when he was a boy it had been too fast for her. They would crawl home from the city on Highway 85, past the canneries and grain elevators of Brighton and Fort Lupton. In the summer they'd stop at a farm in Ione for sweet corn and beans. Kevin liked to think of himself as a realist, and his memories of Pryor were accordingly unsentimental. He had not forgotten the poverty, the dimming of expectations. He'd gone to school with the girl whose parents owned the Ione farm, and he could remember her coming to class some mornings with bright red welts on the backs of her legs. She went an entire winter without gloves. But what Kevin remembered most was his own aching need to get out.

Traffic was sparse, and Kevin made the Pryor exit in just under forty-five minutes. This was my home, he reminded himself as he headed east on the old two lane highway into town. Everything was familiar: the smell of Jorgenson's dairy, the old farmhouses posted along the road, a stand of cottonwoods marking the Platte River in the distance. The car dipped into a creek bottom and rose again. To the left side of the road, where Roy Miller's beet fields had been, were a handful of new buildings, big bland suburban homes with swimming pools and cedar decks. Just beyond Miller's was the turnoff to his grandmother's old place. The house was still fresh in his mind, the grease-stained wallpaper in the kitchen, the outhouse his grandfather had converted into a storage shed, the bedroom he'd slept in for eighteen years.

Kevin went straight into town, turning left onto Main Street, away from a brand-new neighborhood of cul-de-sac homes. When he got to Carl's parents' home he pulled the rental car to the curb and cut the engine.

The Greenes' was exactly as Kevin remembered, long and flat, a brick ranch house with a neat lawn and green tufts of junipers in the flower beds. When Kevin was growing up, Carl's father had been the only doctor in town. His office had been in the house, a converted sunroom with its own entrance from the backyard. There had been no houses then between the Greenes' and the highway, just empty lots and an onion field. From the waiting room you could see the grain elevator and the trains going by and Cemetery Hill, where they used to sled in the winter. Kevin had a vague memory of bony hands under his shirt, the cold circle of a stethoscope pressing into his back, the woody taste of a tongue depressor.

He rolled down the window and sat for a moment in the car, collecting himself. He wished he still smoked, wished he could light a cigarette and waste the time it took to finish it. The grass had just recently been cut and edged. The pattern the lawn mower had made was still visible, narrow swaths crossing the yard on the diagonal, then turning and crossing back again. The driveway and sidewalks were neat and clean, the curtains drawn. It looked as if no one was home—as if, perhaps, no one had ever been at home.

Kevin stepped into the street and made his way toward the shaded porch. Grasshoppers leapt up around him, barraging his pant legs. He knocked on the front door and waited. After a few seconds the door opened and a woman appeared, her hair tucked up inside a net cap, her face quizzical.

"Mrs. Greene?" Kevin said, realizing he had never actually met Carl's mother before. Carl's friends had never been allowed inside the Greenes' home, and all his memories of her from childhood were of a dim figure behind the window.

The woman blinked. Her feet were bare, the skin pale, lined with thick veins. "Yes?"

"I'm sorry to bother you," Kevin continued. "I used to come here when I was a boy—to see Dr. Greene." He gestured toward the back of the house. "My name's Kevin Burns." He waited, hoping for some recognition.

"The doctor passed away quite some time ago," the woman said, her face blank.

"I'm so sorry," Kevin told her. She had her hand on the door as if she was about to close it. "I'm actually an old friend of Carl's. I know it sounds strange, but we were supposed to meet yesterday and he never showed up. I tried calling, but no one answers. I was hoping you might be able to tell me where he lives." He opened his mouth wide and smiled, a young man to be trusted, a friend of Carl's from high school. "I've got the phone number, just not the address."

Mrs. Greene looked past Kevin's shoulder, as if searching for something in the yard or the street. "You don't know?" she asked.

"Excuse me?"

"I'm sorry." She stopped herself and looked up at Kevin's face for the first time. "I'm sorry," she repeated. "Carl's dead."

"O-oh," Kevin stammered, his eyes involuntarily fixed on the old woman. Her skin was loose and sallow. Two dark crescents rimmed her eyes.

"There was an accident," she said wearily, and he knew she'd repeated this same line many times already.

Kevin wrenched his eyes away from her and looked down at the green outdoor carpet that covered the stairs. He could smell junipers, the stony chalky odor of the bricks, and the peppery scent of geraniums. "I'm sorry for your loss."

The woman didn't say anything.

"And Lucy?" Kevin asked.

"She's fine." There seemed to be the faintest edge of bitterness in her voice, anger at the way things had turned out.

"I should see her," Kevin said.

Mrs. Greene nodded. "The house is out Magpie Road, next to Miller's. You can't miss it. It's the biggest one out there."

. . .

The old woman had been right. Even in a cluster of homes remarkable for the width and breadth of their garages, Carl and Lucy Greene's house stood out. A rambling two-story suburban behemoth, it couldn't have been more than five years old. The trees surrounding it were still spindly and awkward, providing only wisps of meager shade. Kevin pulled into the long driveway and parked behind a white Mercedes. Cutting the ignition, he ran his finger along the sweat-soaked collar of his shirt, stepped onto the driveway, and headed up the walk.

The porch was studded with flowers. Gaudy candy-colored impatiens swung in moss baskets from the eaves. Two huge terra-cotta planters were stuffed with waxy begonias. Something, perhaps the wind, had knocked over a pot of alyssum, scattering soil and pottery shards. Kevin stepped over the mess and pressed the doorbell. A chime rang inside and faded to silence. Kevin waited for an answer, then knocked.

The door gave way beneath his knuckles, swinging slowly open on its hinges. Kevin stuck his head inside and called out.

"Lucy?" His voice skipped and echoed across the foyer. "Lucy?" he called again. When no one answered, he stepped through the doorway.

It was cool in the house, still and quiet. The floor of the foyer was creamy marble, its veins conservative shades of brown. A swooping stairway led up to a second floor. An archway to Kevin's right led into a blandly tasteful living room. Another door revealed a hallway and, beyond, part of the kitchen. The walls and carpets and furnishings were unthreatening desert shades: sagebrush, coyote, sunset, dune. Through a third door was what looked like an office. Papers were strewn across a dark cherry desk.

"Lucy?" Kevin wandered through the living room and looped through the dining room, back toward the kitchen. Except for a dozen or so withering flower arrangements, and some prints of shoes on the thick nap of the ivory carpet, the house seemed uninhabited in its neatness.

Several oil paintings, all evidently creations of the same artist, graced the walls. The canvases were large and vividly colored, suggestive of doorways or portals, thresholds pared down to their essentials. Lucy's, Kevin thought, though her style had changed substantially since the last time he'd seen her work, the senior art show at the high school.

The kitchen was luxurious, with a high ceiling and a terra-cotta floor. Tall windows looked out over the pool and yard and the fields beyond. Kevin took in the lavish accessories: the stainless-steel Viking range, the granite countertops, the Italian tiles. He had lived in New York long enough to know the value of these things.

On the front of the Sub-Zero refrigerator was a photograph of Lucy and Carl. They were standing at the base of a ski slope, a long snowy run curving back behind them. The couple was in full gear, ski boots, pants, and puffy down parkas, their skis jammed upright into the snow beside them. Carl was wearing his goggles, and his eyes were invisible behind the mirrored plastic. Lucy had pushed her goggles up on her head, revealing a white halo around her eyes where the skin hadn't tanned. Age and wealth had been kind to her. She had hardened since Kevin had last seen her, moving away from pretty toward beautiful. She was smiling, a smile Kevin fully remembered. It was hard for him to imagine her happy here, or satisfied, and yet she seemed to be. At least she *had* seemed to be.

The glass door slid open. Kevin jerked his head toward the sound, and his eyes lit on Lucy. She'd sneaked up on him, and he felt the surprise in his chest. She stepped up from the patio, warm air billowing around her.

"What the fuck do you want?" she asked. Her hair was matted on one side, tangled and knotted. There was a small cut on her upper lip, a crust of dried blood. She was barefoot, in a white terry robe, and she pulled her hand from one of her pockets, revealing the dark shape of a handgun.

Kevin took a careful step to the right, out from behind the butcher-block island that stood between them. He'd seen her use a gun before, and even unsteady as she was he had no doubt about her proficency with the pistol. Autumns in high school when they'd hunted ducks with Chick out at Burle Reservoir, Lucy always bagged her limit early in the day. Nine times out of ten, Chick or Kevin or both of them would let her take some of their quota as well.

"It's Kevin," he said now, lifting his hands slowly to show he had nothing to hide. "Kevin Burns."

Lucy looked unsurprised. A shadow of recognition played over her face, and she slipped the gun back into the pocket of her robe. "Got any cigarettes?" she asked. Slightly unsteady on her feet, she wavered but caught herself on the door frame.

Kevin shook his head. "I quit," he told her.

"Me too," Lucy said. Then she brought her hands to her face, and Kevin could hear the soft sound of her sobbing.

Kevin took a sip of his coffee and set the mug down on the glass-topped table. Not knowing what else to do, he'd put a pot of coffee on and gone into town for cigarettes. When he came back he'd found Lucy out by the pool. She'd cleaned up some while he was gone. She was still in her robe, but her hair was pulled off her face. Neither one of them had mentioned Carl yet.

"You look good," Kevin said, and he meant it. Worn as Lucy was by grief and fatigue, looking at her still got him like a one-two punch to the gut. She shifted in her chair, and her robe opened around her calf. Her skin was perfectly tanned, smooth and lustrous.

Lucy rolled her glass between her palms, ignoring the coffee Kevin had put before her. He could smell the gin in the tumbler, the odor flowery, like cheap aftershave, though he knew the gin would not be cheap. The glass was cut crystal, heavy and substantial. "Oh, yeah?" she said. "I feel like shit."

Beyond the deep green of the back lawn, Kevin could see what was left of Miller's farm. A troop of migrants had fanned out in the furrows and were steadily working their way down rows of spindly onion tops. Where they had finished picking, the field was dotted with burlap sacks, lumpy and half human, like the bagged heads of abductees, or prisoners awaiting execution.

The last summer they'd worked for Miller, Lucy had been sick most of July. That was the summer before he left for Columbia, and Kevin remembered her huddled in the back of the truck, her face gray and waxen. He remembered walking back through a row she'd worked and seeing the pale stains of her bile in the dirt. He'd left for New York in September, and when he came back for Christmas she was already seeing Carl.

"I'm sorry," Kevin said now, and he meant that, too. He reached across the table and put his hand on Lucy's arm. Where her robe fell from her thigh, the shape and weight of the gun was visible. A form of desperation, Kevin thought, wondering what she'd been planning to do with the pistol, whether she'd meant to use it on herself or someone else.

She moved her arm from under his fingers, drained her glass, and set it down with a clunk.

"I stopped at Carl's mother's house before I came out here," Kevin said carefully, unsure of where to begin. "She told me there was an accident."

Lucy nodded. "They're saying he must have fallen asleep at the wheel." She picked up the empty glass and tilted it to her lips, getting the last few drops. "He was in Seattle, for work."

"You know, he called me in New York. I was supposed to meet him yesterday, in Denver."

Giving up on the empty tumbler, Lucy picked up her coffee, took a sip, and winced. Somewhere inside the house the telephone rang. Ignoring it, Lucy took another drag on her cigarette, then flicked the butt into the plush grass at the edge of the patio. They looked at each other, both waiting for the ringing to stop.

"He wanted to talk about something," Kevin said finally. "He said he had a story for me. Any idea what he was talking about?"

Lucy shrugged.

"He seemed upset," Kevin added.

"Yeah, well, Carl gets upset sometimes." She took a good look at Kevin. He was sweating and the tips of his hair were wet and shiny, as if he'd used some kind of oily pomade. She couldn't understand why he'd come, why he wanted to talk about Carl, and she was too tired to ask. She was thinking about her bottle of Seconal, the dark cocoon of sleep.

Kevin fingered the pack of cigarettes, picking at the seam in the cellophane wrapper. Lucy could tell he wanted one, that not smoking was taking a good deal of his concentration. "I'm sorry," he said again, and Lucy got the feeling he didn't just mean about Carl.

"Me too," she told him.

"You still painting?" he asked, after a moment's hesitation. Raw as Lucy was with emotion and booze, Kevin couldn't see much point in continuing with questions about Carl and the accident.

Lucy took a swig of coffee and thought about what to say. She gestured toward her studio on the other side of the pool. "It keeps me busy," she said with a shrug. She was embarrassed by the question and by what her answer implied: that she was someone's wife with too much time on her hands, that she could do nothing else. She had a sudden desire to be sober, a longing for clarity of mind.

Kevin smiled. "That your stuff inside?"

Lucy nodded, offering nothing else. She took another cigarette from the pack and lit it.

They sat in silence for a moment while Kevin grappled for something more to say, some way to keep her talking, to keep himself there with her. "How's Chick?" he asked finally.

"Did he have the Fort Ward job when you were here last time?" Kevin shook his head.

"Well, I guess you know they shut the plant down. Chick's been caretaker there for a while now." She took a drag off the cigarette and held the smoke in her lungs before exhaling. "He's sick a lot, you see."

"Sick, how?"

"Ever since he got back from the Gulf he hasn't felt right, but it's gotten worse lately. Most of the guys he was over there with aren't doing too well." She could feel herself crossing the line out of inebriation and into fatigue. "Look," she said. "I'm tired."

Kevin nodded. "I could stay, you know, while you get some sleep."

Lucy shook her head.

"It's no problem," Kevin persisted. "I'll keep out of your way."

"No," she told him, "I think you'd better go." She looked up and mustered a weak smile. "I'll be fine, really."

Kevin stood, still reluctant to leave her, and drew his wallet from his pants. "The work number's no good anymore," he said, finding a business card, "but you can reach me on my cell phone. Really, Luce, if you need anything, anything at all."

"You heading back to New York?" Lucy took the card and looked at it, then slipped it into the pocket of her robe.

"Not right away. I think I might stick around for a few days."

Lucy didn't get up. She watched Kevin walk across the patio and disappear around the side of the house. Everything was quiet for a moment; then she heard his car door slam shut and his engine turn over. It was lunchtime, and from out in Miller's field she could hear the faintest sounds of laughter and conversation, a woman's voice and then a man's, the tuneful rhythm of Spanish.

Lucy sat there for a while, watching the breeze ruffle the surface of the pool, letting her mind begin to clear. When she had finished her coffee she got up, walked around to the front of the house, up the steps, and through the front door. She stood in the foyer for a moment and surveyed her surroundings.

To her right was the living room. Through the large arched doorway she could see the TV and stereo, a crystal vase she and Carl had been given for their wedding, a pair of silver candlesticks. Straight ahead, down a wide hall, was the kitchen. Just to the left of the hallway, the staircase swept upward toward the second floor, and on the left side of the foyer, tucked away next to the staircase, was the smaller door to Carl's office.

It seemed a strange choice for an intruder to have made, especially in the dark, when the office door would have been almost invisible, when any of the other options would have most likely seemed more fruitful. Even with the lights off, the streetlamps would have shone through the front windows to illuminate the living room and undoubtedly some of its contents.

Lucy walked to the open office door and peered inside. Papers and files poked out from the half-opened drawers of the filing cabinet. The desk drawers had been opened as well, then closed sloppily, as if whoever it was had been looking for something specific. On the desktop, untouched, were a gold letter opener Carl had inherited from his father and two Waterman pens. Not the crown jewels, but they could be pawned easily and for a fairly good price. And yet they'd been left behind.

Lucy stepped back into the foyer, sat down on the stairway, and looked out the open front door toward the jewel-green lawn and the silk-tasseled horizon beyond. Far in the distance, a white vapor trail headed west across the cloudless sky.

Lucy had been out for her morning run when the pair of sheriff's officers came to tell her Carl was dead. She saw their brown-and-black car in the drive as soon as she cleared the cornfields and knew something was wrong. They must have seen her in their rearview mirror, for they stepped out of the cruiser together and caught her halfway across the front lawn.

"Mrs. Greene?" one of them asked.

Lucy stopped walking. She had propped her hands on her hips and looked around her, at the house, the yard, the begonias on the front porch, the sunflowers that grew along the edges of the cornfields, the fabric of the men's uniforms. Something was very wrong. She felt a sudden need to take everything in before her perspective was changed forever.

"It's Carl," she said.

"We're so sorry, Mrs. Greene," the younger of the two officers told her, solemnly.

I should get used to hearing that, Lucy thought. "What happened?"

The men glanced at each other, and then, as if by silent agreement, the second man cleared his throat and spoke. "There was an accident, outside of Seattle, near a little town called Elwha Beach. They're pretty sure your husband nodded off, ma'am. It was a bad road he was driving, pretty hairy. They're saying he just went right over the edge, no skid marks even where he might have tried to stop."

The younger man took a step toward Lucy and put his hand on her shoulder. The skin on his face and neck was dotted with tiny red sores, a combination of acne and razor burn. "It was late," he said, "and raining. Easy to lose control."

It was a ridiculous thing to say. Lucy had thought so then, and she still thought so. No one who knew Carl would have said such a thing, would have ever accused him of lack of control.

Once, coming back from skiing, she and Carl had driven through a hundred miles of whiteout blizzard, the air so thick with snow she had thought they would suffocate. While she prayed silently to herself, Carl tranquilly sang Bob Marley hits.

Another time, driving home from Denver at night, a doe had darted out in front of them on the little two-lane highway, just a few miles from the turnoff to the house. Lucy hadn't even seen the animal coming, but Carl calmly turned the wheel and pumped the brakes. "Missed her," he'd said, satisfied, not looking back, as they sped on toward home.

Even when Eric had died, when she had lost it in the hospital, Carl had managed to keep himself together.

Lucy tried to imagine Carl that last day in the car, the green of Washington whipping by his window, trees tousled by wind, the road shiny with rain. She saw a place somewhere near the water, the name of the town, Elwha Beach, carved into her mind as deeply as initials in living wood. She tried to imagine Carl as they said he must have been, asleep or inattentive, but she could not.

She leaned back, setting her elbows on the carpeted step above her, and turned her face toward the high ceiling. It felt as if her life was starting to unravel, as if the one knot that held everything together had come undone. *He seemed upset*, Kevin had said. It just didn't make sense. In fact, Lucy couldn't understand why Carl would have called Kevin in the first place. Something was very wrong. Even through the fading scrim of the gin, the cottony fog of the Seconal, Lucy was certain of it.

Chapter four

Darcy Williams grudgingly paid her six-dollar adult admission and walked through the turnstile into Rawhide Bob's Frontier Town. It was almost noon, and the actors who played the townspeople were starting to gather along Main Street for the daily gunfight. A woman in a buckskin dress and Nikes hustled past, checking the time on her digital watch. She was, Darcy thought, wearing a little too much makeup for a nineteenth-century Indian princess.

Darcy hated Rawhide Bob's and dreaded this meeting with the warden all the more because of where it took place. There was too much forced good humor, too many sweaty tourists scrambling along the dirt-packed streets, too many lemonades and lollipops. Not to mention the bad memories the place brought back. Though she figured it could have been worse. When she'd been at the facility she'd heard other women say he'd taken them to the prison museum. Now *that* was definitely in poor taste.

A voice like a low growl boomed from the far end of the street, and the actors settled into their positions along the wood plank sidewalk. A gray-haired woman with a tight bun stood outside the Mercantile, fanning herself distractedly, her mouth working a piece of tough chewing gum. In front of the saloon, a group of red-feathered whores had gathered to watch the shootout. One of them slid a pack of Camels from her corset and offered them around.

"Sheriff Dooley!" a voice bellowed. "Make your peace with God or the Devil!"

Darcy mouthed these words along with the outlaw. The warden especially liked to come at noontime, and Darcy had heard the pre-fight spiel dozens of times. She ducked through the swinging doors of the saloon and glanced around, letting her eyes adjust to the sudden lack of daylight.

In the semidarkness, his girth spilling over the wooden arms of his chair, the warden resembled a slightly slimmed-down version of Jabba the Hutt. He had no neck to speak of, just an unnaturally small head that widened out toward flabby shoulders. He smiled at Darcy, and she felt her stomach turn. Her last year at Canyon Women's Correctional Facility, she and the warden had spent more than a few Sundays together. Their dates always began at Frontier Town; then they'd drive over to Pueblo and have dinner at the Red Lobster. On the way home, the warden would pull off the highway and have Darcy blow him in the back of his big cream-colored Lincoln.

Darcy had been a lot of things criminal, but she'd never been a whore. If she'd been the only one concerned, she would have done her time in solitary rather than spend five minutes between the warden's sausagelike legs, but she wasn't the only one concerned. Her little sister, Angie, was doing a long stint at Canyon on some heavy-duty drug charges, and Darcy and the warden had reached a mutually beneficial agreement.

When she'd gotten out six months earlier, Darcy figured her part of the deal was over, but evidently the warden hadn't agreed. When he called her at home, her first response was *no* to whatever he was asking. Then he brought up Angie, how they were thinking of transferring her, how things could get uncomfortable for a scrawny white junkie where she'd be going.

Darcy had stood there blankly, in the nearly empty one-room apartment she'd managed to rent on the meager pay she got cleaning bathrooms at a truck stop south of Castle Rock. She wanted to get straight more than anything. She wanted not to go back to Canyon or anywhere like it, and she hadn't liked the sound of what the warden was asking. But she suddenly had a clear vision of her sister, the way she'd felt beside her when they were little and had shared a bed. There she was, in a Strawberry Shortcake nightgown, her mouth open against her pillow, one flap of fine hair rising and falling with her breath.

The warden motioned to the chair opposite his and Darcy sat down. From the street outside the saloon came the sounds of gun-shots. Several people screamed. A few ducked inside and stood cowering behind the swinging doors. At least there wouldn't be any of what the warden called "intimacy" this time. Strictly business, he'd said. She'd told herself she'd walk if it wasn't.

"What happened?" he asked, sounding like a disappointed father.

"What happened is the lady of the house woke up and I almost got shot."

The warden took a sip from a tall glass of lemonade. Rawhide Bob's being a family place, the saloon didn't serve liquor. "Unfortunate," he observed. "When are you planning on going back?"

"How's my sister?" Darcy asked.

"She's good, real good." The warden winked, folding his tiny hands across his chest. "She's even got some admirers. I've noticed Odetta's taken an interest in her. There've been some rumors of an adoption."

Darcy winced. Odetta was not someone you wanted to be noticed by. A lifer at Canyon, her version of motherhood was about as far from bedtime stories and milk and cookies as you could get. She'd taken a fleeting interest in Darcy when she'd first arrived at Canyon, and Darcy had spent a good two months wary of every doorway and dark corner.

"I'll go back in the next couple of days," Darcy said.

"Good." The warden beamed. "Can I get you something? Lemonade? Chocolate milk?"

Darcy shook her head. "It's the same thing still, right? TB tests at Pioneer? I'm just making sure, 'cause there's a lot of stuff in that place to wade through and I'm not going back."

The warden nodded silently and uncrossed his diminutive hands. They were pale and smooth and ladylike, the nails shaped into perfect half-moons, buffed to a dull sheen. "I have something for you." He bent over slightly and produced a paper bag, white with red stripes. "Taffy," he said, "from the Mercantile."

"No, thanks." Darcy started to get up.

"Take it," the warden insisted, leaning forward, grabbing her elbow with his free hand. His grip was firm. Darcy remembered how startled she'd been by its power the first time she'd felt it.

Darcy took the bag.

The warden pulled her close to him. "She wakes up again," he whispered into Darcy's ear, "and you take care of her."

Darcy didn't open the bag right away. Most of her wanted to keep believing it was taffy, even though all of her knew it wasn't. She had almost an hour to kill before visiting time at Canyon, so she drove through town and out to the ravine. She got a couple of hot dogs and a Coke at the café in the visitor center and ate them in her Dart.

Even before Darcy's temporary residence in Ophir, she'd thought of it as a strange little town. Ophir had two things going for it, the ravine and the prisons. Despite these draws, the town barely managed to keep its head above water.

Ophir Ravine was pretty to look at, its granite walls deep and sheer enough to inspire vertigo. An aerial tram stretched from rim to rim, the cars bobbing like Christmas lights in a breeze. Rawhide Bob ran a scenic railway out to a vantage point where people could look down at the river roiling through the narrow gorge below. There was a gift shop and nature walks and a suspension bridge. But compared to something like the Grand Canyon or Niagara Falls, the ravine was a grade-B natural feature.

The prisons, on the other hand, were world class, impressive because of their ubiquity, if nothing else. The town of Ophir and its surroundings were home to some dozen different correctional enterprises. The East Ophir Complex alone housed seven different facilities, including the State Penitentiary, Darcy's old residence, and Pioneer, a small facility that had been built in the early eighties as a temporary home for maximum security prisoners while the new State Pen was under construction.

Darcy finished her second hot dog and leaned back in her seat. A tour bus had pulled up in front of the visitor center and a stream of senior citizens was filing out. They stood in the parking lot, blinking and bewildered, adjusting their hats and tennis visors. Darcy took a swig of her Coke and reached across the front seat of the Dart, pulling the bag the warden had given her into her lap.

She had to dig through a layer of saltwater taffy to get to the warden's gift. Beneath the semitranslucent wrappers, each candy was decorated with a different Western icon: an Indian head, a buffalo, a cowboy hat. She felt among the little bundles, her fingers brushing something solid, her hand finally emerging with the black checkered stock of a palm-sized pistol. Darcy looked up instinctively, letting her eyes range across the parking lot. She took in the group of oldies, an obese family of four, some Ophir Ravine employees, all annoyingly bland and innocuous enough.

Cradling the gun in her lap, Darcy squinted to read the words etched into the stainless steel finish: COLT PONY, they said. She felt the base of the stock with her thumb, then popped the magazine out and counted the six bullets in the clip.

This whole business was bad and getting worse. Darcy suddenly felt nauseated, and it wasn't from the hot dogs. She thought briefly about getting out of the car, walking a few yards down the ravine, and pitching the pistol into the river. She thought about telling the warden to go fuck himself.

The alarm on Darcy's digital watch beeped twice, signaling visiting time at Canyon. She stuffed the gun back into the paper bag, shoved the bag under the front seat, and drove east, out of the parking lot and toward the complex.

An ugly, angular, virtually windowless structure, the Pioneer Correctional Center was hidden deep inside the East Ophir Complex. Behind the razor-wire fences of the compound, no one called it Pioneer. Prisoners and staff alike referred to the soulless concrete giant simply as *the Box*.

Darcy had never had the pleasure of seeing the inside of the building. She'd only caught glimpses of the exterior—a corner of the roof visible from the yard at Canyon, a long blank wall viewed through the window of the warden's Lincoln—But these brief impressions had been enough to give her the willies.

As she rolled through East Ophir toward the visitors' parking lot at Canyon, Darcy craned her head, trying to get a better look at the Box. For some reason Darcy didn't know and didn't want to find out, the warden had a deep interest in TB tests that had been conducted inside Pioneer's walls almost two decades earlier. TB, she thought: tuberculosis. She had a vague memory of a grade-school nurse, the prick of a needle on her forearm, anxious checking and rechecking of the spot. Of course she hadn't been sick. No one, it seemed, ever was. Wasn't tuberculosis one of those illnesses that only existed in isolated parts of the third world?

A space opened up between two buildings and Darcy caught sight of the front of the Box: a short walkway, double security doors, brown grass, and an electrified fence. She could feel the warden's hand on her arm, his voice in her ear. "Take care of her," he'd said.

Slowing, she rolled into the Canyon lot and parked the Dart. In a few more minutes she'd be inside, through the patdown, and in the visiting room with the other relatives. Then the doors would click open and Angie would come strolling in to meet her.

Chapter five

Lucy took the gin and the Seconal pills from her
nightstand and poured them down the toilet. Then
she turned the shower in the big master bathroom
on and let it run till it was hot. Maybe it was Kevin's
visit that had done it, or the sudden disequilibrium
of her life, but for some reason she was thinking
about the baby. Of course, he wouldn't have been a
baby anymore. Lucy stepped into the steamy spray,
let the water needle her back, and counted back.
Five years, she thought. Being childless, it was hard
for her to imagine what this might mean. Would a
five-year-old dress himself in the mornings? Would
he tie his own shoes? Would his little fingers have
trouble working the zipper on a winter coat? He'd
be in kindergarten, she was sure of that.

Someday he would forsake her, enter the stage she'd heard parents talk about, the part of his life when adults were nothing more than an embarrassment. But still, she thought, what a relief motherhood would be, a form around which she could wrap herself, a distraction from the pretense of her life.

The phone was ringing when Lucy stepped out of the shower, loud and insistent. For the first time since the funeral, she decided to answer it. Throwing her robe back on, she made her way into the bedroom and picked up the receiver.

"Lucy? Jeez, Luce, I was starting to get worried. You okay?" It was Chick. Lucy heard the faint echo that meant he was calling from work.

"Not really."

"I'm coming to get you," her brother said, and hung up.

Lucy put the phone back in the cradle. The night table on Carl's side of the bed was strewn with things he'd left: a pile of change, mostly pennies; a tiny silver pocket knife; several scraps of paper with notes. And doodles: a crude, hastily drawn picture of a cottage surrounded by pine trees, a rocket ship with smoke billowing up around it. To get away, that's what Carl had wanted. A house in the woods, a trip to the moon. She pictured him as she'd seen him so many times, phone clamped between his neck and shoulder, his pencil scratching out some haphazard design.

She had not loved Carl at first. After Kevin left for school, she'd gotten a job at the poultry plant in Fort Lupton where her father was a machinist. She worked the night shift all that fall and winter, driving back and forth in darkness on the ice-glazed highway. In those few months she'd come to see her life as something stubborn and implacable, each day rolling out as cold and indifferent as the last and nothing to be done about it, and she'd hardened herself to the future as she saw it, to the monotony of feathers and blood, the quick and efficient slaughter.

It was around Thanksgiving when Carl first called. He was home from Boulder for the break, restless and bored with his parents. He was going to CU, living in a dorm, and Lucy was hardly able to conceive of life as he described it. He took her to Boulder on their first date, to dinner at a restaurant downtown, and afterward they walked along the Pearl Street Mall. By Christmas, Lucy was spending weekends with him in his narrow twin bed at CU.

No, she had not loved Carl at first, but she had seen him as a way out and had clung to him with the fierceness and devotion of a refugee. And from the beginning she had known that Carl loved her. She had sensed an incredible earnestness about him, a desire to do even the simplest things well. It was this carefulness that struck her most about Carl, a deliberation that lent a weightiness even to his love.

She lay back on Carl's side of the unmade bed. She had changed the sheets the day after he left and she was sorry now that she'd done it. She crossed her hands over her chest, opened her eyes wide, and stared up at the ceiling. She could feel a headache coming, and the dull craving brought on by the slow draining of alcohol from her system.

The phone rang once more and Lucy picked it up, expecting Chick's voice again, but it was a woman on the other end. "This is Maria, from the Seattle Hilton. Is Mr. Greene available?"

Lucy clutched the receiver to her ear. "No," she stammered.

There was an awkward silence on the line, then, "Is this Mrs. Greene?"

"Yes."

"I'm sorry to bother you, ma'am. Your husband was a guest here last week, and he left without checking out. Is there somewhere we can send the final bill? And there are some personal items as well."

"Personal items?"

"Yes, ma'am. An overnight bag and some other miscellaneous things, I believe."

"Oh." Lucy was unsure of what to say.

"He left a Pryor, Colorado, address. I just wanted to double-check. Shall we send the things there?"

Lucy thought for a moment. She could hear the blood beating against her temples.

"Mrs. Greene? Is everything all right?"

"Yes, everything's fine. You can send them here."

. . .

It was a short trip from the plant to Lucy's house, the road turning at perfect right angles through the patchwork crops. In late summer, when the high corn meant driving blind and the lack of visibility made it necessary to slow at each dusty intersection, the trip took a little longer than usual. Today, Chick's foot was tentative on the Fairlane's accelerator as he headed away from the plant toward Magpie Road.

Lucy was waiting for him on the porch, sitting on the steps with her knees drawn up into her chest and her arms wrapped around her shins. From the road, with the lawn between them and the house looming behind her, she looked small, almost childlike. Thinking she needed some time alone, he had not bothered her right after the funeral, but obviously he had been wrong.

Chick had never really liked his brother-in-law, and now that Carl was dead, Chick felt slightly guilty around his sister, as if his feelings had had something to do with Carl's death. It wasn't that he'd hated his sister's husband, more that he'd felt uncomfortable around the other man. Even when they were kids, when they'd all worked out at Miller's together, Carl had seemed different from them.

Chick and his sister had picked at Miller's out of necessity. Most of what they earned went toward winter clothes and other essentials, whatever their father's wages wouldn't stretch to cover. But Carl Greene didn't have to work at the farm. He did it because his father thought it would give him something to do, thought it would keep him out of trouble and make him a better man. Carl used his summer money to buy himself a car, a beat-up Camaro he drove the five short blocks to school each day.

Chick was gone the fall Lucy started seeing Carl, stationed on a Saudi army base, doing his second of a four-year stint in the military, and he had wondered at his sister's choice. What she wrote of in her letters to him wasn't love but an eerie resignation. He'd felt helpless, always one step behind her jet-lagged correspondence. And when Lucy and Carl finally got married, Chick was angry with himself, mad that he hadn't been there in the beginning.

He hated the new house more than anything, the ugly patio furniture, the expensive beer glasses, the rugs you couldn't walk on. Even the studio Carl had built for Lucy was offensive, the patronizing way in which he talked about her painting, the pleasant hobby it had become. Chick and his sister had always been poor. Chick hadn't forgotten, and he understood Lucy didn't want to go back to that life. But Carl was rich in a way that made Chick want to stay broke, made him proud of their shabby childhood.

Chick pulled in behind his sister's creamy Mercedes and climbed out, keeping one hand on the open door. "C'mon," he said over the Ford's roof. "We'll have lunch."

Lucy stood up slowly and crossed the lawn. She was wearing khaki shorts, an orange T-shirt with capped sleeves that stopped just about the curve of her biceps, and old tennis shoes. The skin around her eyes was dark, almost bruised, and her face was dull and drained.

Chick slid in behind the wheel and backed out of the driveway. "I'm working," he said as he turned onto the road, "but I thought we could have lunch at the plant."

Lucy nodded. "Thanks for coming to get me."

"You been getting any sleep?" Chick ventured, glancing at his sister's tired profile. She had her window rolled down all the way, and her hair was buffeting her face.

"I guess," Lucy said. She thought about the sedatives, the warm black maw of dreamless oblivion. She fought off the part of herself that wanted to crawl back under the covers and sleep. "Someone broke into the house last night."

Chick glanced across the seat at her. "What do you mean?"

Lucy shrugged. "Just what I said. Someone broke into the house. I ran them off with my Glock."

"Shit, Luce, why didn't you call me?"

"It was just a kid, more than likely," Lucy said, using the same excuse she'd tried to sell herself the night before. "Some meth head. I doubt they'll be back."

"You're staying with me tonight," Chick told her.

Lucy shook her head, regretting having told him. She didn't want his solicitude, couldn't stand the thought of going into town. She needed quiet right now, the house all to herself. "Let's talk about it later, okay?"

When they got to the old nuclear plant, Chick climbed out and unlocked the gate; then they parked and headed inside. Chick's office was in the plant's old maintenance room. He'd stuffed a TV, personal computer, couch, and substantial library into the cramped space. One corner of the room held a make-shift kitchen: hot plate, mini-refrigerator, table, and chairs. Online for only a short time before various insurmountable problems shut it down, Fort Ward had been mothballed for quite some time. Chick was the only permanent employee, and his job consisted of little more than watching dust gather.

Chick opened the refrigerator and began rummaging among its contents. There were a half-dozen prescription bottles on the top shelf of the refrigerator, and half a dozen more neatly arranged on the table. Beside them was a haphazard stack of documents, some loosely bound, others stapled, Chick's most recent finds on Gulf War Illness. Lucy thumbed through the top-most paper, a report titled "Russian Doll Cocktails and GWI."

The majority of the information Chick gathered came off the Internet or from other vets. Lucy thought it was mostly mis-information, paranoia, or conjecture camouflaged by medical or scientific-sounding jargon. But Chick scoured everything he found for possible answers. Snake oil, Carl used to call it, and it made Lucy mad, sometimes, the way her brother clung to each new theory.

Chick was sick in small ways before his discharge, but it wasn't until he came home that his health took a real turn for the worse. He'd enlisted in the army with college in mind, and when his four years of service were over he enrolled at CU. Carl and Lucy were married by then, renting a house in Boulder while

Carl finished grad school, and Chick stayed with them during his freshman year.

There were signs of something serious during that fall, headaches that lasted for days, insomnia. Chick would come home from school gaunt and tired, bruises ringing his eyes. By Christmas he was throwing up every morning, complaining of numbness in his legs and constant pain. He struggled through a second semester of school and finally dropped out. That summer, when their father had his first stroke, Chick gladly moved back out to the old house in Pryor to take care of him.

Chick foundered through several years of unemployment. After their father died, he stayed on in the old house in Pryor, mowing the lawns of old ladies around town and taking seasonal shifts at the cannery. The Fort Ward job was a stroke of luck. It paid well and kept Chick busy without demanding too much. And it gave him plenty of time to cruise the Internet for other vets like himself, soldiers who'd been downwind of the Khamisaya weapons depot, or dodging scuds in the Saudi desert, or just inexplicably sick.

To Lucy, the worst thing about her brother's illness was not the physical symptoms but how angry he'd become. Chick had always been a pissed-off little kid. He was a year older than Lucy. He'd taken it personally when their mother left, and Lucy knew he'd spent much of his childhood feeling cheated. But since he'd come back from the Gulf, things had gotten worse. He was angry at the army for sending him, angry at the VA for telling him there was no such thing as Gulf War Illness, and angry at everyone who he thought had a better life.

A part of Lucy understood her brother's rage, the part that knew he was too smart for Pryor, too good for the Fort Ward job. But there was another, colder part of her that knew better than to expect much out of life. Get over it, that part wanted to say.

"How are those new meds working out?" she asked.

Chick shrugged and gave his stock answer. "Better in some ways, worse in others. I'm not falling down as much." He stood up and turned to face her. "You should read that," he said, gesturing to the stack of papers under Lucy's hand. "It's the most interesting stuff I've found in a long time."

"What's a Russian Doll Cocktail?"

Chick set a couple of sandwiches on the table and a bag of potato chips. "Basically, it's when they put one biological bomb inside another, say a small amount of Marburg virus inside an anthrax weapon. Like those Russian dolls, you know, where you keep opening them up and finding a smaller doll inside. It's a kind of camouflage system. Makes it about a hundred times harder to figure out what you're dealing with."

Lucy looked down at the sandwich, trying to remember the last time she'd eaten.

"It's roast beef," Chick told her. "You want a root beer?"

"Sure."

Chick fished in the fridge, producing two frosty brown bottles.

"Kevin Burns came by the house this morning," Lucy said, tearing into the sandwich. The food tasted good. She felt like she couldn't eat fast enough.

"He still working for that news station back east?" Chick set the root beers down and joined Lucy at the table. "CNN, right?"

Lucy shook her head. "Used to be. And it was MSNBC, not CNN. He got fired a month or so ago. He faked some story, on illegal immigrants, I think. It was in the news for a while there."

"What a racket, huh?" Chick said, referring, Lucy knew, to the media in general, another target of his ire.

"He said Carl called him; they were supposed to meet at the Rockies game on Saturday."

"I didn't realize they were still in touch."

"They weren't." Lucy opened the potato chips bag with her teeth. "He said Carl called him last week and wanted to talk to him about something—a story, is what he said."

"That's a long way to come for a baseball game. They couldn't talk over the phone?"

Lucy shook her head. "I don't know. Something's funny. Kevin said Carl seemed upset."

Chick shot her a sideways glance. "Was he?"

"Not that I know of." She paused for a moment. "And then there was that break-in last night."

"What's that supposed to mean? I thought you said it was just some kid."

Lucy shrugged. "I don't know. You come in the front door of our house and there are at least a dozen things worth pawning sitting right in plain view. But whoever it was went straight to Carl's office, straight to his files, didn't touch anything else. It seems weird, doesn't it?"

Chick set his sandwich down. "You know what's in those files?"

"Research, I guess. Work stuff and, you know, financial papers, stuff about the house. I paid the bills each month, but all the investing, all the important financial stuff? Carl took care of all that."

"Was there anything weird going on lately? Money problems? Work problems?"

"If there was, I didn't know about it."

Chick thought for a second. "I don't like this," he said finally. "I want you to stay in town with me for a while."

Lucy shook her head. "I'll be fine."

"Humor me, will you?"

Lucy didn't answer. She took another bite and chewed, finishing the sandwich in silence. When she was done, she looked across the table at her brother. "Chick?" she asked.

"Yeah."

"What if it wasn't an accident?"

Chick laid his arm across the table till his fingers were touching hers. "It was a terrible thing, Luce," he said, "what happened to Carl. But you know, you can't bring him back."

It was late afternoon when Lucy turned onto Magpie Road and started the last half mile to the house. The air was humid, thick with the promise of an evening thunderstorm. The mountains were jagged silhouettes in the distance, black and brooding. Over the ragged tips of the corn, Lucy could see the tops of the first few houses in her development. After lunch with Chick she'd decided to walk the almost four miles home. The rhythmic movement felt good to her, the simple workings of her muscles, her feet hitting the hardpack of the road. Her mind had started to clear, and for the second time that day she caught herself thinking about Eric.

When he was born, Lucy had known something was wrong— even before she saw the silent faces of the nurses, the quick and tidy way they bundled him up and rushed him out of the room. She had known in the way he slipped from her body, passive, quiescent, as if he didn't want any part of what was to come.

He died two hours later, and only then, only when Lucy had raged to see him, did they bring him back, the crevices of his face still crusted with mucus and afterbirth. At first, seeing him swaddled in a blanket, she had not understood what could have possibly gone wrong. He seemed perfect and whole, his tiny fingers curled into angry fists, his face like a wrinkled fruit. But when she took him from the nurse she could feel the sack of spongy tissue at the back of his head, the swollen skin where his skull had failed to come together.

The night before Carl left for Seattle, he had come to bed late. Lucy had been sleeping, but she woke to the presence of him in the dark. He pulled the sheet back and slipped in next to her, the entire length of his body curled against her back. He put his knee between her legs, his hand on the hollow of muscle in her inner thigh, and she slid through his grasp, turning her face to kiss him.

"Honey," he said carefully, "maybe we should try again. It's time to move on."

For an instant she had been unafraid. She had let herself believe that Carl was right; it might be time. Yes, she wanted to say, and then the old terror gripped her, the anguish that had held itself between them for so long. Her body stiffened and she turned away from him for the last time.

The wind picked up and the first raindrops exploded in the dry dirt at Lucy's feet, kicking up dust and bullheads. She quickened her pace, jogging now. She would live with this her entire life, she thought, this final gesture, this simple movement of refusal replaying itself for her.

She pumped her arms, running faster, her lungs working hard, her heart hammering. The side of her house appeared, the green expanse of the front yard. There was a car in the drive, an unfamiliar silver sedan parked behind her Mercedes, its interior empty and dark. Lucy stopped short, propped her hands on her thighs, and struggled to get her breath back. She was certain she had locked the house when she left. But now someone was inside. The windows in Carl's office were lit up bright as the hollow eyes of a jack-o'-lantern.

Chapter six

Lured by a hand-painted sign promising kitch-
enettes and cable TV for thirty-nine dollars a night,
Kevin had pulled off the road south of Brighton
and checked into the Mountain Aire Motel. At least
he thought he was somewhere south of Brighton.
The sprawl of Denver made it nearly impossible to
tell where one town ended and another began. It
was as if the places he knew from his childhood
had been swallowed whole, their borders overrun
by cheap housing and cedar fences. Kevin's memory was no longer accurate, and he'd long since
given up on trying to let it guide him.

His room was neat and clean, in a shabby, well-
worn way. There was a queen-sized bed, a TV, and
a kitchenette, emphasis on *ette*. Kevin took his bag

and his laptop inside and headed to the neighboring King Soopers to get some provisions.

The supermarket had been cooled to a near-arctic chill, and Kevin shivered in his short sleeves and thin pants. He'd forgotten how temperature-controlled the West was, how little time was voluntarily spent outside. Winters were too cold and summers too hot. Whenever possible, people raced from one sealed environment to the next.

It was different in New York, where, in summer, half-naked bodies crowded every inch of available grass. Even in steamy August, New Yorkers ate outside. They spent hours in borrowed cars trying to get to a beach or a campground in the Catskills.

People here were not quite far enough removed from their grandparents' sod homesteads to enjoy outdoor living. They'd spent too much time fighting the land to think of central air and heated pools as anything but their well-deserved birthright. It was something Kevin could appreciate. He could distinctly remember his grandmother's living room in the summertime, the shades drawn to keep out the sun, the old air conditioner gurgling and humming in the window. He could remember coming into that sanctuary after work at Miller's, his pores tightening up, the sweat cooling under his arms, and his grandfather, in a T-shirt and worn Wranglers, reading the newspaper in his favorite chair.

Space here was to be tamed, not conserved. You could see the truth of such a statement in the extra-wide aisles of the King Soopers, the rows of frozen orange juice and microwavable entrees, the acres of breakfast cereal and canned soup, and in the distance people put between themselves and others, the houses cast adrift on the plains like rudderless ships freed from their moorings. Now that safety came in forms other than numbers, now that the marauding Indians and the beasts outside the campfire had been beaten back into the deepest woods, neighbors, like the federal government, were nothing more than a nuisance.

Kevin cruised the unfamiliar aisles, tossing a Stouffer's frozen lasagna, a box of Pepperidge Farm cookies, some doughnuts, and fresh ground coffee into his basket. He paid with his Visa card and walked back across the parking lot to the Mountain Aire and his room.

It was moving toward Sunday evening on the East Coast. Kevin figured he'd call his super first thing in the morning, let him know he might not be back for a while, and ask him to pick up his mail and water his plants. That took care of his responsibilities at home.

Kevin flipped the TV on, trying to block out the silence of the empty motel room. Finding an adapter in his bag, he plugged his cell phone into the wall outlet and stuck the lasagna in the microwave. He pulled the phone cord from the jack, snapped his laptop's line in place, dialed up a connection, and, unable to think of a better place to start, typed in the address for the *Denver Post* web site.

He found Carl's obituary in the online archives, just a couple of terse paragraphs to sum up a life. What few facts the text provided was mostly information Kevin already knew: that Carl had grown up in Pryor, that he'd graduated from the University of Colorado and married Lucy, that he was a researcher for a company called Bioflux. Six years ago, when he had last seen Carl and Lucy, Kevin remembered, Carl had just gotten the job.

Done with the obituary, Kevin left the *Post* site and jumped to a search engine. According to Lucy, Carl had been in Seattle because of work, so Kevin figured it wouldn't hurt to find out exactly what the Seattle branch of his company did. He entered the word BIOFLUX and the monitor flickered, throwing a list of web sites onto the screen: a French site on deep-sea research; an article on energy therapy from the Massachusetts Holistic Health Center; something called the Alien Message Board, which was described as a humorous look at alien visitations; the plant cytometry mailing list; a German site on old-school rave music, whatever that was. Looking for real information on the Internet was like searching for spare parts in a junkyard. Kevin jumped to the next page and let his cursor stop on the first entry. Bioflux Corporation, it said: company profile, research, development, marketing—

The timer on the microwave rang. Kevin clicked on the link to Bioflux and got up and checked his food. He rummaged in a drawer for a grimy fork, rinsed the tines under tepid tap water, and took the steaming lasagna back to the laptop.

The Bioflux Corporation web site was pretty much what Kevin had expected, straightforward and fairly uninformative. There was a lot of medical jargon Kevin couldn't understand, most of it focusing on immune system research and HIV and AIDS. Color pictures showed the Seattle and Denver research facilities, both bland, in business park settings with well-manicured evergreens. Below it was a smaller picture of the Denver production plant, a much larger structure, from what Kevin could tell. There was a brief history of the company from its founding in 1970 and a list of the current board members, a handful of names that meant absolutely nothing to him.

Kevin jumped back to the search results. There were several more entries dealing with Bioflux Corporation: an article from the *New England Journal of Medicine* on a new treatment for allergic rhinitis, mention of the company on a web site for asthmatics, a discussion of potential HIV vaccines.

Kevin scrolled forward, stopping at a link for the Colorado Secretary of State online database. BIOFLUX CORP., the description said, ANNUAL REPORTS, ARTICLES OF INCORPORATION. Kevin clicked his mouse and watched the web page load onto the screen. A list of files appeared, arranged chronologically, and Kevin chose the oldest. Again the screen in front of him flashed away, and a new file materialized, a scanned copy of Bioflux's original application for incorporation. SEPTEMBER 12, 1970, a date at the top of the screen read.

Kevin skimmed through the grainy text. Again, there was nothing very interesting, just stiff business argot, the official workings of the fledgling company. It was a standard form, most likely drawn up by Bioflux's lawyers. Where specific information was needed, the blanks had been filled in by hand. It wasn't until Kevin clicked onto the third page of the old form that something caught his eye. Under the bold heading that read BOARD MEMBERS were a half-dozen blanks. At one time, five names had been penned by hand, but they were no longer legible. Someone had taken a thick black marker to the orginal document and carefully covered them so that all that remained were long dark stains.

Lucy cut across the lawn and headed for the front door. What had started as rain had quickly turned to hail, clattering against the roof of the house, bouncing up from the grass at her feet. She ducked under cover of the porch, quietly swung the door open, and stepped into the foyer.

The door to Carl's office was open. From where she stood she couldn't see whoever was inside, but she could hear their voices over the thrum of the hail. There was a rustling of paper, the sharp sound of a metal drawer slamming closed.

"Shit!" a man's voice said, sounding irritated. "We might as well take everything."

It had been steamy outside, but the air-conditioned cool of the house and Lucy's wet T-shirt made her skin prickle with goose bumps. She thought briefly of her gun in the upstairs bedroom and considered the door she'd just come in.

"You want the hard drive too?" the same voice asked.

Lucy took a step forward, then another, till the luminous rectangle of the open door slid into her line of view. She could see the corner of Carl's desk and a man propped up against it, his head bent in concentration, his dark suit jacket tight across his shoulders. The skin on the back of his neck was white and exposed, dark with a triangle of faint stubble at the nape.

"Christ!" whoever was doing all the talking exclaimed. He was in the far corner of the office, where Carl's files were, still hidden from Lucy's view. "He's got a whole cabinet full of NTD stuff."

"Make sure to take it all," the man on the desk said, setting the manila file he'd been reading from aside. Then he turned his head and looked back at Lucy, casually, carefully, as if he'd been aware of her all along. His eyes locked on hers and his lip curled up into the shadow of a smile.

"Mrs. Greene," he said, as if welcoming her to a social occasion, as if it were his house and she an unwanted guest. "We've just come by to take some of your husband's files. You know he was doing very important research for Bioflux. We wouldn't want to lose any of it."

There was an implied threat in the way he spoke, a confidence born out of sheer power. He motioned for the other man. "I think you know Craig Weldon."

Nodding, Lucy wrapped her arms around her chest and clamped her jaw tight to keep her teeth from chattering. Craig stepped into the doorway and smiled like a school-yard coward whose parents had just bought him a pit bull.

"Lucy," he said, in the same voice he might use to address a child. "Sorry to bother you."

Craig was one of the hot-shot researchers at Bioflux. He was a few years older than Carl, part of the soft-bellied golf-and-martini set at the company, with a wife whose bra size was at least double her IQ.

Lucy looked at the two men. She was outnumbered and knew it. "Make yourselves at home," she said coolly, and turned and headed up the stairs to her bedroom.

It took them a good hour to get everything packed up. The hail let up about a half hour after it started, and through the open door of her bedroom, Lucy could hear Craig Weldon cursing and panting as he humped back and forth from the office to the car. Then the front door closed and the wheels of the sedan crackled down the gravel drive.

When Lucy was certain they were gone, she went back downstairs. They'd taken almost everything from Carl's office. His filing cabinets had been cleaned out, his desk drawers emptied of all but a few stray paper clips. There was a faint outline of dust where his hard drive had been. Only the blank monitor remained, the useless keyboard.

Lucy went into the kitchen and found a pack of cigarettes. The storm had rolled away toward the plains, and beyond the pool the sky was stained with the first dark flush of summer's gradual dusk. She had not known much about the details of her husband's work. At company parties she played along with the other wives, the Mrs. Weldons in their pastel shirts and Bermuda shorts, their cocktail dresses that stopped just short of being sexy. She feigned interest in the jobs they themselves feigned interest in, interior decorating or real estate. She watched them carefully tiptoe around the subject of children when she was around.

But one thing Craig Weldon had said didn't sit right with Lucy, something about a cabinet full of NTD files. And the other man: *Make sure to take it all*. NTDs—neural tube defects—was a subject Lucy knew something about. Spina bifida was an NTD, as was encephalocele, both birth defects. Their son had been born with the latter, and it had killed him. It surprised Lucy to find out that her husband had been doing research on NTDs, that all these years later he still wanted an answer. And for some reason it hurt that he had kept it a secret, that he had never once mentioned any of this to her. It's time to move on, Carl had said. Lucy had always believed in his ability to let his life propel him forward. And yet he had not completely separated himself from Eric's death.

But this what not what worried Lucy. What bothered her was that she could not understand what interest the company might have had in any of this. Lucy was certain that NTDs were not part of Carl's work at Bioflux.

She looked across the darkening yard and felt the hairs along the back of her neck bristle. Someone else had been in Carl's office, someone who, for one reason or another, couldn't afford to come in the daylight. More than likely, they'd been looking for the same thing Craig Weldon had been sent to find.

Chapter seven

September 12, 1970. Kevin scratched the date of Bioflux's origin into his little pocket notepad and turned his computer off. It didn't take a genius to realize that people don't generally go to the trouble of blacking out information unless they want it kept secret. And in Kevin's experience, secrets usually mean someone is up to no good. Kevin's gut told him Carl Greene had known something unflattering about Bioflux. And now he was dead.

Kevin's cell phone rang and he leapt across the room, snatching it from the charger.

"Kevin Burns," he said, snapping the phone open.

There was silence on the line, a moment's hesitation, then, "It's Lucy. Where are you?"

"Brighton. I think."

"I need to see you. Can you come back out?" She sounded clear, sober, and wide awake.

"I can be there in half an hour."

"Good," she said. Then, before hanging up, "Why don't you bring another pack of cigarettes?"

They were on the patio again, at the table where they'd sat earlier that morning. The pool lights were off and the water was black and glassy. Crooked fingers of heat lightning crackled over the plains, the erratic flashes showing glimpses of what lay hidden in the darkness around them, the gnarled branches of a grove of cottonwoods, the geometric silhouette of a barn. The only light in the yard was from the kitchen windows. Millers swarmed toward the glow, their powdery wings fluttering against the panes.

"I thought you didn't know anything about Carl's work," Kevin said, reaching for a cigarette from the opened pack that lay between them. "I thought you were just the wife."

Lucy had just finished telling Kevin about the sudden interest in Carl's office—shown by both the midnight visitor and Craig Weldon and the other man from Bioflux.

"I'm sure about one thing," she said with conviction. "Whatever Carl was doing with neural tube defects was weekend work, strictly personal. I would have known if his work at Bioflux had had anything at all to do with NTDs."

"It seems like a strange hobby."

Lucy shifted in her chair so her face was drawn back into shadow. Kevin could see her eyes, glittering in the half-light, and the white scythe of her teeth.

"We had a child about five years ago, a little boy. He had a type of neural tube defect called encephalocele. He was born with part of his brain outside his body. He only lived for two hours."

"Oh, God, Lucy, I'm sorry. I didn't know."

"How could you have?" she said matter-of-factly, wrapping her bare arms around her shoulders.

Kevin lit the cigarette and leaned back into his chair. He hadn't smoked in years, and the tobacco went straight to his head, making him dizzy and disconnected. He saw Lucy get up.

"I'm going to get a sweater," she said. "I'll be right back."

The patio door slid open, then closed. Kevin turned in his chair and watched her walk across the bright kitchen and disappear down the hall.

He had a sudden memory of her beside him in his grandfather's ugly green Impala. She had on red jeans—he remembered this still—and a pink T-shirt that showed the seams and clasps of her cotton bra. Over her shoulder, out the Chevy's passenger window, Kevin could see the blue light of the television flickering in the front room of her father's house. He leaned closer to her and could smell lip gloss, someone's idea of strawberry or cherry, and the faint, almost imagined, medicinal odor of the clinic.

"I'm sorry," he'd said, and she shook her head. Her face was tired, her shoulders drawn into her chest as if for protection.

She wasn't mad at him, though Kevin wanted her to be. She was changed, sophisticated in the worst kind of way, and Kevin knew that everything would be different between them now. She popped the door, got out of the car, and headed up her father's walk.

Now, in a second-floor window of the big house, a light blinked on, then off again, casting a momentarily perfect rectangle onto the surface of the pool. Lucy reappeared in the downstairs hallway, and it occurred to Kevin that things could have gone very differently for both of them. He watched her open the refrigerator and pull out two beers. Then she walked back out to him, closing the door behind her, ducking to avoid the cloud of moths.

"Here." She set the beers down on the table and handed him a sweater. "It's Carl's."

Kevin pulled the sweater over his head and shrugged into the sleeves. It was a good size or two too big for him, Carl's size. The wool held a faint odor of aftershave.

"How well did you know the Bioflux staff?" he asked.

Lucy shrugged. "We certainly weren't antisocial. We went to all the regular functions—you know, ski weekends, holiday parties.

Of course we didn't know everyone. The research staff was pretty big, and there were all the people at the production plant and then the Seattle people."

"Do you have any idea who started the company?"

Lucy thought for a moment, then shook her head.

"Old company bigwigs? Names people mentioned? Funerals?"

Lucy picked her beer up and cradled the bottle in her palms. "There's a Mrs. Beckwith. Viviane, I think. A company widow, as far as I can tell. She comes to the Christmas party every year, hangs around with the other wives. Not my age group, of course, more of the martini-and-furs set. But there's definitely a kind of cult status about her."

"You have a Denver phone book?" Kevin asked.

"Better." Lucy smiled and stood up. "I've got a *company* phone book."

She ducked back into the kitchen and returned with her finger in the directory.

"Mrs. David Beckwith," she said. "She lives out in Golden. And I just thought of something else. When Carl first started at Bioflux they had this huge retirement shindig. The guy was ancient, and it was not your standard send-off."

"You remember his name?"

"Canty," she said. "Herman Canty."

She stepped back into the light and flipped forward through the directory, her finger scanning each name. She shook her head. "He's not in here. What's so special about these guys, anyway?"

"I ran across a copy of Bioflux's articles of incorporation this afternoon. The names of the original board members were all blacked out."

"Why would anyone do that?" Lucy asked, taking her place across from him.

"I guess that's the million-dollar question."

Darcy had planned to wait a few days before heading back up to Pryor, but her visit with her sister had unnerved her. Angie looked bad, strung out and exhausted. She had the nervous energy of someone who's constantly looking over her shoulder, conscious of what, or who, might come screaming out of the next dark corner. When the bell that signaled the end of visiting time sounded and Angie dutifully swung her legs out from under the Formica picnic table, Darcy was gripped by panic.

"You call me tomorrow night, okay?" She grabbed her sister's hand and squeezed it hard.

Angie nodded, her dull eyes already turning away.

It was a long drive back to Castle Rock, with just grainy AM radio to distract Darcy from her sister, from the heavy click of the door Angie had taken out of the visiting room, the top of her head visible through the meshed glass and then bobbing out of view around a corner.

Darcy had been able to take care of herself inside. She had the physical strength and the keen ability to sense when something was wrong, when it was best just to fade away into the gray background of the prison. But Angie was so small she swam in her jumpsuit, her bruised arms sticking out from the sleeves like kindling sticks. She was a junkie, not a criminal, and she lacked the criminal's knack for survival.

It was early evening when Darcy got back to Castle Rock, and she tried to settle in for the night, but the apartment seemed smaller than usual. Even with the TV on, there was a restless silence, the kind that made her wish she still drank. By nine she had changed into her darks and was headed north on the interstate.

In the years that she'd been actively involved in the profession, Darcy had taught herself a lot about larceny. Except for the time in grade school when she'd pocketed a Snickers bar at the corner store, she'd never been a common thief. There was something shameful about it, something embarrassingly easy that had made her set a higher goal.

Darcy had been a burglar, like Cary Grant on the rooftops of the Riviera. Though she regretted the consequences of her actions, she still couldn't stir up remorse for what she'd done.

She'd grown up in Casper, Wyoming, raised on Hamburger Helper and Kool-Aid. She couldn't see the crime in taking the odd diamond necklace or silver teapot from people who drove Beemers and Range Rovers and who didn't think twice about dropping the equivalent of her father's monthly paycheck on a round of golf.

Besides, she'd liked her work, had gotten a certain voyeuristic thrill out of being in other people's homes. She'd been good at it, too, careful and meticulous. If it hadn't been for her drinking, for the way Irish whiskey had loosened her up and made her jabber like a monkey, she would never have gotten caught.

When the warden first asked her to do the Pryor job, she'd spent a few days scoping the house out. There was just the woman inside, but she had an erratic schedule, and Darcy wanted to make sure nothing went wrong. She still had two years of parole ahead of her, and she didn't want to slip up and get sent back to Canyon. It was an easy house to watch. Like most of these big new places, there was lots of glass, and the surrounding cornfields provided more than enough cover.

The warden hadn't told her anything about the woman or the husband, so she hadn't known at first that he was dead, but after a few nights of watching, she could tell something was wrong. The woman's rhythms were all screwed up. She might go to bed at eight or nine, then get up again at midnight and sit out on the back deck. Later, she stopped getting up at all. Darcy would see an occasional light in the hall, a trip to the kitchen or bathroom, then nothing all night.

A couple of days before she'd gone in, she'd read the obituary in the Denver paper. She recognized the name, Greene, from the mailbox. There was a picture of him, a grainy head shot. He was attractive, younger than she would have imagined. That's how Darcy learned the woman's name, too. *Mr. Greene is survived by his wife, Lucy Greene, of Pryor,* the obituary read. Darcy almost felt as if she knew her now. It was good to put a name to the face, to the lonely figure in the house.

It was past ten when Darcy got to the subdivision, still far too early. She liked to work late, in the stone-still hours between

2 and 4 A.M., when people slip deeper into the sheath of sleep, when the ears shut down and the breath slows closer to death. She rolled past the woman's house and eased the Dart down a dirt maintenance road into the adjacent field. She cut the engine, pulled her gloves and cap on, grabbed her tool bag from under the seat, and slipped the sleek little Colt Pony into her pocket.

Lucy Greene might not have had a routine, but her neighbors did, and Darcy had gotten to know them quite well. The people in the house directly to the west went to bed every night at nine o'clock sharp. The neighbors to the east slept in separate bedrooms. The wife would call it a day at around ten-thirty, but the husband always stayed up to watch the *Tonight Show*. The next house over had kids, two teenagers and a preschooler. They put the little one to bed at eight-thirty; the rest of the house was in bed by eleven, all except the oldest boy, whose computer screen Darcy could see glowing in the window of the westward-facing upstairs bedroom until the wee hours of the morning.

What baffled Darcy about these big suburban dream houses, what had bothered her sitting on every job she'd done, was how infrequently these people actually spoke to one another. No one ever ventured next door, not for an egg or a cup of sugar or a friendly mug of coffee. Even inside their homes, families were oddly disconnected. Dad worked on the computer in his office while Mom watched Emeril in the living room and Janey played Tomb Raider in the downstairs den. No wonder no one noticed that Tommy was building pipe bombs in his bedroom.

They had never been alone in Casper. There was always some neighbor in the kitchen, Mrs. Haywood from next door with her coffee mug of boxed white Zinfandel, or Cliff Sears, her father's friend, who smelled of motorcycle grease and fried onions. And if something had gone wrong, if one of them had died or even gotten sick, the house would have been mobbed.

Maybe it has to do with money, she thought, or the lack of it. Maybe her parents and their friends felt some need to fill their otherwise sparse lives. Maybe there is a level of consumption where other people suddenly become extraneous, bothersome even, where the fear of damage to your hand-knotted rug or suede sofa outweighs your desire for human contact, even contact with your children. Whatever it was, it didn't make sense to Darcy. She'd lived most of her adult life alone and lonely, and she couldn't see the luxury in this kind of separation.

Darcy crept to the edge of the corn and peered across Magpie Road. There was an extra car in Lucy Greene's driveway, a nondescript sedan. Most of the lights in the house were off, but through the glass panels on either side of the front door, Darcy could see a light shining from the entrance to the kitchen. Checking to make sure no one was coming, she bolted across the road and down along the west side of the Greenes' property. The houses were spaced some distance from one another, separated by weedy no-man's-lands. It was a perfect setup for Darcy. As she slipped quietly toward the back of the house, she heard the low murmur of conversation.

The pool lights were off, and the backyard was dark, but the light from the kitchen windows revealed two figures, Lucy Greene and a man, seated across from each other at the patio table. Lucy was smoking, gesticulating while she spoke. The orange coal of her cigarette flitted around her face like a firefly. Darcy was too far away from the couple to hear what they were saying, but their conversation was intense. Several times, Lucy got up and went into the house.

It was after midnight when they headed inside together. Darcy scrambled around toward the front of the house. After a few minutes the front door opened and the man emerged. He got into his car, started the engine, and backed down the gravel drive and out onto Magpie Road. Darcy skirted toward the backyard again. The light in Lucy's bedroom clicked on and her head made a brief appearance at the window, then retreated.

Christ, Darcy thought, wondering if she should call it a night and just drive back to Castle Rock. It was late and she had to work in the morning, but she wanted the whole thing over with. She was tired of this woman's grief, tired of sitting in the Dart waiting for her to fall asleep.

Lucy's light blinked off. Reluctantly, Darcy stretched out on one of the lounge chairs by the pool. It was 12:46 by her watch. At 2 A.M. she'd go in.

Kevin always figured he'd done pretty well for himself. He made good money at MSNBC and even got the occasional baffled look of recognition. Sure, a lot of people mistook him for the hero of that cable show about time travel, but at least the guy was attractive. Kevin had scored more than a few phone numbers because of the mix-up and once, miraculously, a last-minute table at Nobu. He had a car, space in a garage, and, by New York standards, an attractive if somewhat small apartment in a pre-war doorman building in the East 80s.

So it seemed somehow unjust to him that the bathroom he'd just used in Lucy Greene's house was easily twice the size of his kitchen. Who needed that much space? he wondered. There was a settee in one corner. For what, those times when you wanted to entertain in the john? Or when the fatigue of personal grooming caught up with you and you just had to sit down?

When he offered to stay the night, he hadn't really expected her to agree. There had always been a toughness to Lucy, an independence that Kevin often found threatening. Their sophomore year in high school, Lucy had run away three times. Twice she'd gone to Denver and the cops had picked her up in the Greyhound station. The third time, she'd hitched all the way to Las Vegas and then come home on her own.

Kevin had never understood what made her run. As far as he knew, things hadn't been bad at home. Lucy's father was a quiet man who worked the night shift and slept most of the day, leaving Lucy and Chick to their own devices. To Kevin it had seemed as if she'd been running toward something instead of away. Whatever made her go, she'd always been able to take care of herself along the way, and Kevin couldn't imagine she'd want his help now. He was right.

"I'll be fine," she said to his offer, putting her hand lightly on his arm, walking him to the door.

"I'm at the Mountain Aire Motel over in Brighton," he told her, "if you need anything."

"Thanks," she said. "Good night."

He stepped out onto the porch, heard the door lock behind him, and walked across the lawn to his car. He rolled his window down and pulled out onto Magpie Road, turning east onto the highway. Out the windshield a bolt of lightning crackled up from the scrub plains of Morgan County. A train whistled on its way through Pryor, mournful, melancholic, and Kevin was wrested from the dark road to the clean smell of his grandmother's sheets and the bright light of a summer afternoon.

His grandparents had gone to Greeley to see a movie and Lucy had ridden out on her bike. She was there in his narrow bed, her shirt open to reveal her bra, the cotton trimmed by a thin border of lace. Her mouth was bright, chapped and flushed from kissing. She wriggled out of her shorts, looked up at him, and smiled. Her right knee was purple with bruises, sore from where she'd taken a fall off her ten-speed. Even then he had thought of this moment as one to be remembered, the slightly hurried pace of her breathing, the delicate brown of her shoulder, the whiteness where her bathing suit had covered her skin. He put his hand on her stomach, heard something rattle in the back of her throat.

This was what he remembered now, not sex but the brief time before, the physical bargaining and the instant of agreement, Lucy's brittleness softened just enough to let him in.

He put his foot on the gas and headed for Brighton.

Lucy threw her clothes on the back of a chair and climbed into bed. She had told Chick she'd spend the night in town, but she was bone-tired, too exhausted even to think about the short drive. She stretched out on her stomach, letting her arm rest on Carl's pillow. You can't bring him back, her brother had said, but as she plummeted toward sleep she felt her husband's hand gripping hers. They were at Lakeside, cresting the hill on the park's old wooden roller coaster. The cars edged up the track, then caught for a moment. Lucy felt her stomach slip out from under her as they started the long thunderous descent.

It was 4:17 by Darcy's watch when she woke to the sound of the irrigation sprinklers in the field behind the house. She sat up and rubbed her eyes, shaking off the night's cold, the stiffness in her back and legs. She had never fallen asleep on the job before, and it worried her. She figured it was just the price of getting older, another sign that the profession wasn't for her anymore. Swinging herself off the lounge chair, she stood up and headed for the front of the house.

She could have easily jimmied the sliding glass patio doors, but that would have meant breaking the flimsy lock, and she wanted to avoid detection if at all possible. Crouching on the porch, she took her picks and tension wrench from her tool bag. If she was careful, no one would know she'd come in this way. She slipped a pick and the spring-wire tension tool into the lock, wriggling the pick gently until she felt the pressure of the pins against her fingers and the distinctive click of the lock giving. In a few seconds she was inside.

The kitchen light was still on, dimly illuminating the front of the house. Darcy glanced around the foyer, up the curve of the stairway, and into the dark living room. Then, pulling her mini-flashlight from the back pocket of her pants, she turned toward the door of the dead man's office.

Chapter eight

"Rise and shine, Lucy Greene."

Lucy was awakened by a woman's voice in her ear and the cold pressure of metal against the nape of her neck. She rolled over onto her back, her eyes combing the darkness as she tried to get her bearings.

"Where are the fucking files?" the voice asked.

A figure leaned down over Lucy and a gloved hand pressed the thick barrel of a gun against her temple. Lucy heard a soft click, the menacing and unmistakable sound of the safety disengaging.

"What files?" She was wide awake, her heart working double-time.

"The ones in your husband's office, you stupid shit. It's fucking empty, or hadn't you noticed?"

Except for the times when she'd been forced to defend herself, Darcy wasn't a violent person. She'd never before taken a gun with her on a B and E. It had never even crossed her mind. But when the beam of her flashlight had skipped across the empty office, she'd immediately thought of Angie and been gripped by an anger so fierce it had scared her. She was both glad she had the Colt tonight and worried she might use it.

Lucy was worried too. The other woman was so close that Lucy could smell the desperation coming off her, the sour ammonia stink of adrenaline and fear.

"Weldon's got them," Lucy said, her voice clear, sharpened by panic.

"What?" Darcy pressed the gun harder into Lucy's forehead.

"Craig Weldon," Lucy repeated, trying to sound relaxed, hoping her forced calm might rub off on the other woman. "He came by this afternoon with someone else from Bioflux. They took everything." There was another click and the lamp next to the bed was switched on. Lucy looked up at the intruder. Her face was covered by a black ski mask but Lucy could see a look of puzzlement in the eyes.

"What the hell is Bioflux?" the woman asked.

"Carl's company," Lucy said, but she could tell that this meant nothing. "My husband," she explained.

"Get up!" Darcy commanded.

Lucy sat up, her eyes ranging to the bathroom door, to her robe, where she'd hung it earlier that day, the Glock still in the pocket.

"That was you, Saturday night," she said, trying to buy herself some time to think.

"Get up!" Darcy repeated.

Lucy did as she was told. "Who are you working for?" she asked, swinging her legs off the bed and getting to her feet.

The other woman didn't say anything. She seemed unsure of what to do.

"It's not Bioflux," Lucy continued. "Is it another pharmaceutical company?"

Darcy peered down into Lucy's face. She was younger than Darcy had expected, but harder, as if whatever she had to lose had already been taken from her.

"Put the gun down," Lucy said, her hands clenched in two tight fists to keep them from shaking.

Darcy didn't move.

"You want those files?" Lucy asked, and then, without waiting for an answer, "I know where they are. I can help you get them."

Darcy muttered something to herself, a whispered expletive, a curse at her own confusion and the impossible situation. She didn't want to face the warden without those files, couldn't bear to think of what she might have to do if she came to him empty-handed, and what might happen to Angie. And yet she had no reason to believe this woman would help her.

"Jesus," Lucy said. "Can I at least put some clothes on?" She pointed to her robe on the bathroom door.

Darcy took a step back, her arms rigid, her gun still trained on Lucy. "Go ahead," she told her. "Slowly."

Keeping her back to the woman, Lucy walked carefully across the room, took the robe from its hook, and slid her arms into the sleeves. She took a deep breath and closed her eyes. Just one smooth motion, she told herself, steadying her hands. She pulled the sash around her waist and tied it, then slid the gun from her pocket and turned to face Darcy.

"Did you kill him?" she demanded, slamming the Glock up to eye level, sighting down the barrel to the other woman's chest.

Darcy didn't flinch.

"My husband," Lucy added, though she doubted this woman had anything to do with Carl's death. If she had, Lucy figured, she would have finished her off by now as well. Besides, she seemed oddly ill-informed. "Did you kill him?"

"No." Darcy shook her head. Her arms were starting to ache, and her hands were sweaty on the stock of the little Colt.

"Who sent you?" Lucy asked.

"You said you knew where the files were."

"I told you. Craig Weldon's got them."

"Where?"

"My best guess? The second floor of the Bioflux building. Now, who sent you?"

Darcy shifted her fingers slightly, trying to hold off a cramp. "Warden Billings," she said.

"Who?" It was Lucy's turn to be confused.

"Roy Billings. He's the warden down at Canyon."

"You mean the women's prison in Ophir?"

Darcy nodded.

"What the hell does he care about neural tube defects?" Lucy wondered aloud.

"What's a tube defect?" Darcy asked.

Lucy took a step forward. "What are you looking for?"

Silent, Darcy held her ground.

"In the files," Lucy prompted, moving closer still. "What are you supposed to find?" Two eyes stared out at her from behind the dark mask, the lids blinking away sweat. No, Lucy thought, if this woman meant to hurt her she would have done it long ago. "I can help you," she said. Carefully engaging the Glock's safety, she took a chance and lowered the handgun to her side. "I will. But first you have to tell me what you're looking for."

What seemed like a full minute passed. Lucy could hear each hot breath the other woman took. A breeze kicked up and the bamboo wind chimes that hung by the front door of Lucy's studio rattled, the sound as hollow and sepulchral as bone knocking against bone. A full minute, maybe even more, and just as Lucy was about to lose faith, she saw the woman's shoulder relax slightly.

"Why?" Darcy asked.

"Why what?"

"Why help me?"

Lucy took her time, thinking carefully about how best to answer. "Because I want to get a look at what's in those files too."

Darcy nodded reluctantly. "TB tests," she said. "Anything from the Pioneer Correctional Center. That's what I'm looking for." Slowly, carefully, she lowered the gun, then reached up and pushed the mask back off her face.

"TB as in tuberculosis?"

"As far as I know, yes."

Lucy pondered the woman a moment. She looked to be about Lucy's age, her features tough and tomboyish. What, she wondered, did tuberculosis and neural tube defects have in common? The answer was somewhere in her husband's files. "What's your name?" Lucy asked.

"Darcy."

"Well, Darcy, exactly how good a burglar are you?"

Darcy shrugged. "There aren't many buildings I can't get into."

"I tell you what: If you can get us into the Bioflux building, I can get us to those files."

"And anything on TB testing at Pioneer is mine."

"Scout's honor," Lucy said.

They stood there a moment, still keeping their distance, neither woman trusting the other, each hoping not to regret the deal they'd just made.

"Let me get this straight." Kevin speared a piece of pancake with his fork and waved it as if for emphasis. "This woman breaks into your house and puts a gun to your head, but it's okay."

"Let's just say we worked out our differences," Lucy told him.

They were at the Perkins in Brighton, across the street from the Mountain Aire. Lucy had called Kevin around six to say she was on her way.

"We talked," Lucy said. Puncturing the top of her fried egg, she dipped a corner of her toast into the soft yolk.

"About what?"

The waitress came by, refilled their coffees, and hustled off to the kitchen.

"You know, when Craig Weldon and that goon came by the house yesterday, I pretty much figured this had to do with business. Even the kind of work Carl did at the company was super-competitive. A new asthma treatment could be worth millions to Bioflux. And that's small potatoes compared to an AIDS drug."

"You think there's another biotechnology firm involved in this?"

Lucy took a sip of her coffee. "That's what I thought at first. Maybe Carl hit on something really hot before he died, and whoever broke in the night before last was working for another company."

"It makes more sense than anything else."

Lucy shook her head. "I don't think so anymore. It was the same woman again last night. I ran her off the first time, before she had a chance to find what she was looking for."

"Let me guess," Kevin said. "Whatever Carl happened to collect on neural tube defects."

"Nope. She's looking for anything having to do with tuberculosis testing at the Pioneer Correctional Center."

"Another one of Carl's hobbies?"

"Not that I know of. But here's where things really start to get strange. Guess who she's working for?"

Kevin shrugged.

"There's a women's prison down in Ophir, a place called Canyon. She's working for the warden."

Kevin stared at her across the table. "Any idea why?"

"No clue, but I'm meeting her tonight. Maybe I can find out."

"What do you mean, you're meeting her tonight?"

Lucy hesitated a moment, wondering exactly how much to tell Kevin. He wouldn't like what she had to say. "We're going into the Bioflux building."

Kevin laughed. "No, you're not."

"I'm not kidding," Lucy told him. "What happened to Carl wasn't an accident, and I want to know why. I need to know what was in those files Craig Weldon took, and this woman can get me inside."

"You're not doing this," Kevin said, though he knew nothing short of physical restraints would keep Lucy from doing whatever she wanted.

"Yes, I am," she told him.

"We don't even know who this woman is."

"Yeah, well, it's not like we're hiring her as a nanny. All I need to know is that she can get me in and out of that building. I think she can."

Kevin started to protest, but didn't. He told himself he'd try again later.

They finished their breakfasts in silence. When Lucy was done, she pushed her plate aside and looked up at him. "I was thinking we could head out to Golden now," she said, "pay a visit to Viviane Beckwith, and see if she can shed some light on the original Bioflux board."

Kevin took a last swig of coffee and signaled for the check. "I need to stop at my room first. There's a phone call I want to make."

They paid at the cash register and walked across the street to the Mountain Aire.

"This'll just take a second," Kevin said when they were inside. Lucy sat down on the bed while he flipped his cell phone open and punched in Max Fausto's number.

Max Fausto wasn't a person so much as a legend, a superhero of information gathering. Kevin had gotten Fausto's number his first year at the network from an aged colleague he'd fortuitously taken to having drinks with after work. The man was retiring, and for some reason probably having to do more with the quantity of scotch Kevin could consume than the quality of his work, the older man chose him to be the recipient of his one best secret.

Though Kevin didn't like to admit it, the gift had made his career. Fausto's services didn't come cheap, but, as the lucky handful of journalists who used him knew full well, he was worth every penny. No one knew how Fausto did what he did, and no one wanted to know, but it was taken for granted that not all his methods were on the up-and-up.

The phone rang several times on the other end, then a groggy voice picked up. "Yup."

"Max? It's Kevin Burns."

Fausto chuckled, a sort of low gravelly wheeze. "I heard you and MSNBC went your separate ways."

"No shit, Sherlock."

"I thought they taught ethics in journalism school. Did you just sit out that class?"

"I'm gonna pretend you didn't say that," Kevin told him. "Especially since you were the one who hooked me up with that moron in Nogales."

"Hey," Fausto growled. "Buyer beware."

"Listen. I need a favor, and the way I see it you owe me one."

"I don't owe you shit, but since your employment problems are partly a result of my information, and since you're such a good customer, I might be able to look at this as a goodwill gesture."

"I need you to find someone for me."

"Name?"

"Canty. Herman Canty."

"That C or K?"

"C. C-A-N-T-Y."

"Herman," Fausto mused. "He must have taken a lot of shit as a kid. What else you got?"

"I'd guess he spent part of his life in the Denver area; he was on the board of a company called Bioflux in the early seventies. He's got to be sixty-five at least, probably older."

"No birthday?"

"Sorry, man."

Fausto sighed. "I'm not even going to ask for a social security number."

"Shit, if I knew all that I wouldn't be calling you."

"You got a number where I can reach you?"

Kevin rattled off the cell phone number.

"Ta-ta," Fausto rasped as he hung up.

A monument to just how much could be accomplished when one had the money to spare, Viviane Beckwith's house sat perched high in the arid foothills west of Golden. The house was a miracle of modern engineering, sharp angles of wood and glass and natural stone. An entire wing had been built on thin air, cantilevered out over the dry scrub pines and sunbaked boulders of the canyon below.

Viviane was proud of her house. When she and David had it built some twenty-five years earlier, they'd been alone on the hillside. The cost and complication of piping water in had been high enough to discourage neighbors, and the Beckwiths had cherished their solitude. But sometime in the mid-nineties, when the high-tech economy swept into Denver and Boulder, realtors' signs had cropped up in the foothills, as ugly and invasive as non-native weeds.

From the two-story windows in the great room, Viviane could now see at least a dozen other homes, the garish and tasteless creations of twenty-something software designers. Short of hiring eco-terrorists, there was nothing she could do to prevent their construction.

There was a new behemoth going in on the ridge just below her, a marvel of excess and pretension. And worst of all, Viviane would now be forced to share her road. She'd spent the first part of the morning watching the new owner, a goateed twit who'd introduced himself to her as Jason, going over the project with his contractor. Everything about her new neighbor enraged Viviane: the bleached hair, the hipster eyewear, the slightly condescending way in which he said her name, as if he were talking to a senile grandmother.

One well-placed pack of explosives, Viviane thought to herself, as she watched Jason gesticulating to the builder. He shook the older man's hand, got in his Range Rover, and headed down the hill. It wasn't the safest road, and Viviane harbored a secret hope that someday the massive SUV might flip on a corner. But Jason sped safely through the first turn and the second. He reached the bottom of the hill, passed a cream-colored Mercedes that was going in the opposite direction, and disappeared into a stand of trees.

The Mercedes climbed up past the construction site and kept coming. Viviane wasn't expecting anyone, and the car didn't look familiar. They could be lost, she thought to herself as the Mercedes pulled into her driveway. The front doors popped open and a man and a woman got out. Viviane watched their heads disappear beneath the porch roof. A few seconds later the doorbell rang.

Standing in the great room of Viviane Beckwith's house, with the vast sweep of the Colorado foothills spread out beneath her, Lucy was beginning to get vertigo. She felt as if she'd been kidnapped by some large bird and flown to a rocky aerie. When she took a step toward Viviane and the window, her stomach lurched.

"Mrs. Beckwith," she said, "I'm Lucy Greene. I'm sure we've met at some Bioflux function or other." She motioned to Kevin. "And this is Kevin Burns, a journalist friend of mine. He's doing a story on the old days of biotechnology, on some of the industry's pioneers. We were wondering if you might answer some questions?"

Viviane nodded. "Of course, dears, though I don't know if I'll be of any help. May I bring either of you something? Coffee? Tea? Mineral water?"

Lucy shook her head.

"Mr. Burns?"

"No, thanks."

Viviane smiled tersely, as if she'd just taken a bite of something disagreeable. She crossed the room toward the fireplace and a group of heavy mission-style armchairs. "Shall we sit down?"

Lucy watched the older woman settle into one of the chairs. She was at least seventy, but an extremely graceful seventy, perfectly preserved. She had on a black linen shift and simple silver jewelry. A silver and turquoise barrette held her gray hair in a tidy knot. She had been beautiful in her youth, and she was beautiful still.

"Now, what exactly did you want to know?" she asked when Lucy and Kevin had joined her.

"I understand your husband was with Bioflux for quite some time," Kevin said.

Viviane nodded. "Yes. We've been with the company since 1970."

"Was Mr. Beckwith on the original board?"

The woman shifted uneasily in her chair. "Yes," she said, pursing her lips. "Yes, he was."

"Mrs. Beckwith," Kevin continued, "we're trying to find out who the other board members might have been." He smiled, a smile he'd used hundreds of times. Trust me, he hoped it said, I'm your kid brother, your son, your grandson. "We know Herman Canty may have been one of the board members."

Viviane turned to Lucy. "It was your husband who died so recently," she said kindly, ignoring Kevin.

"Yes," Lucy said.

"I'm sorry, dear. It's hard, I know. It'll be almost ten years now that my David has been gone." She shifted her gaze to the tall front window, to the cloudless sky and the heat-raked plains below. "I wish I could help you, I really do, but I didn't know anything about David's business." She looked back at Lucy conspiratorially. "I think you know what I mean, dear."

"Anything at all would be helpful," Kevin told her. "People you socialized with, names your husband mentioned."

Viviane smiled. "I do wish I could help you. It was so long ago. And my memory's not what it used to be."

There was something infinitely implacable about the older woman, something in her smile that told Lucy they could spend all day with her and never learn anything more.

"And Herman?" Kevin prodded. "Do you happen to know where he is now?"

"Let's see. . . . He left Denver some time ago. I suppose he's off fishing somewhere. Herman certainly did like to fish." She looked down at her hands in her lap and fidgeted with the fabric of her dress. "I'm sorry, dears. Like I said, I don't know much."

There was a moment of awkward silence; then Lucy stood. "We'll let you get back to your day, now. Do you mind if I use your bathroom before we go?"

"Of course not." Viviane rose and walked them down the stairs. "The powder room's through there," she said when they reached the main floor hallway. She motioned to a door just behind the stairs and turned for the front foyer with Kevin in tow.

Powder room, Lucy thought, as she stepped into the small space and closed the door behind her. What a ridiculous name. Great care had been taken in decorating the little bathroom. It was a masculine space, bold and rocky, like the rest of the house and the hillside it sat on. Next to the sink, above the designer towel rack, was a black-and-white photograph.

It was a group photo, about three dozen young men arranged in rows by height. The ones in the very front were kneeling. Each man sported the same military haircut. Each wore a white lab coat. It was a stiff picture, but they didn't look unhappy, just serious, workmanlike. It was hard to say for sure when it might have been taken: in the fifties, maybe the sixties. There seemed to be no landscape surrounding the men, no trees or mountains, just a flat dusty background and, in the corner of the picture, part of a large, dark, spherical object.

Lucy looked over the boyish faces again, their earnest expressions, wondering if David Beckwith was somewhere in that sea of white coats.

From her perch by the window, Viviane watched the Mercedes pull out of the driveway and start down the road. She hated to admit it, but she had liked the woman. She was smarter than the other wives at Bioflux. Prettier, too, and without all the props. Dangerous, Viviane thought. The Mercedes careened down the hill, kicking up dust and gravel.

Kevin Burns. She repeated the journalist's name to herself, trying to spark a connection in her brain. He was a TV reporter, she was sure of that, but she couldn't quite come up with his network. She was relatively sure they'd bought the doddering-old-woman routine. But still, Viviane hadn't liked their questions.

A backhoe thrummed to life at the construction site, its one bucketlike claw scrabbling at the upslope behind the skeletal house. The swimming pool, Viviane fumed, imagining bikini-clad trillionaires sipping designer margaritas on a hand-fired Portuguese-tile deck.

Turning from the window, she picked up the phone and punched in eleven digits she knew by heart. The phone rang several times on the other end before a familiar voice answered.

"It's Viviane," she said. "I thought you should know: Carl Greene's wife was just here asking questions. She wanted to know about the original Bioflux board."

"And what did you tell her?"

"I played dumb."

"Anything else?"

"There was a man with her. A news reporter named Kevin Burns."

"You think she was telling us the truth?" Lucy asked, punching the gearshift, accelerating up the on-ramp onto the interstate. She glanced over at Kevin and saw him shake his head. "You think your friend will find Herman Canty?"

Kevin shrugged. "If anyone can, he can." He leaned back into the leather seat and contemplated the Denver skyline, the glass and granite towers flashing and winking in the harsh sunlight.

"Luce," he said, "maybe you should just let this go. I've got a bad feeling. Things could get ugly."

Lucy darted around another car and into the fast lane.

"Maybe it wasn't an accident," he told her. "Maybe it was. Either way, you can't change what happened."

No, Lucy thought, I can't. But she couldn't help remembering that last night with Carl, how she'd lain awake in the dark, her every cell wanting to move toward him. And yet she hadn't. She had let him down. She didn't think she'd be able to live with herself if she deserted him again.

Chapter nine

It was a good ninety miles from Denver to Ophir, but it was mostly interstate, flat and open, and with Lucy driving they made the trip in just over an hour. It was not yet noon when Lucy and Kevin pulled into the parking lot of the *Ophir Gazette*. They were working on a long shot and they both knew it, but they had little else to go on. Kevin knew how small-town newspapers were; if anything funny had happened at the Pioneer facility, anything at all, common sense told him it would have been news.

"Any idea what years we're looking at?" Kevin asked as they walked through the door of the red-brick building.

"She just said TB tests. But I'm pretty sure Pioneer wasn't built until the early eighties."

"Twenty years is still a lot of newspapers to go through." Kevin stopped in the entryway and looked at Lucy. "What's the warden's name?"

"Browning? Bunting? I don't remember. Something like that."

Sliding his phone from his pocket, Kevin punched in the numbers for information. "Ophir," he told the mechanical voice that asked him to specify a city, then, "Canyon Women's Correctional Facility." Kevin waited for the number, then hung up, reconnected, and dialed.

"Canyon Women's Facility," a woman answered.

Kevin put on his most professional voice. "This is Kevin Burns from MSNBC," he said, hoping that if his name did ring a bell it was a good one. His dismissal had been briefly in the news, but it was long enough ago for the memory of his name to have faded. Besides, it was the kind of story that only people in the business, or people who knew Kevin, had paid much attention to. "I'm doing some fact checking for a story," he went on. "Can you tell me your warden's name?"

She seemed disappointed by the simplicity of his request. "Warden Billings," she said, "Roy Billings."

"I'm sorry to keep bothering you, but what year did he become warden?"

"Nineteen-ninety, I believe. That's the year before I started here."

"And he came straight from Pioneer?"

"Yes, sir. I think so."

"Thank you. You've been a big help. Just one last thing. Do you have the number for the office at Pioneer?"

The woman recited the number and Kevin thanked her, then disconnected.

He rattled off his same fact-checking spiel to the man who answered at Pioneer. "When exactly was Roy Billings warden of your facility?"

"I'll have to check," the man said.

The line went silent while Kevin was put on hold. Finally: "Sir? Are you still there?"

"Yes," Kevin answered.

"Warden Billings was here from September of 1986 to March of 1990."

"Thanks." Kevin flipped his phone closed and tucked it back into his pocket. "Fall of 'eighty-six to spring of 'ninety," he told Lucy.

"Jim! Jimmmmmeeee!" The woman at the reception desk craned her head over her shoulder and howled to the open newsroom behind her, then turned back to Lucy and Kevin. "He'll be right with you."

There was movement at a desk by the far wall. A pimple-faced kid stood up from behind a mammoth computer screen and hurried forward.

"These people want to see the archives," the receptionist told him; then, to Kevin and Lucy, "Folks, this is Jim, our intern from the high school. He'll take you downstairs."

Jim looked over at Kevin and blinked. "Follow me," he said. Motioning for them to step behind the desk, he headed toward a door at the far side of the newsroom and down a flight of stairs.

"We've been online since 'ninety-seven," their escort explained, leading them down a dimly lit corridor and through a door marked ARCHIVES. He switched on a bare overhead bulb and directed Lucy and Kevin to a row of dusty shelves. "But anything before that is still paper." He slapped a volume of bound newsprint. "'Eighty-six starts here. Good luck, and don't forget to turn out the lights when you're done."

He started out the door, then stopped short and turned back to Kevin. "What was it like over there? I mean, it must have been intense as shit, the real deal."

Kevin assumed he was talking about the Balkans. The war had been Kevin's first big story. He'd been briefly "kidnapped" by Serb soldiers, and film of him being hustled into Serb headquarters at gunpoint had been shown again and again to riveted viewers in America, who were suddenly interested when one of their own was threatened by the distant war. In truth, the hardest thing he'd had to endure was a few glasses of bad Serbian brandy.

"Yeah," he agreed guiltily, "it was intense."

The kid paused for a moment, his face turning gravely serious. "They screwed you on the immigration story," he said. "I know they did. You never would have made it up. You're too good a journalist for that." He disappeared down the hall before Kevin could think to tell him otherwise.

Kevin watched him go, then turned to Lucy. "How do you want to do this?"

"Why don't you start with 'eighty-six, and I'll work my way back from 'ninety."

Nodding, Kevin set to work on the old papers. There was a front-page story about Pioneer's new warden in the September eighteenth *Gazette*, a glowing review of Roy Billings's life and work. Not surprisingly, he was a devoted family man. He'd had a long career in the prison business and, before that, an army career. Judging from the three or four chins Billings showed in his photograph, Kevin figured it had been some time since the warden had done his calisthenics.

There was nothing unexpected in the article. Like all upper-level managers, the warden vowed to "streamline the system" and "make some much-needed changes." He talked about how happy he was to be in Ophir, how he and his wife would be the newest members of the Redemption Christian Church. Kevin scribbled a few notes and moved on through the rest of the fall of 1986 and into winter.

Ophir was an uneventful little town. Crime seemed to be remarkably uncommon; Kevin couldn't help but wonder if the looming prison complex had an influence on would-be lawbreakers. Guns were cheap and plentiful. Post-hunting-season sales at local sporting goods stores advertised everything from Winchester varmint rifles to Glocks. There was the occasional domestic dispute, and an ongoing debate about whether or not the city needed a traffic light at the corner of Fifth and Olive.

Kevin had gotten about half as much sleep as he needed the

night before, and he struggled to stay awake. The basement was cool and quiet, the only noise the sound of Lucy ruffling through dusty newsprint.

"You finding anything?" he asked as he skimmed the last day of November 1987.

"I found a good deal on compost at the Farmers' Supply. How about you?"

Kevin laughed. "You're doing better than I am."

Lucy was quiet for a moment, then Kevin heard her voice from the other side of the shelves. "What *was* it like?"

"In the Balkans?"

"Yeah."

"To tell you the truth, we spent most of our time in the press hotel, scared shitless and drinking Hungarian champagne. You ever drink Hungarian champagne?"

"No."

"It's like carbonated paint thinner." Kevin leaned back against the wall and thought about the grueling boredom of covering the war, the long stretches of monotony punctuated by sudden flashes of fear and his own inescapable cowardice. He didn't tell Lucy the things he remembered most, like the time he and his cameraman watched while two soldiers beat an old man to death, how they stood there, pissing themselves with fear, and did nothing. Or how surprised he was at the effortlessness with which he let go the barbarity of the day, how soundly he slept at night.

"And the thing in Nogales?" Lucy asked. From some other part of the basement came the sound of the central air cycling on.

Kevin looked down at his newsprint-stained fingers. "I don't know." What he wanted to say was that Nogales, like all the stories he'd covered, had more to do with vanity than anything else. "There was a story there," he told her instead. "I just couldn't get to it."

In late afternoon, Lucy's and Kevin's paths collided in midsummer of 1988. Aside from the original article welcoming Roy Billings to Pioneer and a brief mention of his transfer to the women's facility at Canyon, there had been nothing of note in the four years of *Ophir Gazettes*.

Lucy's hands were black and dusty, her legs stiff from the cold concrete floor. She reshelved the last volume of newsprint and stood, wiping her palms on her jeans. "You ready to call it a day?"

Nodding, Kevin hoisted himself off the floor.

Darcy hosed down the last stall in the men's shower room, locked her cart away in the utility closet, slipped out of her coveralls, and went inside to the office to clock out. She knew how hard any job was to come by with a record like hers, but she still hated everything about the Lazy J. She hated the piss and chemical smell of the men's room, the nests of hair in the shower drains, the fat secretary in the office who kept her purse locked in the back of the filing cabinet. She could feel the woman's eyes on her now, indignant and afraid, as Darcy pulled the little lever on the time clock, put her card back in its slot, and headed for the door.

It was muggy outside, the heat of the day softening slightly as afternoon gave way to early evening. A semi shuddered up the entrance ramp and onto the interstate, picking up speed as it joined the river of cars and other trucks plunging south. Darcy slid in behind the wheel of her Dart, started the engine, and crept forward to the lip of the parking lot. Easing her foot down on the gas, she headed east into Castle Rock. She stopped at the King Soopers, got a couple of frozen dinners and a six-pack of root beer, and drove to her apartment. It was six when she walked in the door, one long hour until her sister would call, time for a shower and something to eat.

Neither Lucy nor Kevin spoke much on the drive back from Ophir. They were both tired, worn down from the day's disappointments: both the fruitless trip to Golden and the wasted hours at the *Gazette*.

"Listen," Kevin said when they pulled up in front of his room at the Mountain Aire, "I know I can't talk you out of going after those files, but I can't let you do something this crazy alone. I'm coming with you."

Lucy shook her head. "Two of us is already a crowd. Besides, I don't want to scare her off."

"You're not going without me," Kevin insisted.

"No way. Two of us going in may be crazy, but three is just plain stupid. Besides, if we get caught, if something goes wrong, I'm going to need your help. I'll call as soon as I get home."

Kevin unbuckled his seat belt. "I don't like this," he said, climbing out of the car. "I don't like this at all."

"You don't have to," Lucy told him.

She put her foot on the accelerator and felt the engine open up as she cruised out of Brighton and on toward Fort Lupton and the old weigh station outside of Ione. She took the northern exit into Pryor and made a loop through town, past the volunteer fire department and the little video store and their old house. Chick's Fairlane was out front, and she thought about stopping. She hadn't even called last night to let him know she was okay, and no doubt he was worried. But she was tired, and she knew there'd be an argument if she did stop. Chick wouldn't want her alone tonight, either, and she just didn't have the strength to fight him on it.

Tomorrow, she told herself, she'd stop at the plant and see him, but right now she needed sleep, rest, and sustenance for the night ahead.

Angie had sounded good on the phone, so good, in fact, that Darcy had begun to worry. Her little sister's voice had the refreshed, slightly manic quality of a junkie who's just gotten a fix. And if Angie was scoring a high in Canyon, Darcy knew someone in Canyon was scoring something off Angie. It was a bad train of thought. Darcy tried to clear her mind and focus on the task at hand.

Through the front window of the Dart, she could see the Bioflux bulding in all its corporate grandeur, a boxy structure with three floors of windows. The building was mostly dark, the in-ground sprinklers hissing into the bushes around the front walkway. There was an unnerving number of cars in the parking lot and a white van labeled SPIC & STAN CLEANING. Except for a man she'd seen come out from the back entrance to the building, get into a gray sedan, and drive away, Bioflux offered few signs of life.

A Mercedes pulled into the parking lot of the all-night Taco Bell where Darcy was parked. It was Lucy, and she was early. She rolled forward into the space next to Darcy's and cut the engine. Stupid, Darcy thought, as she watched the woman climb out and walk around to the passenger door of the Dart. This had to be the stupidest thing she'd ever done. Though if they got caught, she'd be sent back to Canyon where at least she'd be close to Angie. Reluctantly, she reached across the seat and unlocked the door.

Lucy slid into the passenger seat. She was wearing darks like Darcy had told her to, black jeans and a black sweatshirt. "How long have you been here?" she asked.

"A couple hours. I like to get my bearings. There are an awful lot of cars."

"I know they keep research animals on the fourth floor. They must have people here around the clock taking care of them. I can't imagine any of the regular staff would be here this late. Even at his busiest, Carl was always home before midnight."

Darcy looked over at the building. Above the third floor was the windowless fourth story. She didn't need to ask what the animals were for. "I saw someone leave about a half hour ago."

"What about the Spic and Stan crew?"

Darcy looked at her watch. It was almost two-forty-five. "Let's try to wait till they clear out. I'd rather go in after they're gone."

"Sounds good," Lucy agreed.

"There's a back door, right?" Darcy asked, confirming the information Lucy had given her when they'd made a rough plan the night before.

Lucy nodded, trying to remember what she could about the floor plan from the handful of visits she'd made to Carl's office. She didn't tell Darcy that she hadn't actually been inside for several years. For all she knew, they were going in blind. "It's got one of those bars that you push on to open it," she said, fairly sure of this recollection. "There's a sign, you know, it says something like 'warning, alarm will sound.'"

"You said your husband's office was on the second floor, right?"

"Uh-huh. I'm pretty sure there's a stairwell that starts up from the door we'll be using."

Darcy shot her a look of concern. "What do you mean, pretty sure?"

"There's a stairwell, okay?" Lucy insisted. "I'm sure there's a stairwell."

Stupid, Darcy thought again, wishing she hadn't come. She picked up her binoculars and scanned the windows of the building, looking for movement.

"So how much does Warden Billings pay for a job like this?" Lucy asked.

"Nothing."

"What does that mean?"

"It means I've got other reasons for doing it." Darcy set the binoculars on the dashboard. "It means it's none of your fucking business."

"I take it you didn't make each other's aquaintance at the PTA."

Darcy didn't say anything.

"What was it that landed you in Canyon in the first place?" Lucy asked.

"What do you think?"

"I thought you were good at this."

"I am."

"So why are you working for Roy Billings?"

The front doors of the Bioflux building opened and a man in a blue uniform, evidently a security guard, stepped outside. Chatting animatedly, the cleaning crew streamed out behind him.

"You got a sister?" Darcy asked, watching the cleaners climb into their van.

"Brother," Lucy said. "Why?"

"I've got a kid sister in Canyon. I do this for the warden and he keeps an eye out for her."

"I'm sorry," Lucy offered.

"Not as sorry as I am."

The van turned out of the parking lot and the security guard disappeared back inside. Darcy looked over at Lucy. "You sure you can handle this?"

Kevin sat up, dazed and half asleep, trying to decipher his surroundings. A thin beam of light blazed in through a gap in the curtains. He could make out a small desk and a TV. The bed was too big for home, the sheets too fresh and crisp. Somewhere in the darkness, a phone was ringing. He had the fleeting, joyous delusion that he was in one of the oceanfront rooms at the Colony in Miami Beach and the light coming in through the curtains was the moon over the Atlantic. Then his mind snapped to life and he awakened to the disappointing reality of the Mountain Aire.

Flipping the bedside lamp on, Kevin leapt up and fumbled for his cell phone. "Lucy?"

"I've got your man," the voice on the other end of the line muttered. It was Max Fausto. "You ready, amigo?"

Kevin grabbed a pencil and a scrap of paper. "Go ahead."

"Three-two-one-zero-zero Absaroka Road, Homer, Montana. Herman's still alive and kicking, though from what my sources say, barely."

"Thanks, buddy."

"Listen, no calls for a while, okay?" Max lowered his voice a notch. There was a tremble in it Kevin had never heard before. "This is bad shit. Deep and high. You're gonna make some powerful enemies if you're not careful."

Kevin opened his mouth to speak, but Fausto had already hung up.

Christ, Kevin thought, feeling a prickle along the back of his neck, an electric combination of dread and excitement, Fausto had been afraid. Max Fausto, a man who'd once found him a Mafia hit man deep in witness protection, who, for the right price, seemed to know the whereabouts of every single person with an INTERPOL file, had been scared by something he found. Kevin walked to the window and peered out through the gap in the blinds. The motel's parking lot was quiet. His own rental car sat silently in its space outside the door to his room. Across the street, a few heads bobbed in the windows of the Perkins. Nothing was out of the ordinary, but Kevin still felt naked and vulnerable in his boxer shorts and T-shirt.

A real story, he told himself, pulling the curtains tight. He sat down at the desk and turned his laptop on. His hands were shaking as he dialed up an Internet connection and then typed in the address for his favorite map site. *Important,* he heard Carl Greene say. He felt wired, alive in a way he couldn't remember feeling since college, those late and lingering nights at the Hungarian Pastry Shop on Amsterdam Avenue, the low-ceilinged coffee shop electric with earnest conversation.

Graphics flashed onto the laptop's screen, and Kevin entered Herman Canty's information into the site's search engine. A few seconds later a map appeared. Absaroka Road snaked across the screen, the red dot that marked Canty's house the only visible landmark. Kevin clicked his mouse, zooming out, and the town of Homer came into view, one main street and a smattering of ranch roads twisting off into the empty countryside.

It's the middle of nowhere, Kevin thought, zooming farther out, till the towns on the screen became somewhat familiar. Gardiner and Livingston, the edge of Yellowstone Park, and, to the northwest, Bozeman.

Darcy crouched down next to Lucy and set her bag on the cement walkway that led to the back door of the building. The door was set back into the exterior wall, forming a fortuitous box of darkness into which the two women had wedged themselves.

"Any other doors back here?" Darcy asked.

Lucy shook her head.

"All right then." Opening her bag, Darcy handed Lucy a small flashlight. "Hold this," she instructed, taking out her tension tools. "Keep the light on my hands."

"What about the alarm?" Lucy asked.

"It's not on."

"What do you mean, it's not on?"

"I told you, when I was waiting for you I saw someone leave the building. He came from the back, which means he must have come through this door. The alarm's not on."

"That's weird."

"Not really." Darcy pondered the lock for a moment, then set to work. "I'd say three quarters of the time these alarms aren't on. Employees cut them mostly, people who want to be able to sneak out for a smoke or play hooky."

Lucy held the flashlight steady, watching Darcy's hands. She was graceful and delicate with her tools, her fingers moving with gentle precision. "How does it work?" Lucy asked.

"Lots of practice and patience," Darcy said, nodding toward the thin curl of metal that served as an exterior handle. "I want you to pull that for me when I say go."

Lucy put her free hand on the metal lip and waited. Her black clothes were far too heavy for the August night, and she was uncomfortably warm. A trickle of sweat rolled down the length of her spine.

"Go," Darcy said finally, flicking her wrist. Lucy pulled and the door swung open, revealing the building's back stairwell and a gaping hallway beyond.

Darcy took the flashlight from Lucy as they stepped inside. "Someone saved us a lot of work," she said, turning and directing the beam toward the top of the doorway. The flashlight wavered over a tangle of severed wires. "And recently too, I'd bet." Except for a small area around the clipped wires, the wall above the door frame was caked with dust and cobwebs. She flicked the light off and looked over at Lucy. "Where to now?"

The truth was that Lucy didn't know exactly where they were headed. But she was betting the files Craig Weldon and his unlikable companion had taken from Carl's office were somewhere in the Bioflux building. "Upstairs," she said. She had never been to Weldon's office, but she knew most of the researchers were on the second floor. She started up the stairwell with Darcy behind her.

Old habits die hard, and one of the obsessions Darcy had acquired as a result of her years breaking and entering was a preoccupation with exterior and interior dimensions. Over the course of time she'd learned a lot about acquisition, about the ingrained human impulse to keep cherished belongings close at hand. After all, what good is the ten-thousand-dollar diamond necklace if you can't show it off to friends? Most of the homes Darcy worked on had contained some version of the traveler's money belt, a readily accessible hidey-hole in which they could secure items of value.

Space can be dauntingly deceptive. Any amateur decorator knows the tricks that make a small room look larger. But Darcy had learned some tricks of her own, private rules for judging distance, for finding the sealed-up closet, the fake wall, the hidden crawl space. As she followed Lucy down the second floor hallway of the Bioflux building, she had a strong suspicion the architecture was concealing something.

The building's interior floor plan was simple: A ring of windowed offices, connected by a common corridor, hugged all four outside walls. The inside of the same hallway was lined with larger rooms, usually labs, most of which had windowed doors or banks of windows opening onto the corridor. From what Darcy could see, the space these labs and offices occupied didn't come close to matching the outside dimensions of the building. Something was missing from the inside of the structure, something like a very large airshaft. Only if there had been an airshaft, Darcy would have expected to see windows looking out onto it, or, at the very least, vents.

"Are all the floors laid out like this?" Darcy asked. They had just turned a corner and were starting along the front of the building.

"I guess," Lucy said distractedly, her eyes scanning the name plate on the door to each office. "I never really thought about it. But, yeah, I think so."

"And the fourth floor?"

"I've never been up there. It's pretty much off limits because of the animals." Lucy stopped walking, her gaze fixed on the office door in front of her.

"Is this it?" Darcy asked.

Lucy shook her head. "It was Carl's office," she explained. A newly affixed name plate read JANE APPLETON.

From down the hall came the sound of a toilet flushing. Both women froze. There was the rush of water in the pipes, a door creaked open, and a figure stepped into the hall. Putting her arm across Lucy's chest, Darcy flattened them both against the wall. The bathroom door swung closed and the figure paused for a split second, as if deciding which way to turn. Darcy took a shallow breath and held it. Finally, the person pivoted away from them, the footsteps growing fainter as whoever it was disappeared around the far corner of the corridor. The steps stopped; a door snapped open and closed. Darcy exhaled, counting a full thirty seconds before she and Lucy moved away from the wall and started back down the hall.

They finally found Craig Weldon's office near the end of the corridor, just a few doors down from the bathroom. His light was on, a dull glow visible through the frosted glass of the transom. Darcy put her fingers to her lips and motioned for Lucy to step behind her. She dropped down on one knee and carefully put her ear to the door. After several minutes of dead silence convinced her there was no one inside, Darcy started to work on the lock.

"Same thing here," she whispered, as Lucy held the flashlight for her. "You'll go on my signal."

Lucy nodded, put one hand on the doorknob, and waited. It took Darcy longer to pick this lock. Lucy had almost given up when the other woman hissed, "Go!"

She twisted the knob to one side, and the door swung open to reveal Craig Weldon, still at his desk. He was sitting upright, his head thrown back and his mouth wide open, as if he'd fallen asleep in his chair.

Lucy let out a low, hoarse grunt and stepped back into the hall, groping instinctively for her gun. Weldon wasn't asleep. His arms dangled at his side, and his right hand, just peeking out from the side of the desk, held a small silver revolver. There was a hole in his right temple, a wet red gash as big around as a quarter. A thin trickle of blood had snaked over his shoulder, down his arm, and over his index finger and the gun, forming a scarlet pool on the floor.

"Jesus," Lucy whispered. "He shot himself."

Darcy stepped into the office and closer to Weldon.

Chapter ten

"He hasn't been dead long," Darcy said, bending to examine Weldon's head. The wound was fresh, the blood just beginning to darken.

"I don't get it. The cleaners were here, plus we've got someone working down the hall. How come no one heard anything?" Lucy stepped into the office and carefully pulled the door closed behind her. She knew the answer as soon as the words were out of her mouth. The noise of a vacuum or a floor polisher would have easily covered up the pop of the little pistol.

The office stank of urine and feces and blood. Lucy put her hand to her mouth and fought the tide of nausea that swept through her body. She caught a glimpse of her reflection in the window, a pale face with a suburban-housewife haircut and dark clothes. What exactly did she think she was doing, prowling around the Bioflux building in the middle of the night with an ex-con and, now, a corpse?

Darcy had already jimmied the lock on one of Weldon's filing cabinets and was rummaging through the files. "Any idea what mycoplasma is?" she asked, sliding the topmost drawer closed and moving on to the one below it.

"No." Stepping around Weldon, Lucy peered over Darcy's shoulder. The word was vaguely familiar, too vague for Lucy to place. She must have heard Carl mention it, she thought to herself.

"It looks like that was his specialty." Darcy ran her thumb across the plastic tabs that marked Weldon's files. "Mycoplasma fermentatis. Mycoplasma incognito." She read the file designations aloud. "Incognito with HIV env. Whatever that means."

Lucy pulled one of the files out at random and skimmed through it. There was little she could glean from the scientific text.

Darcy nudged her. "Why don't you check those?" she said, pointing across the office to a couple of cardboard boxes. "I was ready to get out of here five minutes ago."

The boxes were a dud. When Lucy lifted the lids all she found inside was clean white printer paper. "I don't think Carl's stuff is here," she said reluctantly, scanning the office for anything she might have missed.

Darcy closed the last file drawer. "There's nothing here, either."

She turned from the cabinet, put her hands on her hips, and contemplated the dead man. His desktop was laid out tidily, mousepad and pencil holder to the left of the computer, daily joke calendar on the right. There were several framed photographs. The obligatory family portrait, a smiling Weldon with his wife and teenage daughter. Another picture of the daughter, this time in her cheerleading outfit. Weldon and the wife in their bathing suits sipping frozen drinks on a sandy beach. The last picture was of Weldon teeing off against the long green of a fairway. He was at the end of his swing. His knee was turned in and his satisfied gaze was directed up toward the trajectory of his ball.

"We should go," Lucy said.

"Do you golf?" Darcy asked.

"What?"

"Do you play golf?"

"Sometimes. And not very well." Lucy was distracted, thinking about Craig Weldon's wife and daughter. She couldn't remember the girl's name. Alyssa, Melissa, something like that. Lucy had never liked the Weldons. It wasn't that they were bad people, just that they had never struck Lucy as deep thinkers. As far as she could tell, their world revolved around fraternity reunions, ski weekends, and the Broncos.

"Show me your golf swing," Darcy said.

"Here?" Lucy looked at the other woman incredulously.

"Yeah." She nodded, serious. "A tee shot, straight down the fairway."

Lucy planted her feet and took a halfhearted swing at her imagined ball. "That what you wanted?"

"Are you a righty or a lefty?"

"Righty."

"And if you were a lefty, you'd stand to the opposite side of the ball?"

Lucy nodded.

"Don't you think it's funny," Darcy said, motioning to the gun in Craig Weldon's right hand, "that someone would write with his left hand, and golf with his left hand, but when it came time to shoot himself, he'd use his *right* hand?"

"You think it was our friend with the wire cutters?"

Darcy blinked. "If I was a betting woman I'd put money on it."

This was as far as she was going, Darcy told herself, as she and Lucy walked back across the Taco Bell parking lot to their cars. Burglary was one thing, but she couldn't afford to get tangled up in murder. In the morning she'd call Billings, tell him someone else had gotten to the files, and hope he was feeling magnanimous.

"As far as I'm concerned," she said, putting her hand on the door of the Dart, "neither one of us was here. Got that?"

Lucy nodded.

"No need to say goodbye, 'cause we never met." Darcy slid into the driver's seat and jammed her key into the ignition. The engine coughed weakly, then fell silent. The Dart had been acting up the last few weeks, and she'd known it would die on her sooner or later, but she didn't think it would pick the worst possible time. She tried the key again, but nothing happened.

It was rotten luck. This whole thing was, really. Just when she was starting to get her life together, the universe decided to take a giant crap on her. At least when she'd been knocking over houses, there'd been no dead bodies to contend with.

She tried the engine one more time, then rolled the window down and waved to Lucy, who was just pulling out. The Mercedes stopped, and the passenger window lowered.

"My car won't start," Darcy called.

"Come on." Lucy motioned.

Darcy climbed out of the Dart and into the Mercedes.

"Where do you live?" Lucy asked.

"Castle Rock," Darcy told her.

An hour there, Lucy figured, and two more back to Pryor. Three long exhausted hours of driving. "I'll take you down in the morning," she said. "You'd better come home with me tonight."

Arlen Krill hadn't felt so bad about an assignment since the incident in Nicaragua when his target had ducked out of the way at the last minute and he'd accidentally killed the man's dog, a beautiful collie named Calypso. It had taken him two weeks, holed up in a Managua hotel with a sixteen-year-old prostitute, to stop dreaming about the animal.

Taking care of Weldon hadn't bothered him. Though he didn't know everything Carl Greene had known, he had enough information to be a problem. Besides, the man was a moron. In the several hours Krill had spent with him, Weldon had talked almost exclusively about the various aspects of the Broncos' passing game, past and present. It was like he was some kind of idiot savant, specializing in John Elway and biochemistry.

But the woman was a different story altogether; it was a shame Krill had to get rid of her. He'd been impressed by her balls that day at the house, the way she sneered at him and Weldon when she found the two of them in her husband's office. Help yourself, she'd said, and he'd wanted to help himself to more than just Greene's files. It wasn't that she hadn't been afraid. Krill knew she was. Most people had the common sense to fear Krill. Lucy Greene hadn't seemed to care.

He'd seen this kind of thing before. Once, in Laos, an old woman had come after him with a rusty hatchet. Krill had just shot her husband and her son, and he figured she must not have given her own life much weight at that point. He shot her in the chest, but not before she carved a wedge of flesh from his right shoulder.

The Greene woman hadn't been home when he got there at two in the morning. Krill had spent the next couple of hours alone in the darkened house, and he felt as if he'd gotten to know her. She was a painter and, as far as Krill could tell in the meager illumination his flashlight offered, a good one. Her canvases were big and richly colored, dusky and sensuous worlds from which all extraneous clutter, both people and things, had been removed.

Despite the oversized suburban manse, there was a simplicity about the woman that Krill liked, a lack of vanity. Her surprisingly spare bathroom told him she wasn't a makeup wearer. Her only artifice was a bottle of orange-scented body lotion. When Krill pressed his nose to her sheets he'd smelled citrus and sweat, the sour odor of restless sleep.

He'd enjoyed waiting up for the woman, something a husband might have done, but it was moving on toward dawn now. Krill was starting to get antsy, and evidently he wasn't the only one. The phone had rung at least five times since he'd been there, echoing through the empty house, and each time, Krill had fought off the urge to answer it.

He stepped to the front window and peered down the road. It was after five in the morning and Lucy Greene still wasn't home. Maybe she was having an affair, Krill thought. The idea excited him. Maybe she was with the reporter. Krill knew that was one job he'd enjoy if the time came.

Past the edge of the subdivision, where the road slipped into the corn, light rippled through the stalks, a car heading in from the west. Krill ducked back behind Lucy's curtains, slid his silenced Ruger from his shoulder holster, and readied himself for his next move.

Chick couldn't sleep. His legs were bothering him. His feet were unpleasantly numb, and from his ankles up his muscles were tingling. But it was worry that was keeping him awake. He knew how stubborn his sister could be, and it hadn't surprised him that she hadn't shown up the night before. But he'd expected her at least to call sometime that day, just to let him know she was okay.

Rolling over, Chick grabbed the portable phone that was next to his bed and dialed Lucy's number for what must have been the dozenth time that night. It was just after five by his alarm clock, and still no answer. Most likely she'd turned her phone off, he tried to reassure himself, but he didn't feel any better. He lay there for another ten minutes, trying to convince himself there was nothing to worry about; then he rolled out of bed and pulled on jeans and a sweatshirt. Padding into the kitchen, he grabbed a carton of eggs and some bacon from the refrigerator and started for the front door. At least he could make her breakfast.

He cruised through Pryor in the Fairlane, crossed over the river, and headed out through the cattle and farmland toward Lucy's. Maybe, Chick told himself, what they both needed was a change of scenery. He'd wangle a few days off from the plant and they could drive up to Copper Mountain or Steamboat, do a little fishing, eat some good food, sleep in a nice bed with sheets changed daily by someone else. Or they could take the tent up to Rocky Mountain National Park and camp.

The highway dipped slightly and Chick watched Miller's old road whip past the window, the dirt track headed out toward what was left of his property. Slowing the Fairlane, Chick turned onto Magpie Road.

Like all the other houses in the subdivision, Lucy's was dark. There was no sign of her Mercedes, but Chick figured she pulled it into the garage for the night. He stopped in the driveway and contemplated the unlit house, debating whether or not to go in. Let her sleep, he told himself, she needs it. But something else told him he should get out of the car, that there was an urgency to his visit. Cradling the breakfast provisions in his right arm, he opened the car door and stepped onto the driveway.

Suicide had seemed like the obvious choice when Arlen Krill was first thinking about how to handle the woman. It would be quickly dismissed as the natural result of a young wife's grief. But suicide had its problems. Overdose was exceptionally difficult to fake, since it normally took a willing participant to swallow the required pills. Unless you could get close to the target without suspicion, as had been the case with Craig Weldon, gunshots could be messy and hard to stage.

In the end, Krill had decided to go the standard home intruder route. True, it lacked imagination, but it had never failed him before.

When he saw the headlights in the corn, Krill made his way into the front foyer. His intention was to get the woman as she came in the door. This way things would be quick and clean. He'd smashed through the flimsy lock on the patio doors and rifled through the bedroom drawers earlier, just to make everything look authentic. If it all went smoothly he could be out the door in ten minutes.

Krill tugged his watch cap down over his ears, pressed his back up against the wall of the foyer, and peered through the tall mottled glass panels that flanked the door. The headlights swung into the driveway and the car stopped, idling for a moment before the lights blinked off and the engine cut out. A figure came up the walk, dark and blurred. Krill ducked back out of sight, took a deep breath, and shifted his Ruger to his left hand.

"Back up," Darcy said, craning her neck as the Mercedes hurtled along Magpie Road, kicking up a cloud of dust and gravel. She wasn't sure, but she thought she caught a glimpse of another car as they passed her familiar parking spot. "Stop the goddamn car and back up!" The urgency of her own voice surprised her.

It surprised Lucy, too. She put her foot on the brake and skidded to a stop. "What's wrong with you?"

"Just back the car up, okay? I think I saw something."

Lucy jammed the shifter into reverse and rolled backward.

"Far enough," Darcy said, popping the passenger door and stepping into the road.

Lucy rolled her window down and stuck her head out. "What is it?"

"There's a car back in there." Darcy started down the dirt utility road, disappearing briefly from Lucy's view.

"Turn your lights off," she said when she came back. "And cut the engine. Leave the key in the ignition."

"What's going on?"

Darcy opened Lucy's door. "Get out," she told her. "We're walking the rest of the way."

Footsteps sounded on the porch, and Krill heard the unmistakable rasping of a key fumbling to find its way into a lock. Finally, there was a click, and the door swung open. It wasn't easy, surprising someone like this. The goal was to immobilize the person with your right arm to their throat, then get a quick and well-placed shot off with your left hand. The trick to the whole thing was knowing exactly how much force to use. It was a matter of intuition, of judging your target's strength.

As soon as Krill got his arm around the figure in the doorway, he knew he had seriously fucked up. For one thing, the person he had in his grasp wasn't Lucy Greene. It was a man, close to Krill's size. He'd been carrying something in his arms, but he'd dropped it when Krill grabbed him. Now the package was wadded up beneath Krill's feet. Krill took a step back, trying to get some purchase, but the soles of his shoes hit something slick and shot out from under him. He fired blindly and heard glass shatter. By the time he struggled up, the man was out the door.

Krill thought about letting him run, but his instinct said there would most likely be one hell of a mess if the man got away. His best course of action would be to take care of this loose end before it unraveled.

The corn blocked out a substantial portion of the artificial light that normally brightened the prairie. It was dark on the road, the sky above Darcy and Lucy spattered with stars. From somewhere deep in the adjacent field came the *drip-drip* of a leaky irrigation pipe. As they neared the edge of the corn, Darcy slowed her pace, and Lucy fell in behind her. They could see the front yards of the subdivision now, the grass bathed in the harsh light of streetlamps so that each blade seemed coarse and bristlelike.

"Whose car is that?" Darcy asked, pointing to the Fairlane in the Greenes' driveway, but before Lucy could answer, a figure burst from the front door of the house.

"Chick!" Lucy called, starting forward.

Chick looked up, his eyes seeming to focus on the two women. He threw his hands out and waved furiously as he lumbered across the lawn.

"Chick!" Lucy yelled again.

Lunging after her, Darcy grabbed for her waist and pulled her back.

Behind Chick, the menacing shape of a pistol in his right hand, was another man. He stopped on the porch, brought the gun up, and fired soundlessly.

"Get back," Darcy hissed to Lucy, trying desperately to keep a grip on the other woman.

The first couple of shots missed, striking the dirt around Chick's feet. But the third bullet caught him just below his left shoulder. He stumbled, pitching forward onto the dew-glazed turf.

The shooter strode quickly down the steps and across the lawn, stopping briefly to put one more bullet into the back of Chick's head. Then he looked up and headed toward the two women at a controlled run. Out of the shadow of the porch, his face was familiar to Lucy. He was the same man who'd come to the house with Craig Weldon.

"C'mon!" Darcy growled. She jerked Lucy toward her as the corn to their right exploded.

Lucy looked back at her house, at the limp shape that had once been her brother sprawled on the neatly landscaped lawn. The shooter fired again. This time Lucy heard the bullet, a whisper in the air like breath in the neck of a bottle. She wrenched herself out of Darcy's grip and lunged forward.

"Chick!" Lucy screamed, desperate now.

Darcy stood there for a split second. Just a few yards ahead was the refuge of the Mercedes, the chrome bumper shining like a beacon on the dark road. All she had to do was get in the car and drive away. Behind her, frantic and unarmed, Lucy stumbled headlong across the yard, toward the man with the gun and the crumpled figure in the grass. Run, Darcy told herself, just go, but her feet refused to move, would not let her leave the other woman to die.

The shooter fired once more and missed, and Darcy heard his magazine click empty. He released the clip and fumbled in his coat pocket. Darcy turned back toward the house and sprinted for Lucy.

"C'mon!" she yelled, catching Lucy, wrenching her backward. "You can't help him."

"No!" Lucy beat at the other woman's arms, but Darcy held on tight.

"You want to die here?" Darcy asked.

Lucy looked back at the shooter. He drew a fresh clip from his coat and jammed it up into the stock of his gun. No, Lucy told herself. She looked over at Darcy. "Let's go." And they ran.

Several more shots rang off the rear bumper of the Mercedes as the two women slid inside. Lucy cranked the engine and reached under her seat. "Here." She handed Darcy the Glock and hit the accelerator. The rear wheels spun against the dry pack of the road; then the rubber caught and the Mercedes leaped forward.

Darcy leaned out the window and fired twice at the car behind them, trying to see the driver in the car's dusty wake. Another bullet hissed by, catching the edge of the sideview mirror and shattering the glass. The Mercedes curved away into the corn, and the road behind them disappeared.

They emerged onto the paved highway and Lucy put her foot on the accelerator, hurtling them forward into the darkness. With their headlights still off they were nearly invisible.

"It was him," Darcy said, breathless, "our backdoor friend from Bioflux."

Chapter eleven

Kevin tried desperately to fall back asleep, but in the end his efforts were futile. His eyes braced open by exhaustion and unease, he lay on his back in the bed, watched the ghosted lights of passing cars skate across the ceiling, and thought about that first phone call from Carl. They'd spoken for only a few minutes, but it had been long enough for Kevin to sense the authenticity of Carl's fear, the slight breakdown in his composure. Carl had mentioned a story Kevin had done several months earlier, a piece about an army reservist who had refused inoculations and was being court-marshaled.

Kevin strained to recall the man's name: Soames? Stiles? Carl had remembered it. *That was a nice piece you did a couple of months ago,* he'd said. Goddamn it, Kevin thought. It was Stykes; no, Sykes, that was it: Earl Sykes. He'd been a bit of a nutcase, a little too paranoid for Kevin to take seriously, but the story was interesting. And really, who could blame the guy for not wanting anthrax shot into his bloodstream?

Could Bioflux be making the vaccines? Kevin wondered. If they were, it certainly wouldn't be a secret. No, there was something else going on here, something worth killing for, and somehow the warden was tangled up in it. Kevin rolled onto his side and stared at the alarm clock. It would be morning soon. Why hadn't Lucy called?

There was a jump in activity at the Perkins across the street, the sounds of doors slamming and sleepy conversation that signaled the start of the early morning rush. A car drove into the Mountain Aire parking lot; its headlamps poured through Kevin's curtains like a spotlight, before blinking off with the engine. Kevin heard one door close, and another, then muffled movements outside his room. He tensed and sat up in bed, Max Fausto's warning replaying itself for him. *This is bad shit.*

Someone knocked, quietly at first, then louder. Kevin felt his stomach contract.

Whoever it was paused for a moment, then knocked again. "Kevin!" The voice was urgent. "It's Lucy. Open up!"

"I'm coming," Kevin called. Fumbling with the bedside lamp, he leapt up and scrambled for the door.

Lucy's face was wan and pinched. She had the edgy stare of someone who'd long ago reached emotional exhaustion. "I need your car," she said, brushing past Kevin.

There was another woman with her, close to Lucy's age and just slightly less haggard. Lucy was far too harried to bother with an introduction, but Kevin assumed her companion was the woman who'd broken into her house, the one who'd helped Lucy get into the Bioflux building. There was blood on the woman's neck, a burst of small wounds, as if from fine shrapnel. She followed Lucy inside and closed the door behind them.

"They shot Chick," Lucy said, her voice washed out, frighteningly calm. "We need to get out of here."

Kevin let the words sink in. "Who?" he asked dumbly.

"Jesus, did you hear me?" she barked, stepping to the front window, parting the curtains slightly, and surveying the parking lot. "Get your shit together so we can get out of here."

When Lucy turned her back to him, Kevin could see her gun, the butt hooked securely over the waistband of her jeans.

"Where are we going?" he asked, pulling a pair of pants on over his boxer shorts.

"I don't know," Lucy said, still facing the window. "We'll take Darcy down to Castle Rock. From there, I don't know."

Kevin shrugged into a T-shirt. "I found Canty."

"Where?" Lucy snapped her head around.

"Montana. South of Bozeman."

The sun had come up by the time they rolled out of Brighton, leaving Lucy's Mercedes in the parking lot of the Mountain Aire. They took the toll road east, skirting Denver's morning traffic. Kevin was driving, with Lucy beside him in the front seat. Darcy sat in the back, her cheek pressed against the cold glass of the window, and watched the plains roll by. Out on this side of the city there was still prairie, sprawling grass and grazing land interrupted here and there by newly erected battalions of single-family homes, the tracts uniform as soldiers in a Roman phalanx. Beyond the brown swell of hills, Darcy caught a glimpse of the new airport, the white cones that formed its roof lustrous as firelit tents.

The car hummed along, its shadow racing after them. Lucy had regained some kind of emotional equilibrium and was describing the night's events to Kevin. Darcy considered her next move. Whatever the warden was into was some pretty serious shit. If it was as serious as she thought, the information he'd wanted from the Greene house might be worth a lot more to him than just a cushy work detail and a friendly cellmate for Angie.

A green highway sign skated into view, announcing the Castle Rock exit. Up ahead, just off the highway ramp, was the Flying J: fetid mop water, weekly piss tests for her parole officer, scowling secretaries; that, Darcy told herself, was the rest of her life on the straight and narrow.

Kevin put the blinker on and slowed the car.

The rest of her life and the rest of Angie's life, the two of them meeting in the visiting room at Canyon each weekend for the next ten years. If they were both lucky they might go back to Casper and work at the refinery with their father. And that was the *good* version of the future, the one in which Angie made it through her ten years at Canyon in one piece.

The car headed down the exit ramp. Darcy sat up and put her hand on Kevin's shoulder. "Get back on the interstate," she told him. "I'm going with you."

Kevin glanced up at the rearview mirror. "You're getting out here," he said, pulling into the parking lot of a Conoco station.

"Look," Darcy said, "nothing's changed. All I want is the testing records for Pioneer. Chances are you're going to need my help again before this is all over. Look, you said you're heading up near Bozeman. Well, I've got a friend up there, a safe place where we can crash."

Kevin shook his head. "This is a bad idea," he murmured.

Darcy turned to Lucy. "You owe me this at least."

Lucy thought about the night before, how they'd fought each other, how Darcy had kept her from going back to Chick. She'd be dead now if it weren't for Darcy.

"She's not coming," Kevin insisted.

"It's my kid sister," Darcy said to Lucy. "What would you do?"

Lucy looked up toward the highway above them. "Get back on the interstate," she told Kevin.

"Do you really think we should do this?" Kevin asked, cupping his hands around his coffee mug. "I mean, we don't know anything about her."

They had pulled off at a truck stop just south of Cheyenne to get gas and something to eat. Darcy was in the bathroom.

"What if your first guess was right?" Kevin continued. "She could be working for another biotech firm. As far as we know, she could be the one who killed Carl. All this stuff about Warden Billings might just be bullshit. I mean, we couldn't find anything on him. And this crap about her sister? Come on."

Lucy took a swig of her coffee and lit a cigarette. "I don't know," Lucy told him, "but she saved my life when she didn't have to. She could've gotten herself killed, too. Besides, what she *has* told us doesn't exactly make her look like Mother Teresa. If I was lying about my past I'd pick a better profession than ex-con. She was right when she said we might need her again. I saw her work, and she can pick a lock in less time than it usually takes me to find my keys."

Kevin rubbed his eyes with the heels of his hands. "I still don't like it," he said, looking up to see Darcy emerging from the bathroom. "I don't like it at all."

Darcy came forward and slid into the chair next to Lucy's. She had cleaned up, but the tiny cuts remained.

"What happened?" Kevin asked, motioning to his own neck.

"A bullet hit the sideview mirror of the Mercedes," she explained, bringing her coffee to her lips. She wasn't sure what to think of Kevin, but she could tell he wasn't crazy about her.

"Ouch," he said.

A waitress appeared with their breakfasts, overloaded platters of eggs and sausage and pancakes.

"Okay," Kevin said when she was gone, "what exactly do we know?" He doused his pancakes with syrup and took a bite. "We know Carl was doing weekend research on neural tube defects, something Craig Weldon and our friend from last night happen to be interested in. Now Carl and Weldon are both dead, and it looks like someone wants you that way too. And you guys found nothing in Weldon's office?"

Lucy shook her head and pushed her food away. All morning she'd managed to stay in control, but now she kept seeing Chick, his legs splayed out in the wet grass, his body jerking when the man leaned over him and fired. She thought she might be sick.

"When Carl called me in New York he mentioned a story I'd done, a piece about this reservist who was court-marshaled for refusing the standard biological warfare vaccinations."

"And you think the story has something to do with all this?" Lucy asked, managing a sip of coffee.

Kevin shrugged.

"There's something funny about the Bioflux building," Darcy interjected. It was the most she'd said all morning.

Kevin looked across the table at her. "What do you mean?"

"It's this thing I've learned to do. When I was working I was always looking for hiding places. It's like there's a big space that's unaccounted for in that building." She paused, fumbling for the words to describe what she meant. Her two companions looked confused. "Like a false bottom in a suitcase. Only big, really big. The entire core of the building."

She speared a sausage from her plate and bit off the end.

"You know, I was thinking about this whole Pioneer thing. Last night, driving out to Pryor, Lucy told me you guys couldn't find anything unusual in the Ophir paper during the time Billings was warden, right?"

"Uh-huh." Kevin nodded.

Darcy uncapped a bottle of Tabasco sauce and shook an alarmingly large amount onto her eggs. "Well, the warden's all worried about TB testing. Now, TB's a disease, and a disease is something that might not show up right away." She took a bite of the eggs and looked from Kevin to Lucy, waiting for them to catch on. Neither one of them said anything. "What if something *did* happen when he was there," she went on, "only no one knew about it until later?"

"Oh, shit!" Lucy exclaimed, but not in response to what Darcy had said. Her attention had turned to the TV that hung over the lunch counter.

Darcy looked up and Kevin turned in his seat. On the screen was a picture of Lucy's house, the yard and driveway cordoned off with yellow crime tape. In the foreground was a reporter from one of the Denver stations, an attractive brunette. The sound was off, but the closed captioning had been activated. Lucy squinted to read the words: . . . NEIGHBORS FOUND THE PRYOR MAN DEAD THIS MORNING . . . UNIDENTIFIED EYE WITNESS . . . POLICE ARE LOOKING FOR THE MAN'S SISTER . . . WANTED FOR

QUESTIONING. A snapshot of Lucy flashed onto the screen, lingering there for what seemed like an eternity; then the reporter reappeared, the house behind her.

A group of men stepped out the front door and onto Lucy's porch: Pryor's one officer of the law, three guys in brown sheriff's uniforms, a couple of detectives in cowboy hats. In back of the group, lurking almost intentionally behind the others, was a man in a dark suit. He was pale and wiry compared to the others, his face grim and businesslike.

Darcy slowly lowered her fork to her plate. "It's him," she whispered.

Lucy's eyes locked on the man's face. "From last night, at the house," she stammered. "What's he doing there?"

Darcy scanned the restaurant. Several faces were focused on the television screen. "Get up," she whispered to Lucy, "and go out to the car."

"We need to go to the police," Lucy said. "We should have gone this morning. I wasn't thinking."

"Go to the car," Darcy repeated, gripping Lucy's wrist.

Lucy stared incredulously at the other woman. "It'll be fine. I'll explain what happened."

Darcy shook her head. "He's *with* them," she hissed, releasing Lucy's arm. "Go, and keep your head down on the way out."

Lucy looked over at Kevin, as if for confirmation. Again he thought of what Max Fausto had said. *Deep and high. You're going to make some powerful enemies.* In all the years he'd worked with Max, Kevin had never once known him to lie. "She's right." He nodded, reaching into his pocket and handing her the car keys. "We'll be right behind you."

Rising slowly, Lucy threaded her way through the Formica tables and vinyl-covered chairs to the door. She kept her eyes on the floor in front of her. The other customers passed through her peripheral vision: a baseball-capped trucker, an old man in a straw cowboy hat, a woman with a baby. Wasn't this what she had always wanted, something to take her out of her life, a tide on which she could be swept away? Her eyes stung and her vision blurred. She blinked away tears and kept walking.

Chick was dead, the boy who'd walked her to school each morning, who'd shown her how to wriggle through the hole in the old junkyard's back fence. Chick, her brother, was gone, and Carl was gone, and the life she had lived was gone forever. Putting her hand on the front door, she pushed her way out into the parking lot.

"Where exactly are we going?" Darcy asked, when they had re-assembled at the car. She had bought a road atlas inside. Now she opened it on the hood of the car and put her finger on Cheyenne.

Kevin scanned Montana, picking out Bozeman and then the crooked line of the Yellowstone River, the Paradise valley, and the tiny dot that marked Homer. "Here."

"We can go straight up through Wyoming. It's about three hours to Casper. I know a place there where we can stop and get a change of clothes. How much money do we have?"

Kevin pulled his wallet out. "About fifty bucks, plus credit cards."

"About the same here," Lucy said.

Darcy shook her head. "It's better not to use the plastic," she said; then, to Kevin, "There's an ATM inside. Go take out as much as you can. We'll gas up the car."

Chapter twelve

On a map of Wyoming, Casper stands out, the only city in the center of the state, a welcome patch of black ink on an otherwise frighteningly white page. So there's a certain amount of expectation for anyone traveling toward Casper. Driving south through the no-man's-land of northern Wyoming, or north through the southern no-man's-land, you look forward to a break in the monotony, something besides snow fences and antelope, the glacial sweep of the Rocky Mountain front looming in the distance.

It's a misguided expectation, as anyone who's ever been through Wyoming will tell you. The reality of Casper is nothing more than a slight bend in the interstate, a seemingly random ten-mile drop in the speed limit, and a cluster of worn-down houses and chain motels.

It was just before noon when Lucy, Darcy, and Kevin descended from the interstate into Casper's dusty downtown. Lucy was asleep in the backseat. Darcy directed Kevin through a neighborhood of older, shabbier dwellings, railroad houses with rotting porches and peeling paint. Pit bulls snapped at each other through chain-link fences. Disemboweled Fords and Chevys littered the streets like decomposing bodies.

"Home," Darcy said, pointing to a small house with a noticeably sagging roof. It was a neat residence, if slightly the worse for wear. It had been yellow once, but most of the paint had flaked away, revealing gray clapboards beneath. Flower baskets hung off the lopsided porch. The yard was green and freshly cut, scattered with brightly colored plaster gnomes and hand-painted signs that read WILLIAMSVILLE, POPULATION 4, and CAUTION, LITTLE MEN AT WORK. Whirligigs spun furiously in the stiff wind: a man in a flying machine, a farmer milking his cows with superhuman speed, a little girl frantically waving an American flag. A chain-link fence corralled the chaos.

"I know what you're thinking," Darcy said. *"No wonder she turned out the way she did."*

Lucy sat up in the backseat and stretched. The sleep had done her no good. She was groggy and sore all over, her eyes swollen, her face puffy. "Where are we?" she asked.

Darcy looked back at her. "Casper. My parents' place."

Lucy scanned the cluttered yard. Something moved inside the house, a large flowered body flitting across a gap in the curtains. The front door swung open and a woman stepped out onto the porch. She was short and squat, her housedress splattered with giant red roses. Her hair was dull gray, plastered to her head, the comb marks set with grease.

"Hey, Mom!" Darcy called, getting out of the car. She opened the front gate to step into the yard, and two little black dogs came tearing out from the back of the house.

"Elmer!" the woman yelled, clapping her hands together. "Annabelle!" But the admonition only seemed to make the dogs bark more loudly. One of them snapped at Darcy's ankle and got a snoutful of sock.

Darcy looked back at the car. "Don't worry," she said, motioning for Lucy and Kevin to follow. "I'll run interference." She climbed up to the porch and gave her mother a hug.

"Mom, this is Lucy and Kevin, some friends of mine." She released the woman and motioned to the two of them.

The mother peered suspiciously at the visitors. "Why aren't you working? I thought you worked weekdays."

Darcy smiled reassuringly. "I got the day off. I decided to bring my friends up, show them around."

Kevin climbed the first step and stuck his hand out. "Nice to meet you, ma'am."

"Yeah," the woman remarked, her eyes looking Kevin up and down, taking in the pleated khakis, the cotton shirt. "I guess you'd better come in," she said, turning on her heel. "I'll fix you some lunch."

It was dark inside, the curtains drawn to keep out sun and heat. The TV was on in the living room. A family of soap opera actors gathered around a young woman in a coma, her hair perfectly coiffed, her lipstick muted to suggest illness. The house was crammed with trinkets, porcelain curios, cheap plastic dolls, framed photographs of Darcy at various ages, and pictures of another child, a delicate girl with wispy blond hair.

"Is this your sister?" Lucy asked, pointing to a snapshot of the blond girl.

Darcy nodded. "C'mon, let's see if we can find some clothes."

The two women disappeared into a back bedroom, and Kevin lingered for a moment, studying the photographs, the two sisters in Halloween costumes and team uniforms. If Darcy had something to hide, Kevin told himself, she wouldn't have brought them here. And yet he was still dubious about having her along. All I want is the testing records for Pioneer, she'd said, but Kevin doubted there'd be any neat way to accomplish that, to separate what she wanted from whatever else they learned.

"You know how to shuck corn?" Darcy's mother poked her head out of the kitchen, one eyebrow raised skeptically.

Kevin nodded.

"Good." She thrust a lumpy paper bag out to him and pointed to the front door. "You finish this and then I'll find you something else to do."

Seemingly untouched for what Lucy guessed was the last decade, Darcy's bedroom was a sort of makeshift reliquary, a shrine to the childhoods that had been lived there. The twin beds were dressed in matching pink comforters, flowered pillows, and lacy dust ruffles. Tom Cruise smiled down from one wall, his thumbs hooked into the waistband of his jeans. An army of teddy bears perched on top of a bookshelf, a glass-eyed, plush-furred force poised for some silent attack. A beat-up dresser was littered with lip gloss and eye shadow, little gouged-out boxes of plum and periwinkle.

It was, Lucy thought, the way her own room might have looked if her mother had lived. But of course she hadn't, and Lucy had never quite managed to get girlhood right. For the longest time she hadn't cared to. She'd been happy with Chick's castoffs and the fierce competition of boys. She was better than her brother at many of the things he valued, physically braver, a better shot, a more patient and skillful fisherman. But she had failed to learn the subtle social rules of female friendship, the tools and tricks of the trade.

Darcy pulled open a dresser drawer and took out a couple of T-shirts and two pairs of shorts. "Here," she said, handing one set of clothes to Lucy. "I think these'll fit you."

Lucy nodded. "Are these yours?" she asked, pointing to a shelf of trophies next to the door.

Darcy shook her head. "I was the fuckup of the family. Those are Angie's."

"She was a runner?"

"Cross-country. She took State her senior year." Darcy smiled, proud as any parent.

Lucy looked up at the trophies, at the gold and silver figurines of young women caught in mid-stride. In the middle was a photograph of Angie, her delicate face turned slightly upward, her back straight, her legs long and muscular, working toward an unseen finish line.

"She's beautiful," Lucy said. She had a sudden memory of her brother, the two of them out on the Platte River fishing the morning rise.

Lucy closed her eyes and watched Chick take a step into the current, carefully mending line as his fly dipped into a riffle and headed downstream. He waited a moment and then lifted his rod, and the fly took to the air, rising and falling, its winged shadow skipping across the river. That was Chick, she thought, not the best but the most graceful, the one who carried her love the most easily. And in the end she had not been able to save him.

Kevin stepped onto the porch and sat down in a cheap plastic lawn chair. He could hear the dogs in the back, their sustained yapping. Across the fence, in the adjacent yard, a woman was sunning herself on a chaise lounge while a dirty toddler played in the dust nearby. A radio was on in the house next door. The soft patter of a baseball game on a grainy AM station drifted out an open window.

It was hot and dry, and even in the porch's shade Kevin was sweating. He took the corn out of the bag and piled it on the boards at his feet. The ears were fresh, moist and grassy smelling. When he peeled the first husk back, the silk beneath it came away to reveal perfect kernels, smooth and even as teeth.

How many times had he done this for his grandmother, and always on the back step? She'd taught Kevin to be meticulous, to work over every ear until not a single silk remained.

He'd been thinking about what Darcy had said earlier, how any problems at Pioneer might have been slow to manifest themselves. They couldn't go back to Ophir, but Kevin had another idea. He finished the corn, pulled his cell phone out of his pocket, dialed Ophir information, and asked for the number of the *Gazette*.

"Can I talk to Jimmy?" he asked, when the newspaper's receptionist answered.

There was a sigh and then a click as the woman put him on hold. A Muzac version of "Eye of the Tiger" played softly, the vocals replaced by a muted horn. Kevin hummed along: . . . *it's the thrill of the—*

"Hello?" It was the kid.

"Jim, it's Kevin Burns, from MSNBC. I was there yesterday looking at the archives. You helped me, remember?"

"Mr. Burns. Wow. Sure, I remember."

"Listen, I need your help again. I need you to do some research for me. Can you do that?"

"Uh-huh."

"Okay, here's what you do. You go through the archives, starting in the spring of 1990, and look for anything out of the ordinary that might have happened at the Pioneer Correctional Center in Ophir. Especially anything where people might have gotten sick."

"You mean like the Pioneer Plague?"

Kevin pressed the receiver closer to his ear. "What's the Pioneer Plague?"

"That's what my dad calls it. He used to work out there, before he got sick."

"How'd he get sick?"

"I don't know. At first it was just prisoners who were sick, but then some of the guards started to get it. It makes you feel bad all the time. My dad's always tired, and he falls down sometimes. His arms and legs feel strange—you know, like when you lie wrong and part of you goes to sleep."

"You remember when this started to happen?"

Jimmy thought for a second. "I was little, maybe in third grade, so, eight–nine years ago, I guess."

"Are there a lot of other guards with the same problems?" Kevin asked.

"Some. I don't really know. And, like, there's this whole thing with the babies, too."

"What thing?"

"Like this guy Dad worked with at the prison. He wasn't sick or anything, but he and his wife had a baby and there was something wrong with its spine, like it was leaking out. Spinal something. I can't remember the name, but there've been a few babies born that way."

"Spina bifida?" Kevin asked.

"Yeah, that's it."

"Aren't people upset?"

"I guess."

"What do you mean, you guess?"

Jimmy hesitated for a second. "Everything in this town runs off those prisons: the schools, the grocery stores, even this paper. No one here wants to say anything bad about Pioneer or any of the others. It's like my dad. They gave him some money, plus he's got his pension and disability. He figures, What more can they do?"

Smart kid, Kevin thought.

"Mr. Burns?" Jimmy asked. "Does this have something to do with that woman's brother getting killed up in Pryor? I recognized her picture."

Kevin didn't say anything, even though he knew the kid would take his silence as a yes.

"Mr. Burns?"

"Yeah."

"Do you still need me to go through the archives?"

"No, Jim, but thanks. Just one more thing. Do you remember your dad ever talking about getting some kind of inoculation or tuberculosis test?"

Jimmy pondered the question. "I don't know. He could've."

"What's your last name?" Kevin asked.

"Hagen. Jim Hagen."

"I owe you one, Jim. You ever need anything, you come to me, okay?"

"Okay, Mr. Burns."

Kevin hung up and tucked the phone back in his pocket. The toddler in the yard across the way had gotten the hose out and was making a series of canals in the dirt. The woman had rolled over onto her stomach and appeared to be sleeping. The sun glared off her white back, the skin vulnerable and exposed like meat on a spit. Kevin gathered the denuded ears of corn, stood up, and headed into the house.

Lucy and Darcy were at the kitchen table, hunched over a bowl of snap peas. They looked up from their work when Kevin opened the door.

"I think we should go," he said quietly. He set the corn down in front of them.

"What's wrong?" Lucy looked up at him. Both she and Darcy had changed into shorts and T-shirts.

Kevin shook his head.

"Mom," Darcy said. She got up from the table and crossed to the kitchen sink, where her mother stood, mixing tuna salad. "We gotta go, Mom. We can't stay for lunch."

The woman turned toward Lucy and Kevin, disappointed, accusatory. "Whadda you mean?"

Darcy shrugged. "My friends have to get back to Castle Rock. It's a long drive."

Lucy smiled as she rose from the table. "It was nice to meet you," she offered.

"You've got a nice place here," Kevin said stupidly.

Darcy put her arms around her mother. "I'll call you, okay? Next time you talk to Angie, you tell her everything's gonna be all right. This is important, Mom. You tell her I'm working on something. Tell her to hang in there, okay?"

"Okay."

"You promise, Mom?"

"I promise."

"And tell Daddy I love him. Tell him I'm sorry I couldn't stay till he came home from work. And I love you too."

Mrs. Williams nodded, but she didn't seem convinced. Her eyes were cold and savvy. She didn't walk them to the door.

"What's going on?" Lucy asked as they headed away from the house. Darcy was driving now, her face intent on the road before her. Kevin was in the backseat.

"I was thinking about what Darcy said earlier, about things not showing up right away at Pioneer, so I called that kid at the *Ophir Gazette*," Kevin said. "I was going to ask him to do a check of the papers after 1990."

"And?" Lucy prodded him.

"It turns out there's something called the Pioneer Plague. You ever hear anything about this?" Kevin asked, directing the question to Darcy.

She shook her head.

"Around the early nineties, prisoners and some guards at Pioneer started getting sick: sleeplessness, constant fatigue, numbness in their arms and legs. Sound familiar?"

"Same as Chick," Lucy said.

"That's not all."

"The kid at the paper told you all this?" Lucy asked.

Kevin nodded. "His father was a guard at Pioneer. He's so sick he had to quit working. But get this. Besides the sickness, the kid says there's been this little cluster of birth defects. Guess what kind?"

Lucy turned her head and stared at Kevin. "Neural tube?" she offered.

Kevin nodded. They had left Casper and were heading north toward Bar Nunn and the interstate again. "Yup. Spina bifida."

When they stopped for gas in Sheridan, Darcy turned the wheel over to Lucy and climbed into the backseat.

"It'll be late by the time we get there," she said, studying the atlas. She passed the map to Kevin and lay down, her knees curled up into her chest. "If I'm still asleep when we get to Livingston, wake me up. We can stay with my friend tonight."

Lucy set the cruise control and they headed into Montana, up through the Crow Reservation, following the Little Bighorn River through Lodge Grass and Hardin. A front had rolled in, and by the time they got to Billings the temperature had dropped significantly. The sky was dark with thunderheads, faraway storms that slipped by them, heading east.

Kevin leaned back in his seat. "You remember that old MG Chick got his senior year?"

Lucy smiled. "He spent more time working on that thing than he did driving it."

"All we saw of him for three months was his skinny legs sticking out from under that car."

Lucy had thought him so old and sophisticated. He'd started working at the cannery in Fort Lupton, making a real paycheck. None of them had ever ridden in a convertible before. "He was going out with that girl from Johnstown; what was her name?"

"Micheala," Kevin said fondly.

"That's right, Micheala. I couldn't stand her."

"I wanted to drive that car so badly. Remember? We weren't even allowed to touch it."

"He let me drive it, once."

"You're kidding!"

Lucy shook her head. "Nope."

"How was it?"

"Amazing," she said. She hadn't thought about that drive for a long time. They'd gone out past the Pryor cemetery toward Burle Reservoir. Lucy had gotten her license a year earlier, and the only thing she'd ever driven was their father's old pickup. When she punched the MG's accelerator and the little convertible leaped forward across the Weld County scrubland, she was overwhelmed by a sense of freedom. She'd felt glamorous, full of possibility.

They were both silent for a long while. Lucy lit a cigarette and watched the blacktop disappear over the horizon. There wasn't another vehicle in sight.

"Luce?" Kevin asked, finally.

"Yeah?"

"Do you ever think about us—I mean, how things might have been if I had stayed?"

Lucy shifted her body, stretched her fingers out on the wheel, and thought about those last few weeks before Kevin left, the hot tail end of summer: the smell of Miller's field, turned earth and sweat. She thought of that last trip they'd made to Greeley,

Kevin behind the wheel of his grandfather's old green sedan, how relieved he was to set her down in front of the clinic and drive off. It seemed to her there hadn't been much left between the two of them to salvage by the time he went away.

"You mean you working a gas crew out in Morgan County and me butchering chickens?" she said. "It doesn't sound like much of a life to me."

"No," Kevin agreed, "I guess it doesn't."

Lucy took her eyes off the road for a moment and looked at him. His face was turned to the side window, his back and shoulders partly to Lucy. She had a sudden impulse to reach across the seat and touch the bare skin at the base of his neck, to allow herself this one small act of affection. But she didn't.

Arlen Krill worked on a need-to-know basis, and he liked it that way. The less information he needed, the better. Krill wasn't a patriot. He worked for the money, and as long as the money kept coming he did his job and kept his mouth shut. He'd done some corporate Civilian Military Assistant work in the past, troop training in sub-Saharan Africa, and a stint in Central America, but he'd never liked taking direction, and he preferred working on his own.

Krill's services did not come cheap. He'd already guessed that the mousy-voiced man who'd hired him when the Carl Greene job first got botched, the man who called him now with updates and instructions, was not his true employer. No, there were deep pockets behind this job, people who had better things to do with their time than get their hands dirty with messy details. People who could arrange to slip him in with the local law enforcement as a Fed. He'd enjoyed that little charade, playing investigator on the shooting in Colorado, getting to see how the small-town cops worked.

Krill didn't know exactly what had happened in Seattle, only that someone had screwed up, and it was his job to fix things. It seemed unlikely the Greene woman had the files, but she was nosy and sooner or later she'd start putting the pieces together.

She already knew more than could be comfortably allowed. Whoever was calling the shots didn't want to take any chances. And after the gaffe with her brother, it had seemed doubly important that Krill take care of her.

It wouldn't have been Krill's choice to involve the media, but the deep pockets wanted her found fast and anything she might say discredited early. At least that's the way Krill's caller had explained it.

"Who knows?" the mewling voice had said. "Fugitives die in altercations with the authorities all the time. This could be a nice tidy way to end things."

Chapter thirteen

"What the hell is this place?" Kevin asked as Darcy pulled off the highway and headed across the river toward the dark foothills and the hulking range of mountains beyond. It was long past sunset, the sky fading from deep blue to black above them. Dozens of tepees glowed in the distance, a whole field of flickering canvas skins, like lamps set out for a giant's party. Just ahead, lit by the phosphorous glare of several utility lights, were the hulking shells of some dozen trailers, connected end to end to form one long snaking structure.

"It's a retreat," Darcy explained. "A friend of mine runs it with her boyfriend. They're activists, Earth-first types. You know, soy burgers and hemp sandals. They're harmless."

Kevin was skeptical. He'd been in Quebec and Genoa and had seen the havoc "harmless" Earth-firsters could wreak.

"It looks like we may be interrupting something," Lucy said. As they neared the compound, a big open tent came into view. Several dozen people were grouped under it, most seated at long tables. "Are you sure this is okay?"

"I'm sure," Darcy observed, pulling into a cow pasture that evidently served as the ranch's parking lot. "Look, we need to spend the night somewhere, and nobody in their right mind is going to look for us here."

"You're right about that," Kevin agreed, stepping out of the car and onto the spongy grass. He stretched and turned, surveying their surroundings. Back toward the highway, electric lights dotted the riverside. The air was cold, touched with the first hint of early fall.

"C'mon," Darcy said, setting off. "It looks like they're having dinner."

She was right. As they approached the tent, the threesome could hear the clatter of cutlery and the murmur of conversation. Except for a few aging hippies, it was a mostly young group of mostly white middle-class kids in loose clothing and Birkenstocks.

"You see your friend?" Kevin asked as they stepped into the lights of the tent.

Darcy scanned the crowd. "Not yet—" she began, but before she could finish, a head of wild red curls popped up in the back of the tent.

"Darcy!" a woman's voice yelled jubilantly, and Darcy saw her friend Shappa hustling forward through the maze of tables.

Beneath her shift, Shappa was trim and pert, her small body compact and utilitarian. Her feet were bare, her toenails painted candy-apple red. When she reached Darcy she threw her arms around the other woman and gave her a lingering hug. "What are you doing up here?" she asked.

"We're just driving through," Darcy said, stepping back to get a better look at her friend. It was the first time, Darcy realized, that they'd seen each other out of their prison blues.

Shappa had been Darcy's cellmate her first year at Canyon. A doctor's daughter from Long Island, Shappa, who'd been born Rachel Lowenstein, was doing a two-to-four-year stint for trying to blow up the machinery that ran the chairlift on Vail mountain. Eco-terrorism was what Shappa called it, and she spent most of her free time in their cell devising elaborate plans for the destruction of various logging and mining operations around the West.

She'd driven Darcy crazy at first, with her half-baked Native American philosophy and her constant ranting about the animal products they were fed in the prison mess. "We're all creatures of the moon mother," Shappa would say. But she was the kind of person who grew on you, and eventually her endearing naïveté and optimism wore Darcy down.

Darcy had gotten a few letters from Shappa after she got out of Canyon. She left Colorado and worked her way through the Pacific Northwest, chaining herself to old-growth cedars and playing the part of a rock-throwing salmon at the World Trade Organization meeting in Seattle. It was in Seattle that she'd met Jeremy, and six months later they were living in Montana.

Darcy smiled, motioning to her two companions. "Lucy, Kevin, meet Shappa."

Shappa took a little bow. "Welcome to our feast," she said. "Any friends of Darcy's are friends of mine."

"We were hoping we could crash here tonight," Darcy said.

Shappa beamed. "Of course!" Then, tugging at Darcy's hand like an impatient preschooler, "Come meet Jeremy!"

"The locals don't know what to think of us," Jeremy explained as Shappa ladled some kind of stew onto plates and set it in front of them.

"I hope you like tempeh." Shappa beamed. "Brown rice for everyone?"

"They know we're kooky tree-huggers," Jeremy went on, fiddling with his matted beard. His hair was snarled into long dreadlocks. Kevin figured he was about twenty years too old for the white-Rastafarian look and at least fifteen years too old for Shappa. "Which in this neck of the woods is worse than being convicted murderers. But they also know we're training people for antigovernment activity. Which pretty much elevates us to the level of saints."

"We're not ideological," Shappa elaborated. "Well, *we* are. But the program's not. We just give people the tools."

Kevin looked down at the contents of his plate. "And just how much do people pay for these tools?"

Shappa started to say something but Jeremy interrupted her. "We live simply," he said, putting his arm around Shappa's waist, "but a place like Sheep Mountain Ranch doesn't run on good intentions. We charge people a fair price for the kind of knowledge and training they get."

Kevin glanced at Lucy skeptically. Beneath the naturally dyed clothing, Jeremy seemed slick as a used car salesman. No doubt their host was making a good living off the ranch.

"Eat up," Shappa directed cheerily. "I'll get you guys settled in after dinner."

Jeremy excused himself after finishing his vegan apple brown Betty, saying only that he had a "session" to host. Kevin watched him walk away from the tent and fade into the darkness, his bear-claw necklace rattling against his chest.

"You look familiar," Kevin heard Shappa say. He turned to see her watching him. "Were you in Quebec?"

"What?"

She rolled her eyes. "Summit of the Americas, April 2001."

"No," he said. Actually, he *had* been there, covering the protests for MSNBC, but he doubted they would have run into each other at the Hilton.

"Oh, well," she said, shrugging her shoulders helplessly. She finished her chamomile tea and rubbed her hands together. "Why don't I take you to your tepee. You must be beat."

They followed Shappa out of the mess tent and along a well-trodden footpath toward the camp's main structure. "The

Worm," their guide said fondly, motioning to the makeshift building. "It's made entirely from scrap. We found the trailers at an old junkyard down by Gardiner. We try to reuse as much as we possibly can; our tepee skins are recycled fibers. Unfortunately we haven't found a way to get off the grid completely, but we're generating about a quarter of our energy, either from the sun or the wind. You guys don't have sleeping bags, do you?"

Darcy shook her head. "Sorry."

"It's okay," Shappa told them. "We've got some spares inside."

They reached the nearer end of the structure, and Shappa climbed up onto a small wooden porch, opened the door, and motioned for the three of them to step inside.

"This is our reception area," she said, sweeping her arm across the unexpectedly large room. Except for the LEGALIZE MARIJUANA! poster, it could have been any office. There were potted ficus plants in the corners, two desks and two state-of-the-art computers, a bank of filing cabinets, and a small waiting area.

"Believe it or not," their guide explained, "there's a lot of competition in this business. You've got to look professional."

Most of the rest of the Worm's trailer sections were well-equipped common areas. There was a small cramped library with titles ranging from *Silent Spring* to *The Monkey Wrench Gang*. Two cobbled-together trailers served as a meeting area and classroom.

"We only run the training sessions during the summer," Shappa said, "so luckily we don't need much indoor space." She opened a locked door that led into what Kevin figured must have been the tail end of the building. "This is where Jeremy and I live."

Shappa flipped a light on, revealing her cramped residence: imitation Oriental carpets, a worn futon, an old lamp with a red scarf draped over it. A pair of skin drums sat in the center of the room. A poster on one wall read OHM. Another said LIVE SIMPLY SO OTHERS MAY SIMPLY LIVE.

"When I first met Jeremy he was living out of a school bus." Shappa laughed, a little nervously. She opened a large closet and pulled out three tightly packed sleeping bags. "His father owned some big construction company in Pennsylvania. He died right after we met in Seattle. That's how we got the money to start this place." She stopped talking and looked at the threesome. "God, I can go on."

Lucy rolled over on her cot and stared into the darkness. Kevin must have fallen asleep before his head hit the hemp-and-buckwheat pillow. His breathing was deep and rhythmic. He stirred slightly and his sleeping bag rustled. From outside the tent came the shrill singsong of crickets, the distant rumble of drums, and the throaty, slightly off-key sound of people singing.

It was like summer camp, Lucy thought, though she'd never been to summer camp. Or like the migrant camps that appeared around Pryor during the harvest, ragtag caravans of beat-up vans and old Chevys crammed with household belongings, babies squeezed in between stacks of sheets and towels, women cooking masa and beans over Coleman stoves.

When they were small, she and Chick had sometimes slept in a tent in the backyard. She remembered this still. The way dew gathered on the fabric overnight, and how if you touched the inside of the tent in the morning your hand would come away wet. Or the long trek to the bathroom in the middle of the night, crossing the dark yard in her nightgown and entering her own house as a burglar might, through the mud room, through the kitchen, down the hall past her father's bedroom door, to the little bathroom they all shared.

Lucy turned onto her back, trying to sort through the scattered pieces of the last three days. At the top of the tepee, where the lodge poles came together, a small patch of sky was visible, a cluster of stars. If the kid at the Ophir paper was right, something very much like Gulf War Illness had spread through the Pioneer Correctional Center. Spread. It was an unpleasant word. Could Chick's sickness have spread? she wondered. He'd been living with them in Arvada right before she got pregnant with Eric. Biologically speaking, Spina bifida and encephalocele were closer than kissing cousins.

And what was Bioflux's role? Were they the ones producing the TB tests Warden Billings was so anxious about? Carl had known.

He had something on them, something Weldon and his companion had come to the house to find. Whatever was going on, Craig Weldon knew enough about it to get himself killed.

Lucy unzipped her sleeping bag, swung her legs off the cot, and groped for her tennis shoes in the darkness. She made her way to the narrow slit of light that marked the tepee's doorway and stepped outside. Across the field, a group of people had gathered in the mess tent, singing. In the other direction were the lights of the men's and women's bathhouses.

Lucy threaded her way between the tepees, heading for the junkyard hulk of the Worm.

"Okay, Darcy, what's really going on here? I know the guy's some kind of journalist." Shappa pulled a decidedly nonorganic Sara Lee cheesecake from the refrigerator. "God, I get so fucking tired of this vegan crap."

Darcy shook her head. They'd taken Lucy and Kevin to one of the tepees and gone back to Shappa's to talk. "You remember Warden Billings from Canyon?"

"How could I forget?" Shappa said. She took the cheesecake from its box, set it down on the table between them, and handed Darcy a fork. "I must admit, I was kind of hurt I never got taken to the Red Lobster. I always figured it had something to do with me being born a Jew, like it's contagious or something. That or he thought I was a lesbian."

Darcy smiled. "My little sister got sent down to Canyon a couple of months after they discharged you. She got herself all messed up on speed, methamphetamines, and tried to rob a Seven-Eleven with a steak knife."

"Shit, girl." Shappa wagged her head. "I'm sorry."

Darcy fiddled with her fork. "She's not like us, you know. I'm afraid for her in there."

Shappa sat forward in her chair and picked at the cake, serious now, while Darcy told her everything that had happened, from the first phone call from the warden to their arrival at the ranch.

"Here's the thing," Darcy said, when she had finished filling her friend in. "Everyone's looking for something Carl Greene left behind: Warden Billings, the guy who killed Weldon and Chick and took shots at us last night, and whoever the guy's working for. There's no doubt about that. But I don't think anyone has found it yet. When I was at the house the first time I got a pretty good look at the husband's files before Lucy interrupted me. There wasn't anything on TB testing or Pioneer or any of this stuff. I thought I must have missed it, but now I'm sure I didn't."

Darcy paused to carve off a forkful of cheesecake.

"What are you thinking?" Shappa asked.

"The warden wants those files bad. He's already way out of his league here. This isn't just a trip to Pueblo and a blow job. If I can get my hands on these I might be able to work something out for Angie. Who knows? People walk off work details all the time."

"And get caught."

"Not always." Darcy hesitated a moment. "But I'm going to need help."

Shappa got up, lit a burner on the stove, and set a teakettle on to boil. "I've got some friends," she said solemnly, her eyebrows knit together in concentration, "from the old days."

Shappa had given them warmer clothes to supplement the shorts and T-shirts Darcy and Lucy had taken from the house in Casper. But Lucy was still cold as she made her way across the compound in the hand-knitted sweater and frayed jeans. Most of the ranch's guests still seemed to be up and about. The ones who weren't singing in the mess tent sat talking in small groups, spread out on the grass or inside tepees, their silhouettes wavering against the backlit skins.

She was doing nothing wrong, but still Lucy felt slightly suspect, an outsider among these earnest people. She nodded to two young women as she passed the last tepee, and they looked up at her, their faces blank.

Shappa hadn't needed a key to get into the office, and Lucy was hoping no one had locked the door since their tour of the building. She stepped into the glare that illuminated the Worm and up the wooden steps and gingerly tried the knob. The door opened.

In the last few years, Chick had spent a good portion of his free time on the computer. Lucy knew that was where most of his information on Gulf War Illness came from: the newest herbal cure that seemed to be working in England, testimonies from other veterans, the Pentagon's latest official tally of how many soldiers had been exposed when the weapons depot at Khamisaya was blown up. She had half listened as he explained these things to her. Now she wished she had paid closer attention.

Closing the door, Lucy took a seat behind one of the desks and turned the computer on. The machine burped to life, the Windows logo flashing onto the monitor. Lucy waited for the desktop to appear, then scoured the icons for an Internet provider. In a matter of seconds she'd connected middle-of-nowhere Montana to the rest of the digital world. She typed GULF WAR ILL-NESS into the home page's search engine, hit ENTER, and waited.

A handful of web sites popped onto the screen: American Gulf War Vets. Office of Special Assistant for the GWIs. Capt. Nancy Bellamy: One Veteran's Story. And at the bottom of the list, in smaller print, SITES 1-9 OUT OF 3,127.

Lucy sat back in her chair. There was no way she could pore over three thousand web sites, especially with little or no idea of what she was looking for. She replaced GULF WAR ILLNESS with NEURAL TUBE DEFECTS. No, she thought, watching the cursor blinking expectantly, she needed something even narrower. Deleting NEURAL TUBE DEFECTS, she keyed in the single word MYCOPLASMA. Heck, she told herself, it was worth a shot.

The monitor flashed, and a new list of web sites appeared: Mycoplasma in Swine. Mycoplasma Genitalium. New York City Department of Health—Communicable Diseases—Mycoplasma Infection (Walking Pneumonia). Her field had broadened from huge to overwhelming; the search engine listed almost seven thousand sites on mycoplasma. Shit, she thought, you can get lost out here in the vast world of cyberspeculation.

Lucy scrolled down through the site descriptions, hoping something would catch her eye. Most of the information seemed highly technical, directed at medical professionals, but on the bottom of the second page she found a link to an article titled Facts on Mycoplasma and Chronic Fatigue that looked slightly less intimidating.

What is mycoplasma? the text asked cheerfully, and went on to describe the organism as "the smallest and simplest subclass of bacteria." According to the site, mycoplasma actually had the smallest genome of any bacteria capable of replicating independently of host cells. What distinguished mycoplasma from other bacteria, however, was the fact that it lacked a cell wall, enabling it to invade tissue and even white blood cells. Its special talent was to activate the immune system and then hide from it within the body's own immune cells. And, unlike bacteria, mycoplasma did not respond to antibiotics.

Lucy scrolled down through the article. The rest of the text talked about Chronic Fatigue Syndrome, immune deficiencies, and the prevalence of mycoplasma in the blood of patients with chronic fatigue. At the very end of the article were various links, sites dealing with information the author thought pertinent or at least interesting. A couple of Chronic Fatigue Syndrome support groups were listed, some articles on fibromyalgia, various mycoplasma web sites, and then, near the bottom of the list, two links that got Lucy's attention: a Gulf War Veterans resource page and another titled Mycoplasma and Gulf War Illness. She clicked on the second title.

Arlen Krill had settled in for the evening. He was just finishing up his take-out fried chicken and flipping through the Holiday Inn's pay channels, looking for some bedtime entertainment, when the call came.

"We've found them," the man whined. "They're up in Montana."

"You're going to have to do better than that," Krill said, selecting a preview of a film titled *Cherry Poppins*. "Montana's a big state."

"They're at some hippie training camp south of Livingston. Place is called Sheep Mountain Ranch."

Christ, Krill thought, these guys were everywhere. Though it wasn't the norm, Krill often worked for unknown employers—or employers who liked the illusion of being unknown. After a few contacts, he could generally figure out who was running the show. In this case, though, he still wasn't sure. He'd ruled out Intelligence early in the game, but he was starting to rethink this decision. They'd certainly screwed up enough to be Intelligence. And they had one hell of an information network.

"I'm on my way," Krill told the man.

Chapter fourteen

"Wake up. C'mon, you guys, time to rise and shine."

A hand touched Kevin's shoulder through the sleeping bag and shook him gently. Still half asleep, he lifted his head and saw the dim figure of Darcy's earth-woman friend as she crossed the tepee to where Lucy was sleeping.

"C'mon, now. Time to get up," she whispered forcefully.

Groaning, Lucy pulled her bag tightly over her head and rolled over.

"What's going on?" Kevin asked.

Shappa put her finger to her lips and came over to his cot. "We had a little problem last night, an informant in the Oregon group."

Kevin rubbed his eyes. "What does that mean?"

"The Feds send them all the time," Shappa explained. "Just keeping tabs on us. You figure there's always one in each group. Jeremy took him into Livingston."

"Before or after dinner?" Kevin asked, Shappa's point starting to come into focus in his groggy brain.

"After," she said, adding, "The three of you were hard to miss."

Darcy had stirred from her bag and was sitting up in her cot blinking at them.

"What time did he leave?" Kevin asked.

"Just after dinner. I'm sure he called the mothership right away. It's only a matter of time before they put two and two together and realize you guys are here." Shappa looked at her friend. "Sorry, babe. I really think you should go."

Nodding, Darcy swung her legs off the cot and shuffled over to Lucy's sleeping form. "Time to get up," she murmured, pulling the sleeping bag back. "You can sleep in the car."

Kevin dug in his pocket for the address Max Fausto had given him. "Any idea where this is?" he asked, handing the slip of paper to Shappa.

She squinted to read his handwriting. "I know where Homer is, but I'm not sure about the address. Jeremy's got a gazetteer in the trailer. You guys get yourselves together, and I'll meet you at the car with directions."

Steam rose off the Yellowstone and lingered in the cottonwoods like some indolent water nymph, too lazy to head for higher ground. A handful of fishing dories were already on the water, gleaming drift boats filled with soft-bellied Brad Pitt wannabes, shadow-casting CEOs from Houston and Indianapolis in five-hundred-dollar waders. Most of the valley was still grazing land, rickety ranch houses, and cattle, but along the river the million-dollar summer cabins were common as flies on a cowpie. The Gallatin Range loomed above everything, the mountains' crags and drainages accentuated by the sideways light of early morning.

They stopped at a gas station in Emigrant, and Kevin disappeared inside, returning with three steaming coffees.

"It's about ten more miles to Homer," Darcy said, consulting the rough directions Jeremy had written out to Herman Canty's address.

Lucy stretched in the backseat, rubbing her eyes. Across the highway, under a low bridge, fish surfaced to feed, their mouths kissing rings onto the calm dark water.

She took a sip of the too-hot coffee and felt it burning as she swallowed. "I found out what mycoplasma is," she said as they pulled back onto the highway.

Kevin gave her a puzzled look in the rearview mirror. Darcy shifted so she could peer into the back.

"Remember," Lucy said to the other woman, "when we were in Craig Weldon's office? All his research was on mycoplasma."

Darcy nodded.

"I couldn't sleep last night. I was thinking about Ophir and this thing at Pioneer. It sounds so much like the way my brother's been sick. And a few years ago I lost a baby too." Lucy stopped to take another swig of coffee. "So I went to the office back at the ranch and got online. Chick spent hours on the computer talking to other vets. Every kook's got a story, you know? But that doesn't mean some of them aren't true."

Darcy dipped her head again in agreement. "And you found something?" she prompted.

"I thought it was worth a try, so I did a search. It's a microorganism, like a small bacterium, only it doesn't always react to antibiotics. It's got a way of hiding in the immune system. Walking pneumonia's a mycoplasma infection. And chronic fatigue. They've been finding it in Persian Gulf vets, ones like my brother, with symptoms of Gulf War Illness. Only here's the thing: It's not your garden-variety mycoplasma. Someone's been fucking with its genome."

Darcy looked lost. "What does that mean?"

"Biotechnology," Kevin interjected. "Genetic engineering."

Lucy smiled grimly. "The house specialty at Bioflux."

"And what does all this have to do with tuberculosis testing?" Darcy asked.

"Good question," Lucy said, catching Kevin's eye again. "What do you think the chances are that Bioflux was manufacturing the tuberculin for the tests?"

"About as good as the odds on their making biowarfare vaccines for the military."

To call Homer a town was a huge overstatement. Even saying it was a wide spot in the road was misleading. The road actually narrowed, squeezing itself onto an old bridge that spanned the Yellowstone, then snaked up into the arid foothills. Just past the bridge was a tackle shop and a tiny white clapboard building labeled, simply, BAR.

The summer homes had thinned toward this end of the valley, but they had also grown larger and more obscene. Six-thousand-square-foot log monstrosities clung to the riverbank, their garages big enough to accommodate a family of Range Rovers.

"I think this is it," Darcy said, pointing to a cluster of mailboxes on the far side of the bridge.

Kevin slowed the car. CANTY was neatly painted on one of the boxes.

"Here," Darcy told Kevin.

He turned, following a gravel lane across a hay field and then back along the river, toward what looked to be the only house on Absaroka Road.

Darcy whistled as they drew closer. "Nice place!"

On first glance, Herman Canty's house looked more like some kind of fishing lodge or dude ranch than a private residence. The walls were rough-hewn logs, with windows that spanned from floor to high ceiling. The house was angled to face downriver, and a covered wooden porch wrapped around two sides of the building, its roof supported by lodgepole pines.

Kevin slowed the car a little and pointed toward the back of the house, where a bank of windows shone from within. "It looks like someone's up."

"You think this is a good idea?" Darcy asked as they pulled in through the split-rail fence that marked Canty's yard. "I mean, Lucy's not exactly Miss Popularity right now."

Kevin eyed Lucy in the rearview mirror.

"If Shappa was right," she said, sitting up and propping her arms on the seat in front of her, "our whereabouts aren't much of a secret anyway."

They parked in the driveway and climbed up the stone steps to the porch. Lucy rang the doorbell, and a chime sounded inside the house.

"How much do you think this little slice of paradise is worth?" Kevin asked, looking out at the Yellowstone, the water sparkling and shining where it rippled over a wide shallow stretch of river-bed. Out in the yard a meadowlark whistled and another replied.

"Too much," Darcy said, unimpressed. The house seemed lonely and cold to her, someone's misguided idea of luxury. She'd been inside too many of these houses and seen too many draw-ers stocked with Valium, too many gin bottles tucked away in shoe boxes or toilet tanks, to want one herself.

"Should I ring again?" Lucy asked. There seemed to be no sign of movement inside.

Darcy cupped her hands over her eyes and peered in one of the windows. A woman appeared from the back of the house and made her way toward them, her solitary form dwarfed by the massive front room. "Someone's coming," Darcy reported, stepping back.

A minute passed, and the door swung open, revealing a frail gray-haired woman. "May I help you?" she asked.

Kevin jumped in. "Mrs. Canty?"

The woman nodded. She was wearing slippers and a fleece sweat suit. A bright Indian shawl was thrown across her shoulders.

"Sorry to bother you this early." Kevin held out his hand and smiled easily, as if they were old acquaintances, just needing a quick reintroduction. "I'm Kevin Burns. I work for MSNBC." Pulling his wallet from his back pocket, he produced a business card. Then, indicating Darcy and Lucy, "These are my produc-tion assistants."

The woman took the card and peered out at the rental car, as if it might confirm what Kevin had said.

"We're actually here to talk to your husband, Mrs. Canty. I'm doing a story on the biotechnology industry, and I understand Mr. Canty was one of the pioneers." Kevin pressed on. "We'll just take a few minutes of his time."

The woman took a step back, seeming to indicate that they could come in. Kevin only hesitated a moment before stepping across the threshold.

"My husband's not well," she explained when Lucy and Darcy had joined him. "Some days are better than others, but he has advanced Alzheimer's disease." She closed the door and started off, motioning for them to follow.

The house's front room seemed even larger from the inside. Darcy tipped her head back and looked up at the graceful tangle of rough-hewn pine rafters that buttressed the vaulted ceiling. A second-floor gallery surrounded the room on three sides, and a mammoth stone fireplace, deep and wide enough to roast a large elephant, occupied the center of the space. The room's furnishings—leather chairs, heavy wood tables, and antler lamps— seemed Lilliputian in scale.

"We spend most of our time back here," the old woman explained, leading them through a door at the back of the great room, down a long corridor, and into the kitchen.

Darcy could see why. Despite the intimidating appliances, the stainless refrigerator and commercial range, the kitchen seemed built to human scale. There was a breakfast nook with a simple pine table, a sunny sitting area with wraparound windows, a modest fireplace, an overstuffed couch, and a couple of chairs— a home within the senseless sprawl of the house.

"Herman?" Mrs. Canty said. She turned to the three of them. "He was just here." She shuffled toward the sitting area. "Herman?" she called, her voice rising a notch. Peering out one of the windows that faced the river, she rapped on the glass with her bony knuckles. "Herman!" she called, loudly now, trying to make herself heard through the glass.

Darcy took a step forward, craning her head to see out the

windows. Out where the lawn met the riverbank, his face turned up to the sun, his eyes closed in the ecstasy of the moment, was an old man in a blue and white striped bathrobe. A boatload of fishermen were passing, their lines catching the morning light as they cast lazily toward promising water.

"Herman!"

Herman Canty opened his robe, exposing his wrinkled belly to the river. The fishermen stopped casting, their eyes moving to the half-naked man on the bank, his midriff like a pallid raisin.

"Bastards!" he yelled, shaking one fist in the air. Holding his old-man dick in his free hand, Canty peed into the bright waters of the Yellowstone.

"Get the boat ready, Alice!" Canty said excitedly.

The four of them had managed to get him inside, but he didn't seem too happy about it. He kept looking out toward the river, pointing downstream.

"I think you'd better go," Mrs. Canty said. "I'm pretty sure you won't get much out of him today."

Lucy looked desperately at Kevin. They had nowhere to go from here.

"Maybe you can help us," he said. "We understand your husband was on the original board of the Bioflux Corporation. Is that true?"

Nodding, the woman put her hand on Canty's shoulder.

"The boat, Alice!" he said, waving her off furiously.

"We've been having trouble finding any of the other board members," Kevin went on. "I'd love to be able to talk to some of them, find out what it was like in the beginning. It's a fascinating field."

Mrs. Canty eyed Kevin skeptically.

"We've spoken with Viviane Beckwith," Lucy interjected, hoping the name might lend them some credibility, even though she hadn't told them anything.

Herman Canty's eyes snapped to attention. "Where's that bitch?" he said feverishly. "Is she here? Alice?" He glanced up at

Lucy and Kevin and Darcy, as if noticing them for the first time. "Who are these people?"

"Herman and Viviane never got along," Mrs. Canty explained. She turned to her husband. "They're here from the news. They want to do a story about you."

"Well, tell them to sit down," Herman bellowed. "They're making me nervous!"

Mrs. Canty motioned for them to sit and pulled a chair up next to her husband.

"He never should have married that money-hungry sour-puss," Canty went on. "I told him, too. Not that it made any difference." The old man's head drooped slightly. He lifted it back up and stared out the window.

Mrs. Canty cleared her throat. "They want to know about Bioflux, dear."

Canty looked confused.

"Viviane," Lucy reminded him.

He nodded. "She was a secretary at Raleigh. A goddamn secretary, acts like she owns the world. Never mind she had the nicest ass on the base. Perfect."

Mrs. Canty flinched; Lucy pretended not to notice.

"They don't wear skirts anymore," Canty grumbled, looking at Kevin for sympathy. "But back then, she shimmied around in those tight little suits and heels. Goddamn legs like a racehorse. Beautiful."

"Herman and David worked at Fort Raleigh together," Mrs. Canty translated.

"In the army?" Kevin asked.

The old woman shook her head. "They worked for the army, but they were both civilians."

Canty stood up. "C'mon," he said to Kevin. "I'll show you."

The old man's leather slippers flopped against his heels as he led them through the kitchen and back down the same corridor they'd traversed earlier. Just before they entered the great room, he ducked through a doorway and up a flight of stairs.

Lucy lagged a few feet behind, with Canty's wife. She couldn't hear everything Canty was saying, but she could tell he was still talking about Viviane, alternating between praise and vitriol. They reached the second floor and started along the mezzanine, traversing the width of the great room below. At the far end of the gallery, Canty led them through another doorway into a dark-paneled office.

Crossing the room, he opened the top drawer of an antique writing secretary. "Here," he said. Rummaging among the drawer's contents, he produced a faded photograph.

Kevin crossed to where Canty stood. Lucy and Darcy followed. Viviane Beckwith stood alone in the picture, a purse tucked under one arm, gloves draped languidly over an upturned palm, her skirt clinging to her thighs. She was some fifty years younger than the woman Lucy and Kevin had met, but there was no mistaking that they were the same person. She was looking straight into the camera, confident and full-lipped, her hair pressed into luscious curls.

Canty withdrew the picture and stared at it privately. "Fuck," he said, shaking his head in awe or disbelief. Setting the snapshot aside, he reached for another in the open drawer.

There were two people in this picture, Viviane and a man. She was wearing a dress this time, and white gloves. In her hands was a small bunch of flowers—lilacs, it looked like. She was smiling, smirking even, her lip cocked seductively to one side. The man was more serious, slightly older. He looked uncomfortable in a suit, starched shirt, and tie. Their wedding day, Lucy thought.

Canty jabbed at the man with his finger. "Bastard," he said.

Lucy watched the old man reach into the drawer one more time. He pushed aside the loose photographs, searching. Then, half covered by another picture, something caught Lucy's eye.

"What's this?" she asked, separating the print.

Canty glanced at it.

It was a group photo, several rows of young men. It was almost identical to the one she'd seen in Viviane Beckwith's bathroom, only there were two men in this picture who hadn't been in Viviane's, two figures in dark suits.

"The white coats at Raleigh," Canty said matter-of-factly. "There's David, and that's me." He pointed to the two figures in suits.

Lucy ran her finger over a funny dark form at the edge of the photograph, a shape like a crescent, part of a large sphere. "What's this?"

Canty shook his head and went back to pawing the contents of the drawer.

Nudging his arm, Lucy showed him the picture again.

He looked at it dubiously, and his face became suddenly agitated. "The eight-ball," he said, and started to cry.

Mrs. Canty showed them out. "Like I told you," she said apologetically, her voice echoing as they crossed the great room, "some days are better than others."

"What was he talking about?" Kevin asked, when they reached the front door.

"Work he did at Raleigh, I guess. It troubles him sometimes."

"I hate to ask any more questions," Kevin said gingerly, "but is there anyone you remember from the old days at Bioflux? A name, even?"

The woman shook her head. "Herman and I didn't meet until 1985. So you see, I really can't help you with any of this."

Nodding sympathetically, Kevin stepped out the door, with Darcy not far behind him.

"Thank you," Lucy said. She took the woman's hand and they stood for a moment contemplating each other.

There was a hat rack on one wall of the entryway, a trout with pegs along its back. Above the trout was a mirror, and Lucy could see herself in the glass as she stood facing the old woman. On the wall behind her back, reflected in the mirror, was a watercolor, a pastel rendering of a little cabin in the woods. A much nicer place than this, Lucy thought, a familiar place, and comfortable.

"Thank you, Alice," she said again.

"Oh, no," the woman corrected her. "I'm Marjorie. Alice was the first Mrs. Canty. Some days it's the only name Herman remembers. I'm never sure if he thinks I'm her or if it's just the name."

Lucy turned, pausing to get a better look at the watercolor. A familiar place. "Marjorie?"

"Yes?"

"Is Alice still alive?"

"Oh, yes, very much so."

"Where does she live?"

"Right there," the woman said, taking a step forward so that she was standing next to Lucy. "I mean, not *right* there. She lives in Washington, with Herman's granddaughter." She pointed to the watercolor. "That's their cabin." Mrs. Canty paused. "I can never remember the name of the town. It's something Beach. Near Seattle."

"Elwha Beach," Lucy said.

"Yes!" the woman exclaimed. "On the Olympic Peninsula. Have you been there?"

Elwha Beach. Lucy repeated the name to herself, once again imagining the landscape she'd envisioned so many times. A place lush and green, the place where Carl had died. And now she knew why the picture was so familiar, the little cabin with its sloping roof and screened-in porch. Carl had been there. On the day he died, perhaps, and sometime before as well. How many other times? Enough to remember the place, to sketch it hastily on a note pad, to think of it in their bedroom in Pryor.

Chapter fifteen

"Elwha Beach, Washington," Lucy said, pointing to the small black dot on the northern edge of the Olympic Peninsula. She handed the atlas to Darcy in the backseat.

Darcy contemplated the map. "It looks like at least a fourteen-hour drive."

"We can drop you in Bozeman," Lucy said. "Get you a bus ticket back to Colorado. No one except Billings knows you're involved in any of this, and I doubt he'll be talking."

Darcy set the atlas aside and looked out the front window at the blacktop ribbon of the two-lane highway disappearing beneath the hood of the car. A flock of magpies leapt up from a rancher's barbed-wire fence and winged across the road, on the lookout for something to scavenge. If she left soon enough, she could be in Castle Rock by morning. She'd missed two days, but she was pretty sure she could talk her way back into the job at the Flying J. Lucy was right, it was not too late to slip back, unnoticed, into what had been her life.

And what did she have now, hurtling west with these two people she didn't know and wasn't even sure she could trust? The promise of a different existence? The possibility, slim as it was, that there could be something better? It was hardly worth the risk, and yet it was. At some point, the odds had to turn in her favor. No, she wasn't going back.

Darcy and Lucy were both asleep when they crossed the Continental Divide and started the long descent into the mine-scarred, wind-blasted basin that cradled Butte, Montana. It was midday, hot and dry, late-summer sun battering the latter-day boom town. A Greyhound bus passed, heading in the opposite direction, and Kevin thought briefly of his mother, of her life as he'd always imagined it, her long journey away from him.

What did he remember about her? She'd taken him out to eat once, at a fancy supper club in Greeley, and ordered crêpes suzette and champagne for her dinner. He'd been embarrassed, ashamed by the spectacle of it, the stiff waiter with his white shirt and long apron, the flourish with which he touched the match to the pan. He'd been angry and, he decided now, disappointed by the choice he'd made, the breaded prawns and soggy baked potato they set before him.

Up and run off with a bunch of hippies. His grandmother's words had always conjured up some kind of dirty circus, greasy-haired clowns and trapeze artists with unshaven legs and bad teeth trooping from small town to small town. And yet she could have become anybody: a farmer, a lawyer, even a mother. That was the trick, Kevin thought, to find the thing that electrified you, a force of grace. Like the instant when the acrobat's body reached the point of perfect momentum, and the hands swung free of the bar.

Lucy stirred and turned her face toward him. Her eyes were wide open, bright with the false alertness of the newly awakened. "Where are we?" she asked, stretching her right arm over her head.

"Butte."

"God, what a dismal place."

Kevin looked out at the mangled hills, the bedraggled houses of the residential subdivisions south of town. "You sleep okay?"

Lucy smiled. "Like a baby in a paint mixer. You want me to drive for a while?"

"I thought we'd stop in Deer Lodge and get gas. You can take over then. Would you do me a favor, though? Something's been bothering me ever since we left Canty's place." Kevin tilted his head toward the backseat. "You see my laptop on the floor back there?"

"Uh-huh."

"There's a little spiral notebook in the front pocket of the carrying case."

Releasing her safety belt, Lucy reached over the seat, unzipped the pocket, and slipped the notebook out. "Got it."

"Okay, my handwriting's terrible, but the last notes in there are from the *Ophir Gazette.* Can you find them?"

Lucy flipped through the notes till she came to the final entry. "Yeah."

"Roy Billings's bio said he was in the army. Did I write down where?"

Lucy's finger skimmed across the careless script. "Here it is: Fort Raleigh."

Kevin glanced over at her. "Are you starting to see a pattern here?"

The American military had never been Kevin's specialty. In fact, the Earl Sykes piece had been a fluke, passed on to him by Sylvia Graham, a senior colleague who was heading to Saint Croix when the story broke. So besides the fact that Herman Canty, David Beckwith, and Roy Billings had all spent time there, Kevin knew nothing about Fort Raleigh.

The batteries in his cell phone had long since gone dead, so when they stopped in Deer Lodge for gas, Kevin made a beeline for the pay phones out front of the Exxon station. He punched in the main MSNBC number, followed by the four-digit extension for Sylvia Graham's office.

"Ms. Graham's out on assignment," a voice informed him.

"Marisa?" Kevin asked, recognizing the voice of Sylvia's assistant.

"Yeah."

"It's Kevin Burns."

"Kevin!"

"You miss me?"

"Every day, baby, every day. So watcha been doing?"

"Just bumming around. Freelancing some, working on a novel. Listen, I really need to ask Sylvia something. She in the office?"

"Sorry," Marisa said. "She's up in Alaska working on a story."

"You got a cell phone number?"

"I got it, but I don't know if it's gonna do you much good. She's out of range about eighty percent of the time."

"It's worth a try," Kevin said.

Marisa rattled off the number. "They're supposed to be shooting in Fairbanks tomorrow. You should be able to reach her then."

"Thanks."

"No problem. You take care. And good luck with Sylvia."

Kevin hung up, shoved another handful of coins into the phone, and dialed the number Marisa had given him. Sylvia's voice mail answered. A recording instructed him to leave a message, with the assurance that Sylvia would call him right back.

Kevin put the receiver back in its cradle. He'd try her later.

"I don't know," the old woman said nervously.

Krill couldn't blame her for lying. There was nothing about him that suggested any good might come from his inquiry. But still, he was starting to get irritated. Krill had driven all night to get to Montana. When he finally arrived at Sheep Mountain Ranch, the Greene woman and her friends were long gone.

Even when Krill threatened to have the outfit shut down, the little redhead who ran the place refused to talk. If it hadn't been for the spinelessness of the dreadlocked boyfriend, Krill might have left empty-handed. As soon as Krill mentioned the IRS, the pasty, wannabe Rastafarian opened up like a clam in a hot frying pan.

And now Krill had backtracked south, down the spine of the Paradise Valley, to talk to some rich gray hair who thought she could play him for an idiot. This was his last U.S. job, Krill decided. He'd said it before, but this time he meant it. Who needed the headache of domestic ground rules, when in any developing country a few hundred well-placed American dollars could produce the same tidy results? There was too much pretense of righteousness here, too much time spent whitewashing corruption for the evening news. And Krill knew as well as anyone he'd be the first dirty little secret cut loose if the shit ever hit the fan.

Krill put his hand on the woman's shoulder, the pressure of his fingers just hard enough to suggest what kind of damage could be inflicted.

"See," he told her, "I think you *do* know where they went."

The old woman tried to move away, but his grip stayed with her.

Darcy got out of the car and stretched. They'd made good time. It was just after seven in Seattle. The city towered above them, windows flaring in the early evening light. A stiff breeze blew off Puget Sound, cool and salty. The ferry was coming in, engines roiling the water into foam as it neared the dock.

It was not the ocean as Darcy had imagined it, blue and inviting, the surf curling onto white sand beaches. No, this sea threatened. Black waves split into dirty froth. Rain-soaked hills reared up like the humped backs of green-scaled sea monsters.

They were parked near the end of a long line of cars waiting to make the crossing to Winslow, on a blacktop slab built out into the bay. Kevin had gone up to the terminal to make a phone call.

Lucy lay across the hood of the car, smoking, her left arm flung over her head, her midriff bared to the cold sunshine.

She finished her cigarette and flicked the butt onto the asphalt, then lifted herself up and opened the back door of the rental car. Darcy watched her slip the Glock from underneath the driver's seat. She popped the near-spent clip out and shoved a fresh one up into the stock: ten new bullets. Lucy checked the safety and slid the gun into the back of her jeans.

There was, at times, a fearlessness about the other woman that scared Darcy, a vacant resignation she'd only seen before in some of the long-timers at Canyon. It had been there that first night at the house, when she'd looked up to see Lucy naked, framed in the doorway of Carl Greene's office.

The ferry groaned as it settled into its slip, chains clanging, metal shuddering against wood. How does it happen? Darcy wondered. How does it come to this? Parents dead, a child, a husband, a brother, and finally the soul goes as blank as the eyes of a sleepwalker. And yet she had a feeling that a portion of this absence had always existed in the other woman.

From the bank of pay phones on the second floor of the terminal, Kevin could see the flow of traffic on the sound. The ferry was coming in, the maw of its lower deck packed with cars.

Somewhere in Alaska, Sylvia Graham's cell phone rang: once, twice, three times.

"Pick up, goddamn it!" Kevin muttered.

Five rings, six, then a woman's voice. "This better be good!"

"Sylvia? It's Kevin Burns."

"Shit. What the fuck do you want?"

Kevin heard a male voice in the background, a muffled complaint of "Where you goin', sugar?"

"What do you know about Fort Raleigh?" Kevin asked.

"Call me back in the morning. Okay, kiddo?"

"I need to know tonight."

Sylvia sighed. "Where should I start?"

"Give me the abridged version," Kevin said. The ferry was starting to dock.

Lucy looked up at the balcony of the terminal and started the engine. The ferry had unloaded, and the lines of waiting cars were beginning to roll forward.

"You see him?" Darcy asked.

"No," Lucy said, shaking her head. It was another hour and twenty minutes till the next crossing, and she didn't want to wait.

The flagman up ahead signaled their lane to go, and Lucy crept ahead.

Darcy craned her neck. A few stragglers were hustling along the second-floor walkway toward the pedestrian gangplank, but there was no sign of Kevin.

"We're getting on," Lucy decided. "If he doesn't make it, we can wait at the other side."

Krill had driven hard across Montana and Washington, hoping to close the gap between himself and the threesome. From what the old woman said, Krill guessed he was a good hour and a half behind them, but he figured they'd be sticking to the speed limit, trying to play it safe.

Krill careened across Lake Washington toward downtown Seattle, navigating the highway labyrinth. Swerving to avoid the hulks of urban SUVs, he found the exit for the waterfront. They were heading across the sound; slow as it was, the ferry was the quickest way Krill could see to Elwha Beach. He turned onto Alaskan Way and headed north, following the signs to the terminal.

"The government opened Raleigh during World War Two," Sylvia explained. "It was the Los Alamos of biological weaponry. A bunch of civilian scientists with the military's toys and money at their disposal. They were producing souped-up anthrax and plague and other nasty products of nature right up until 1970."

That was the year at least two of those scientists started Bioflux, Kevin thought. "What happened in 1970?" he asked.

"Aside from my ill-fated first marriage?" Sylvia quipped. "God, you make me feel old. You weren't even born yet, were you?"

Kevin thought for a moment. "I could have been post-conception."

Sylvia laughed. "On Valentine's Day, 1970, Dick Nixon formally extended the official ban on bacteriological weapons he'd signed in 'sixty-nine to include all toxic agents. That was the end of the U.S. germ warfare program."

Kevin looked out through the terminal's glass windows toward the upper deck of the ferry. Most of the walk-on passengers had already boarded. "You know anything about a company called Bioflux?"

"Nope. You working on something?"

"Kind of," Kevin said. "I may have something on Gulf War Illness. You know anyone who might be interested?"

"I'll tell you a story," Sylvia said. "A couple years ago I got a line on a GWI piece. A bunch of soldiers who'd been stationed at the same base in Saudi all said that a missile, a Scud or something, exploded over them one night. They're saying they were told to suit up. The chem alarms on the FOX vehicle were ringing like crazy. There's a fireball the size of a house bouncing across the desert. Their skin's burning, their eyes. And whatta you know? Now they're all sick. Only here's the problem."

Kevin eyed the ferry nervously. He couldn't see the cars from where he stood, but he hoped Lucy and Darcy had gotten on without him.

"The next morning the XO tells them it was a sonic boom. They didn't see anything. And now the VA says they're not on the official list of soldiers who were exposed to chemical weapons. A week before I was going to run the piece, the network decided to cut it."

"I've got to go, Sylvia."

"Hold on. It took me two weeks to get a straight answer about why they killed my story, but it turns out the Pentagon called. I don't know what they said exactly, but the basic message was that if MSNBC ran the piece we'd never have a front-row seat at a war again."

The ferry sounded its horn, a loud mournful wail that made Kevin jump. He slammed the phone down and sprinted out onto the pedestrian walkway, his eyes searching the dock for the rental car.

Krill could see the ferry from Alaskan Way. What a piece of luck! he told himself as he turned onto the docks. He wouldn't even have to wait. But when he stopped to pay the car fare, the woman in the tollbooth looked down at him impassively.

"You missed it," she said.

"But it's still there." Krill had a strong and sudden desire to take out his gun and shoot her.

"Not for long."

The departure horn sounded, scattering a flock of pigeons that had landed on a neighboring pier. Krill took his ticket and rolled forward, under the terminal and out onto the now-deserted asphalt slab.

The ferry was still in its slip, but the car ramp had been withdrawn. Several yards of cold Puget Sound water separated him from the lower deck of the boat.

The horn sounded a second time, and Krill looked up toward the passenger level. He wasn't the only latecomer. A frantic figure tore down the walkway, gesturing madly. He disappeared from view for an instant, concealed by the covered gangplank, and then Krill saw him emerge onto the deck of the ferry.

Chapter sixteen

Kevin rested his hands on his knees and gasped for breath, his heart rattling against his ribs like a jackhammer. The deck beneath him lurched and the ferry slid forward into Puget Sound. Please let them be on board, he thought. Stumbling into the warmth of the passenger cabin, he headed forward, scanning the crowd for Lucy or Darcy.

"You stay here in case he comes," Darcy instructed. "I'll go look upstairs." She opened her door and got out. Lucy watched her thread her way between the other cars and disappear into a portal. They were driving into the wind. The gusts caught Darcy's hair, whipping it around her face.

Lucy put her sweater on and stepped out of the car. The craft was riding close to the waterline, and spray misted across the open deck. Lucy turned so she could watch their wake churn out behind them, the water greening in a sun break. A gull dove past her, skimming the spume, riding the ferry's draft. Carl came this way, she thought, on this same boat, perhaps, in the final hours of his life.

What did it matter, really, how Carl had died or why? What was she going to do? Once they docked, it was just another hour to Elwha Beach. And from there, what? Carl was dead, and Chick. Lucy felt tender inside, as if there were a bruise deep within her, a dark wale no one else could see. There could be no tidy ending to this, nothing that would let her return to the house in Pryor, to her life as it had been, the rudderless hours.

Something would happen. Something had to happen.

It was loud on the open lower deck. Kevin called out, but his voice was lost in the clamor of the wind and the pulsing whine of the engine. Lucy's back was to him, her face turned to the receding Seattle skyline. He made his way through the parked cars and stood behind her, close enough to touch.

"The nurses wouldn't let me see Eric at first," Lucy said. For a second Kevin assumed she was talking to herself; then she turned and looked at him, and he realized she had known he was there all along. "These things happen," she continued, as if reassuring herself of this truth. "You know these things happen. Children are born sick or crippled, and there's nothing anyone could have done about it. But you still wonder if it was somehow your fault, if it was some choice you made or didn't make."

A strand of Lucy's hair was caught between her lips, and Kevin wanted desperately to put his hand on her cheek and brush it away. He wanted this tenderness between them. He took a step forward and brought his hand to her face. Her skin was cold, her cheeks red from the slap of the wind. Her lips were rimed with a thin film of salt.

"I'm sorry I left," Kevin said.

Lucy shook her head. "We were just kids. It was the right thing to do."

"I could have stayed."

"No," Lucy insisted. "You couldn't have." She stopped for a moment and looked down. "We think we get so many chances, but sometimes there's just the one, and you have to take it."

Kevin nodded, though he wasn't sure what she meant, whether she'd been talking about them, or Carl, or something else altogether. He lifted her face up to his, leaned down, and kissed her. For an instant he felt her body go slack, her mouth loosen against his; then she made a noise like an animal trying to free itself from a trap.

"Darcy," she whispered, taking a step back, her gaze fixed over his shoulder.

Kevin turned to see the other woman coming toward them. She sidled between two bumpers and stopped on the other side of the rental car. There was a moment of awkward silence. What did it matter that she had seen this? Kevin thought. They had done nothing wrong. Still, he felt as if he'd been caught in a deception.

"We're almost there," Darcy said.

The ferry slowed as if on queue, and the town of Winslow slid into view, beach and houses and verdant hills. People were starting to return to their cars.

"I talked to my friend," Kevin said.

Clouds had moved in, and there was a light rain falling by the time they reached Port Angeles. They took the narrow highway along the coast, out toward Cape Flattery and the old Makah whaling camp at Neah Bay. A misty dusk had settled over the Strait of Juan de Fuca, making it nearly impossible to tell where the gray water ended and the steely sky began. Far in the distance, Canada was an unbroken line of green, the densely forested shore of Vancouver Island shimmering like an inverted mirage, an oasis of sylvan land in the numbing expanse of sea. The light was liminal, deceptive. Houses winked from the woods, bright windows hidden behind waxy thickets of rhododendron, cedars soft with moss.

The cabin was on the far side of Elwha Beach, set back from the road on a squat fist of land that thrust out into the waters of the strait. It was dark when the rental car turned onto the gravel driveway, its headlights raking across the neat fence that enclosed the rain-glazed garden. Climbing roses grew thick as brambles against the white pickets, pink blossoms bursting from the unruly foliage.

Kevin shut off the engine and they sat for a moment with the windows rolled down, each of them listening to the soft hiss of the rain, the rhythmic suspirations of the sea breaking somewhere in the darkness.

A figure appeared at the front window of the cabin, a woman in a bathrobe, her hand cupped over her eyes to better see out, her gray hair pulled back into a neat bun. She was small and grandmotherly, her back just slightly rounded with age.

Lucy got out of the car, made her way to the garden gate, and lifted the latch. The woman moved away from the glass, disappearing briefly from view, and then the front door swung open.

"Alice Canty?" Lucy called, heading up the walkway.

"Yes?" The woman squinted from behind the screen door. "Is something wrong?"

Lucy stopped at the bottom of the porch stairs. "I'm Lucy Greene," she said. "I need to talk to you."

Alice Canty nodded. "Yes. Your husband was a friend of my granddaughter's."

Lucy blinked.

"Well, don't just stand there," Alice Canty said, looking past Lucy toward the figures of Kevin and Darcy in the driveway. "Come inside, all three of you."

Arlen Krill fought his way west toward the outer tip of the Olympic Peninsula. There'd been only a light drizzle falling when he left Bainbridge Island, but now the rain was coming down in sheets, making the crumbling seaside highway nearly impassable. A car sped by going the opposite direction, two blurred headlights barreling from around a blind curve, and Krill had to swerve to keep from hitting it. He felt his wheels slide onto the gravel shoulder, and for a brief instant he was afraid they wouldn't find the blacktop again.

Costa Rica, he promised himself. Once this was taken care of he'd fly down to San José and hire a couple of girls to keep him company. A road sign slid into his high beams; Krill squinted through the watery *flip-flop* of the wipers to read it: ELWHA BEACH 9.

Alice Canty closed her eyes and gripped the arms of the rocking chair with her age-speckled hands. "I was nursing at the Blanchard Academy in Virginia when I met Herman. I was thirty-four, an old maid. That was 1954. Blanchard was originally an all-girls' finishing school. The army requisitioned it during World War Two," she explained. "They used it as a hospital for wounded soldiers."

Lucy took a sip of the hot tea Alice had put before them. There was a fire going in the fireplace, and it was warm and cozy in the cabin's tiny living room.

"It was a beautiful place," the old woman marveled. "Like a palace. There was a ballroom with crystal chandeliers, and a library all paneled in oak. And, my God, the garden! There was an English folly, and a little Japanese pagoda, and a shed built to look like a French château. Though the soldiers didn't like it much. They didn't want to be reminded of the places they'd just been. Of course, by the time I met Herman, the war had been over for quite some time and all those men had gone home. They were using it to house the white coats—"

"The white coats?" Lucy interrupted.

"Seventh-Day Adventists," Alice explained. "They're not allowed to fight, you know, so a whole mess of them worked there as guinea pigs, testing out vaccines and new germ agents for the bio-weapons program. They knew going in that some of them would get sick, and some of them did. I remember one boy got so sick from tularemia we thought he might die, but we never lost any of them."

The picture, Lucy thought, the one she'd seen at Viviane Beckwith's and then again at Herman Canty's house. Boys in white coats, a dark sphere in the background. "Your former husband said something about an eight-ball."

Alice Canty shuddered visibly. She touched the tips of her slippered toes to the wood planks of the floor and rocked slowly backward. "That was David's invention: a horrible thing. Looked like some kind of big round spaceship. I was never allowed to see it except from the outside. It was a containment facility, for gassing the animals. They put those boys in there as well."

Kevin leaned forward. "Mrs. Canty, what happened in 1970? After Nixon shut Raleigh down?"

"Of course the wives weren't supposed to know any of this, but Herman loved to talk. He was sharp as a tack, I'll give him that, but he couldn't keep a secret to save his life. He had to tell someone, and I guess he figured better me than anybody else. Everyone had a piece of Raleigh by then. It wasn't just the army's project. It was TSS especially who didn't want to go."

"What's TSS?" Kevin asked.

"The CIA's technical support division," Alice explained. "Who's the old man in those James Bond movies? U? S?"

Kevin smiled. "Q?"

"Yes"—she grinned—"like Q, only slightly more inept. Exploding cigars for Castro. Poisoned umbrella tips. They'd invested a lot of time and money in Raleigh, and Nixon told them everything had to go. For Herman and David, it was a lifetime's worth of work, their whole scientific careers."

"So they started Bioflux?" Kevin said.

"Cupid's Baby," Alice said. "That's what TSS called the new operation, because it was Valentine's Day when Nixon shut the bio-weapons program down. The CIA and the Defense Department took all the money they'd had for Raleigh and buried it, a little here, a little there. Vaccine research, a couple of arms shipments, a new helicopter. That's how they funded Bioflux."

Lucy set her tea down. "You're telling me Bioflux is really the United States biological warfare program?"

Alice Canty nodded. "Not all of it. There's a legitimate front company there too, but essentially, yes. It happens more than you think, mostly in the arms business. The military funnels personnel into the private sector all the time, and the private sector funnels them right back into the government. The Soviet bio-warfare program ran as a private pharmaceutical company for twenty years after the Biological Weapons Convention, and we didn't have a clue. They hid the bio-weaponry project *inside* the company's buildings, like those Russian nesting dolls."

Darcy glanced over at Lucy, thinking, The unaccounted-for space at Bioflux!

"Alice?" Kevin asked.

"Yes."

"What did you mean by that: *The private sector funnels them right back into the government?*"

She folded her hands in her lap and looked down at them, as if looking for the answer there.

"There were five people on the original board of Bioflux," Kevin prompted. "David Beckwith and your husband were two. Who were the other three?"

The old woman gathered herself from her chair and shuffled out of the room. They could hear her rummaging for something in her bedroom. She reappeared holding a photograph, another faded print from Raleigh, the faces the same as the ones in the pictures they'd seen in Montana. Viviane and David Beckwith. Herman Canty.

Alice pointed to a pretty young woman in a sensible suit and gloves. "That's me," she said.

Next to the young Alice were four other people, three men and a woman, all well-groomed and confident. "This young fellow here was in charge at Deseret. That was the testing facility out in Utah. Lovejoy," she said, tapping her fingernail on the serious face. "Bill Lovejoy. And this girl next to him was his wife. They played bridge with us that night. He's retired now, used to work for the State Department."

She handed the photograph to Kevin. "The man next to the Lovejoys was the commander of the Special Ops division on the base. Phil Sumner."

Kevin looked up at her. *Deep and high.* Max Fausto hadn't been kidding. "You mean Philip Sumner, the former Secretary of Defense?"

Alice nodded. She looked pleased with herself. "You recognize *him*?" she asked, pointing to the last man.

Kevin peered at the time-faded face, the relaxed grin, the well-tailored suit: a son of East Coast ease.

"The baby of the bunch," Alice said. "He was head of TSS at Raleigh."

Kevin knitted his eyebrows.

"He's got a nice-looking résumé. National Intelligence Council. Director of Central Intelligence. He did some private consulting after that. Now he's back on the federal payroll."

"Joseph Auburn!" Kevin whispered, still staring at the boy in the picture, the face so familiar now, the eyes unaltered, a young man who would one day be vice president of the United States. *Deep and high.*

Lucy twisted herself to peer over Kevin's shoulder. "My God," she said.

The old woman lifted her head, staring past Kevin and out the cabin's wide front window, suddenly transfixed. "There's someone out there," she whispered.

Lucy turned, her stomach fluttering the way it did in the last few seconds before she dropped down the face at Vail mountain. She could see nothing but their reflections, the faint outlines of wind-tossed foliage.

"A man," Alice Canty insisted. "Out by the fence."

"The lights," Darcy said, dropping her teacup and reaching for the lamp nearest her. "Get the lights!"

Now there were four, Krill thought, counting the heads in the front room of the cabin and measuring his next move. If Krill had learned one thing from his thirty-odd years in this business,

it was that the complications associated with a job rose expo-
nentially as the number of targets increased. He knew he should
hold out for a cleaner opportunity; he'd be taking a chance with
all four of them there, and things could turn messy, but he was
tired of waiting. He wanted this job over with. He wanted to take
his pay and head south.

If he played his cards carefully, he could make it work. After
all, he'd done harder hits before, under less hospitable circum-
stances. He could pick off two or three through the window
before the others even knew what was happening. Pulling the
brim of his hat down against the rain, he strode along the road
to where he'd left his car, took his sniper rifle from the trunk,
and headed back toward the cabin.

The Greene woman first, Krill decided; then the woman who
was traveling with her, the one who'd shot at him two nights
ago; then the man. Last, the old woman. Luckily, the isolation
and the thrumming of the rain meant he wouldn't have to worry
about noise.

Krill stopped at the edge of the garden and squinted up
into the wind-tossed trees. The porch lamp was on, and in the
shadowy light he could just make out the dark spinneret of
the phone line arching toward the cabin's eaves. Hopping the
picket fence, he crossed the side yard and scanned the outer
wall. Even in his raincoat and hat, he was drenched. Water
oozed in through the seams of his shoes. Krill reached into his
soggy pants pocket, pulled out his Swiss Army knife, and deftly
cut the telephone wires.

These were the moments he liked to savor, the last seconds
before a job when only he knew what was about to happen.
Shielding himself as well as he could from the rain, Krill stepped
under the cavelike branches of a rhododendron and watched the
warm tableau inside the cabin. The old woman was speaking,
the other heads all turned her way, oblivious to his presence in
the garden.

And who wouldn't prefer this kind of ignorance? Despite all
he'd seen, or maybe because of it, Krill himself was terrified of
death. When his time did come, he could only hope it would

sneak up on him, that he'd be alive one minute and gone the next. That there would be no chance to contemplate the great gaping breach. They were lucky, really, he told himself, lifting his rifle to his shoulder. He swung the stock and brought the Greene woman into his sights.

Krill put his finger on the trigger and took a deep breath. No, this wouldn't be easy: lovely neck, lovely shoulders. And then, suddenly, she turned toward him, her eyes wide, searching, her skin flushed as if lit from within. He had her in the crosshairs for only an instant. Then the window went dark, and her face was extinguished.

The first shot hit the glass and kept right on going.

"Get down!" Darcy yelled as the bullet screamed into the room.

Reaching for her Glock, Lucy flung herself to the floor. The porch light was still on, the fire casting a somber orange glow. In this meager light, Lucy could see Kevin beside her, his knees drawn into his chest, the whites of his eyes darting feverishly around the room.

"Kevin?" she asked, rolling toward him. "You okay?"

His hand was clamped tight on his right shoulder. Lucy reached for him and felt the viscid warmth of blood on his shirt.

"It's all right," he rasped unconvincingly. "Just a scrape, I think."

A second crack exploded from the garden, shattering the windowpane completely, sending a torrent of glass into the cabin. Waiting for the explosion to pass, Lucy lifted her head and scanned the room. Near the far wall, Alice Canty had squeezed herself partway under a small table. She was rolled in a tight ball, her hands clasped behind her neck. Darcy was crouched under the front window, her Colt gleaming in the half-light.

Lucy turned back to Kevin. "Can you move?"

He nodded.

"If we buy you thirty seconds," Darcy asked, motioning with her head to Alice, "can you get her in the back?"

"I think so."

"I'll give you a three-count," Darcy told him. "As soon as we start shooting, go and don't look back." She waved Lucy over.

"How many shots in there?" Lucy asked, releasing the Glock's safety, ducking under the window.

"Six," Darcy said, hugging the wall. "Plus your ten makes sixteen. We're going to have to make them count."

Lucy nodded in agreement.

"Alice!" Darcy hissed, her voice raised a notch to carry across the cabin's living room.

The old woman raised her head.

"Is there a back way out of here?" Darcy called softly.

"Through the kitchen," Alice croaked.

"Okay, then," Lucy said, catching Darcy's eyes, "let's go on three. Just enough to keep him occupied."

Darcy brought the Colt up in front of her chest. "Ready," she said.

"One," Lucy counted. She took a deep breath and imagined a fall day at Burle Reservoir, the smell of wet leaves and first frost, the clamor of ducks winging in overhead. There was her father, and Chick hunkered down beside her, her father's hand signaling that they should wait. "Two." Steady, she told herself, though every muscle ached to move. She looked up, craning her head to peer out of the blind, and she could see the birds coming, each powerful breast working in rhythm with the next, the wings beating with perfect grace. "Three," she heard Darcy say. She sprang up around the corner of the window frame and shot once, the bullet whizzing into the rosebushes.

Darcy squeezed off her first round and one of the wooden pickets exploded.

Lucy glanced back to see Kevin struggling to help Alice up, his arm hooked under her shoulders. Counting her remaining bullets, Lucy fired again. Eight. Seven. Six. She ducked back under the sill and rested her back against the smooth plaster of the wall.

Except for the relentless droning of the rain and the sound of the two women breathing, everything was dead quiet.

"Where the fuck is he?" Darcy whispered.

Lucy raised her head slightly, peering around the jamb. Something flickered through the bushes and was gone, a dark figure, almost invisible through the scrim of the rain.

"The back door," Lucy said, rising out of her crouch.

"Go," Darcy told her. "I'll cover the front."

Lucy scrambled through the dark kitchen, groping blindly around furniture and cabinets. Her thigh slammed into something heavy and hard, the thick top of the kitchen table. A burst of wind whined across the side of the cabin, hurling the back screen door open and closed. Rain needled at the windows. Lucy pivoted once, then again, her arms rigid, her fingers tight around the Glock, the muscles in her forearms trembling. The wooden floor planks sighed beneath her weight.

A figure skated across the back window and Lucy squeezed the Glock's trigger. Five bullets left, four, three. But it was only the tousled shadow of a wind-whipped dogwood.

Darcy breathed deeply and shifted her feet, steadying herself. Broken glass crackled under the soles of her shoes. She closed her eyes and strained her ears. She could hear Lucy fumbling in the kitchen and the cascade of water off the eaves. The wind reared up and a door slammed somewhere in the back of the house. Darcy waited, blood thundering against her temples.

Something sounded on the porch, a hollow thump on the weathered boards. Darcy edged closer to the window. Another thump, quieter this time, then the deafening sound of gunshots from the kitchen. One, two. Standing, Darcy turned to go help Lucy, but a bullet whistled past her right ear, hitting the brick fireplace with a loud crack. She sank down again, hunkering below the sill, and let go a couple of blind shots. One left, she told herself, if she'd counted right. She could hear the shooter on the porch, the snuffle and scrape of his shoes. The front door rattled and shook, then the cabin fell briefly and deeply silent.

One bullet, Darcy repeated to herself, gasping to catch her breath, her eyes glued to the square of light that marked the front door. She was sweating, and the Colt's stock felt slippery against her palm. Silence, silence, then a muted shuffling. The door burst open and a dark figure stepped into the room. Wait, she told herself, carefully checking the Colt's sight. Make it count. The man raised his rifle to his shoulder and swung toward her, combing the darkness. Now, she decided. The muscles in her finger tensed and she felt the trigger depress. The gun clicked, weakly pronouncing her miscalculation. She was out of bullets.

Kevin clamped his jaw tight and closed his eyes. The pain in his shoulder had spread through the rest of his body. He felt claustrophobic, sweaty, and nauseated.

"It's just a flesh wound," Alice told him, putting her reading glasses on to better examine the laceration. "But you're going to need stitches."

Shots sounded from the front of the cabin, and Kevin swung his head anxiously in their direction. "You gonna be okay here?" he asked the old woman.

Alice nodded. She was strangely calm, beatific even. She opened the top drawer of a small dresser and pulled out an old revolver. "Here," she told Kevin. "Take this."

Another round of shots rattled the cabin, and Kevin stepped into the hallway, closing the door behind him. Carefully, slowly, he made his way toward the firelit living room.

Lucy heard the front door slam open, and the sound of measured footsteps. She skirted through the kitchen, her grip still tight on the Glock. A man stood just inside the entryway, his back to her, his gun raised. Beyond him, crouched where Lucy had left her, was Darcy. She held the Colt out in front of her like a shield. Her hand shook as she worked the trigger, the firing mechanism producing nothing but a feeble click.

The man took a step toward Darcy and Lucy followed behind, one step, then another. She bought the Glock up and sighted for his neck, but before she could fire, her foot squealed on the old wood floor, and the man wheeled around, his gun turned on her now, the barrel just a few feet from her face.

From the dark depths of the hallway Kevin could see two profiles. To his left, unmistakable to him even in silhouette, was Lucy. Her feet were wide apart, her stance solid, her chest pitched slightly forward. Her rigid arms ended in the blunt outline of a gun. From where Kevin stood, the pistol seemed almost an extension of her flesh, her hands turned into a figure of angry destruction. To Kevin's right, his head on a perfect line with the Glock, was a man. A rifle was slung over his back, and his hands held another gun, smaller but no less menacing.

Neither Lucy nor the man moved. They stood as still as two predators might, two animals, each waiting for the other to attack. Kevin could see Lucy's chest rising and falling. She was breathing hard, her right knee trembling.

Kevin felt the old woman's gun in his own hand, the sheer power of the metal. Silently, he raised the revolver in front of his face and peered across the barrel. Just this one small action, he thought, laying his thumb down, easing the hammer back.

Lucy took a deep breath. Her knee had started to shake, and her forearms ached under the weight of the Glock. A log fell in the fireplace. A tree branch scraped along the cabin's eaves. From the dark back hallway came the slow whine of an exhalation, then the explosive click of a hammer engaging. The man jerked his head around, involuntarily pivoting toward the noise. His eyes left Lucy for a split second, and she fired.

The shot caught him like a right hook might. His jaw snapped back and his fingers loosed their grasp on the gun. Lucy fired a second time, and a third. In each flash from the Glock's muzzle she could see Kevin out of the corner of her eye, the pale moon of his face visible, invisible, then visible again.

Chapter seventeen

Neither Lucy nor Darcy could see the water, but they could hear it as they drew closer, the boom and rush of the surf slamming to shore. Darcy was shivering, her pants soaked through by the water-logged underbrush. Her foot caught on the slick knob of a cedar root and she pitched forward, losing her grip on the dead man's legs, stumbling into a stand of wet ferns.

"You okay?" Lucy asked, bending to set the man's torso down.

"Yes," the other woman gasped, but Lucy could tell it wasn't true. Darcy doubled over, retching into the bracken.

The moon was above them, winking through the dark canopy of boughs and leaves, the shifting clouds. In the dim sooty light, Lucy saw Darcy rise up slightly, the back of her hand wiping at her mouth, and take the legs again. Darcy was looking straight at her, her eyes shining in the darkness, and for an instant Lucy saw herself as she must look: a dim shape in the underbrush, a creature of anger, a figure driven by fear.

Bending, she hooked her arms around the man's shoulders, and they went on, through the thickets of vine maple and madrone, through the dark woods, out toward where the cliffs would be. She was tired, and the weight of the body felt like an impossible burden, strangling and claustrophobic, something from which she might never be free. Just these last few yards, she told herself, and all this will be over. Then the trees thinned and the land tumbled breathlessly to the Strait of Juan de Fuca, the moon's thin wake flaring off the water as if off steel.

Just a place, Lucy thought, setting the body down, like how many other miles of coastline? Like the place Carl's car had left the road, the wheels catching air then tumbling down the embankment. She stepped to the edge of the cliff and peered down into the thickets of five-fingered fern and trillium. Except for a few scars in the foliage, the broken limbs of a mahonia bush, dark earthen wounds where wild ginger would have been torn loose, nothing would mark what was about to happen here, the passage of a man, the transference of a life.

A light moved out on the dark water, a boat heading across the strait toward Canada. An easy way out, Lucy thought, watching the craft like a star, like a comet falling across black sky, steadily working its way toward the opposite shore. The largest part of her wanted to head north too, out through the currents of the strait, out into the dark waters. But in reality, nothing was over with. What loomed out there was much harder, a beginning, a chance to live within the country of her own body, to fashion some kind of life.

Kevin drifted through a haze of discomfort. Even with the painkillers Alice had given him, he could feel the needle going in and out, the thread tightening against his skin. What the

pills mainly did was make his head heavy, make him too sleepy
to resist.

"You're going to be just fine," Alice said.

She looked down at him and smiled, her needle poised at the
highest point of its arc, and Kevin had a brief but lucid memory
of his mother. It was winter, dark early morning in his grandmother's kitchen. She had a needle in her hand, the thinnest
splinter of silver trailing a length of red thread. What had she
been doing? he wondered. Sewing a button on his coat? It
seemed such an unlikely task for her to undertake. And yet he
was certain that's what it was. The coat had been a Christmas
present from her, a puffy down parka that he'd worn all through
first and second grades. And it wasn't a button she was fixing but
the zipper, the bottom of which had come away slightly.

Her face was serious. She finished the last stitch and bit the
thread off with her front teeth, bending close to him, as if bow-
ing. He could see the smooth top of her head, the white line of
scalp where the hair parted.

"You'd better hurry," he heard his grandmother say, "or you'll
miss the bus."

His mother looked up and nodded, kissing him once on the
cheek. "Go on, now," she said.

In an instant he was out the door and down the back steps, his
lungs sore from the cold, his coat rustling as he ran down the
snowy drive toward the freshly plowed road. He could see the
bus, the solitary shape gliding along the highway past the winter-
flattened fields. I'm going to miss it, he thought, but it pulled to
a stop in front of his grandparents' mailbox and the door opened.
Kevin could see the driver inside, old Mrs. Kendrick, who had
probably been no more than thirty. She was waving to him and
smiling, her face round and soft beneath a pink knit hat.

Fine, he thought. I'm going to be just fine.

Lucy lifted the sheet and swung her feet onto the floor, moving
carefully so as not to wake Darcy. Kevin was dead asleep on a
trundle bed in the corner of the room, wheezing slightly as he

exhaled and inhaled. It had taken several hours of tossing and turning for Darcy to succumb to exhaustion, and Lucy didn't want to disturb her delicate slumber. She waited for a moment, counting the other woman's rhythmic breaths, and then got up, slipped her shoes on, opened the door, and stepped quietly into the hallway. Tired as she was, she had slept only briefly. She was grateful to see morning, relieved at the excuse not to wrestle her insomnia any longer.

Quietly, she made her way through the house. Dawn was coming on fast. Out the cabin's shattered front window, the sky was a lucid cerulean blue. The storm had blown away and the pinprick of a planet glowed through the treetops. On the mantel above the fireplace was a picture Lucy hadn't noticed the night before, a recent snapshot of a man and a woman. They were sitting on the front steps of the cabin, faces flushed and gleeful, rubber boots crusted with sand and mud. Each held a bucket, the mouths of which were tilted slightly to the camera, revealing a bounty of freshly dug clams.

The woman looked very much as Lucy might have expected Alice Canty's granddaughter to look: same lips, same eyes. Her long dark hair was tied back in a ponytail, and she had a smear of gray mud on her right cheek. She was a pretty woman, not stunning but solid, attractive in a tomboyish way.

Though the man beside her was Carl, it took a moment for Lucy to recognize her own husband. The Carl in the photograph was so obviously happy, so flamboyantly joyful, that she had trouble making sense of his features. His face was turned slightly to the woman, so there was no mistake about the source of his delight.

Lucy leaned closer to the picture, the reason for Carl's visits suddenly clear, the thing she had known all along yet refused to know. They had discussed her, she thought suddenly, the breadth and depth of her grief. They had talked about Eric, even, about all the private pain Lucy had hoarded.

"Couldn't sleep?" a voice asked.

Lucy spun around to see Alice Canty. "No." She shook her head.

"Me either," the old woman said, scanning the room, the broken window, the furniture in disarray.

"I'm sorry," Lucy offered, though the words were meager condolence for the violence they'd unleashed on this woman's home.

The night before, after they'd finished getting rid of the body, Darcy and Lucy had driven the man's car out to a beach about twenty miles up the coast, far enough away that Lucy hoped the local cops wouldn't nose their way back here.

Still, Lucy was worried for the old woman. "There may be questions," she said.

"He would have killed us all, you know," Alice remarked, starting toward the kitchen. "C'mon. I'll fix us some coffee."

In the dim morning light, the kitchen was quaint and inviting, with lace curtains and a pine table and wallpaper with faded cabbage roses. Alice took the coffeepot to the sink and filled it with water.

Lucy sat down and propped her elbows on the table. "How many times was Carl here?" she asked, rubbing her eyes with the heels of her hands.

"A few," Alice said matter-of-factly, filling the coffeemaker, spooning grounds into a filter. "My granddaughter comes out most weekends. She must have brought Carl with her at least half a dozen times."

"How long had they been seeing each other?"

The old woman shrugged. "I don't know, really. Eight–ten months, I think. He was here before Christmas this year. I remember, because they put my tree up."

Before Christmas. Lucy thought back to December, trying to remember him being gone. He spent so much time away that his trips became indistinct. An allergy conference in Cleveland. A seminar in Dallas. Not to mention trips to the Seattle facility. How many of his absences, Lucy wanted to know, had had nothing to do with work? And the ones that had, what had she really known about them? Which Bioflux had Carl worked for?

"They met through the company," Alice said, as if anticipating Lucy's next question. "She's a researcher. I knew he was married.

I never said a word to Dora about it. She's the kind of girl who's always made her own way. Always been determined to ignore any advice she's given." Alice set a cup of coffee on the table and then put her hand over Lucy's. "I'm sorry," she offered.

Lucy contemplated Alice's fingers on her own. "It's no one's fault," she said. "We had problems." She paused to take a sip of the coffee. "We had baby a few years ago who died in the hospital."

Alice nodded, as if she truly understood this, the loss of a child and what it might do to two people, how it could come between them forever. A thing so powerful it was useless to try to explain.

"And last week?" Lucy asked. "Before he died. Was Carl here then?"

Alice shook her head. "He was on his way out to meet Dora when it happened. She was frantic when he didn't come."

Dora. Lucy said the name to herself, the two syllables so sturdy, so concrete. "There was more to what Carl knew than just the Cupid's Baby project, wasn't there?"

The old woman knitted her eyebrows together and nodded slowly.

"I need to talk to Dora," Lucy said.

Alice contemplated Lucy for a moment. Then she crossed the kitchen, picked the phone up, and dialed. "It's Nana," she said, to the person on the other end; then, "I'm just fine, dear. Sorry to call so early, but I wanted to catch you before you left for work. I'm coming over to the city today. Can you meet for lunch? . . . Yes, one would be fine. How about Myrtle Edwards, the fishing pier? I'll stop at the market and get us a picnic."

From the end of the fishing pier, Lucy could see all of Elliott Bay: the rocky seawall that meandered north toward Ballard and Magnolia; to the south, the skyline of Seattle and the great gray ribbon of the elevated highway. Beyond the city, the port loomed like an apocalyptic rendering of the future, civilization given way to machines. Orange shipping cranes crowded the water-front like faceless titans. Tankers bobbed just offshore. The day was hot, the sky cloudless. The breeze coming off the water smelled of salt and kelp.

"There she is," Alice Canty said.

Lucy put her hand up to shade her eyes and squinted across the park, scanning the black band of the footpath, the parade of walkers and runners.

"By the grain elevators."

"Yes," Lucy said, picking out a solitary figure, a woman, still featureless from that distance. "I see her."

Dora Canty was a good seventy-five yards away, and it took her some time to reach the pier and start toward them. It seemed fitting to Lucy somehow, the slow resolution of the other woman, her body and face gradually coming into focus. She stopped at the end of the asphalt footpath and hesitated a moment, contemplating the three strangers with her grand-mother, and then stepped out onto the wood planks.

Carl had loved this woman, Lucy thought, watching her approach. And yet, that last night in bed he'd turned to her, Lucy, wanting something. Absolution? One more chance? Lucy shivered, thinking of their bedroom in Pryor, the feel of Carl's fingers through the cotton of her nightgown, a curtain, like a lung filling and emptying, billowed by the breeze.

Dora came forward until she was just an arm's length away. She stopped walking and thrust her hand out, as if she'd antici-pated this meeting many times, as if she'd rehearsed exactly what to say. "You must be Lucy," she said.

Lucy stared down at the outstretched hand. She had a sudden flawless recollection of Carl in a drawing class they'd both taken at CU, one of those rare first glimpses of the person who would become her husband. It had been Carl's idea for her to take the class, and when she hesitated he'd enrolled both of them. In her memory, he stood near the front of the room, face determined to do correctly and well this thing he was just learning. His elbow moved as he sketched, fingers careful with the dark wedge of charcoal, eyes skipping from the stooped model to the paper and back. How, Lucy wondered, did one unlearn love? Unless it wasn't love that was forgotten, but forgiveness.

They found an empty picnic table outside the Happy Hooker, the little bait, tackle, and espresso shop that served the pier. Dora was sitting with her back to the water, and over the other woman's shoulder Lucy could see an old Filipino fisherman gutting his catch. He was deft with his knife, the metal of the blade flashing through the silver-white bellies of the fish.

"What happened to my husband?" Lucy wanted to know.

"I met Carl a couple of years ago," Dora explained unapologetically, "at a seminar in Denver. A group of us went to dinner one night, and I ended up sitting next to him."

She scanned the faces of her audience. She had been discreet enough, or perhaps indifferent, not to ask how Kevin and Darcy fit into the story.

"We didn't see each other for another year. Then I ran into him one day up here, out at the company. There was nothing between us at first, just coffee and a sympathetic ear. I think what Carl really needed was someone to talk to."

Lucy winced, thinking about the long silent dinners in the cavernous kitchen in Pryor, the scrape of cutlery on plates, and the nightly battles against intimacy. It was not the physical nature of Carl's relationship with this woman that bothered Lucy but what she imagined they had spoken of, the betrayal of this loss that was hers alone to claim. Yet, how could she not forgive Carl, when she had broken faith in so many ways herself?

"He was on his way to see you that last day," Lucy said.

Dora nodded. She set her hands on the table in front of her and looked down at them.

"I want to know what happened," Lucy continued. You owe me that, she thought, though she didn't say it. You owe me at least the truth.

Dora cleared her throat and looked at each of them. "We had plans, for our future together. Carl wanted to deal with what had happened"—she hesitated and looked at Lucy—"before we went any further. About six months ago he started going to a support group in Denver, for parents of babies born with neural tube defects. That was when he first realized how many parents of NTD babies were Persian Gulf vets. According to him, almost half the people in that group had some connection to the war."

"And the rest?" Kevin asked.

"Normally," Dora explained, "defects like spina bifida and encephalocele can be traced to a vitamin deficiency. You don't see them so much in this country anymore. He told me there were a couple of parents in the group whose children seemed to have acquired the defect naturally, if you can call poverty and malnutrition natural. The rest came from Ophir."

"The tuberculosis tests," Kevin posited.

"Supplied by Bioflux," Lucy said, "just like the army's biological warfare vaccines." She looked at Dora for confirmation, but the other woman refused to meet her gaze.

Alice Canty made a noise in the back of her throat. "Tell them the rest," she said fiercely.

"You don't understand," Dora protested. "You can't understand."

"Tell them," Alice repeated, "or I will."

"Mycoplasma was developed as a weapon to be what we call a nonlethal incapacitator." Dora looked at the blank faces of her listeners and sighed, as if she were attempting to explain calculus to a group of kindergarteners. "Like the flu," she said, "or a bad case of food poisoning, something that makes the enemy really sick, too sick to fight, without killing them. Remember that cult in Oregon that smeared salmonella on the town's salad bars to keep people from voting in the local election? That's a perfect example of a nonlethal incapacitator. When you think about it, it's not so bad, really. I mean what's worse, a bad case of dysentery or a nuclear bomb?"

Lucy shook her head. "And the inmates at Pioneer were the first lucky guinea pigs?"

"Look," Dora said. "You can only use animals for so long. Eventually, if you really want to know how something's going to work in the field, you need to test it on a more compatible species."

"You mean another human being," Lucy translated.

Dora shot her a look of disdain. "It's easy to be smug when you don't know the facts, but we're talking about national security here. The truth is there's a whole world of bio-weaponry out there—things like anthrax and smallpox and Ebola are just the tip of the iceberg—and most of it belongs to people who don't think of us as friends."

Darcy spoke up. "And that makes what you did at Pioneer okay?"

Dora looked exasperated. "The Pioneer trials were on death-row inmates," she said, as if this fact were absolution in itself. "The researchers knew there would be some contagion, but mycoplasma had no history of long-term side effects in the lab."

"But there were," Kevin said.

"We now know there are some negative effects," Dora conceded coolly. "But that wasn't apparent until several years later."

"By then," Lucy interjected, "you'd already run a whole new set of trials."

Dora shifted slightly. "A very small group of soldiers received mycoplasma with their vaccinations. We still had no idea at that point about the rate and duration of contagion, and we certainly didn't know about the other problems."

Other problems, Lucy repeated to herself, thinking about the way Eric had felt in her hands, about Chick stumbling through their old house in Pryor. "What the fuck is wrong with you?" she asked.

"I had nothing to do with any of the testing," Dora protested. "When I took over the mycoplasma project four years ago, those people were already sick. There's nothing we can do for them, and I'm sorry, but that's no reason to let the research go to waste."

Alice Canty shook her head wearily. "Just like your grandfather," she said.

"You don't understand, Nana." Dora sighed, leaning back from the table.

Lucy clenched and unclenched her fists. She took a cigarette from the pack in her pocket and lit it. "That last day," she said. "What happened?"

Dora greedily eyed the newly lit cigarette. "May I?"

Lucy tossed the pack on the table between them.

"You should know, the work Carl did at Bioflux was strictly aboveboard. Like a lot of our employees, he knew nothing about any of this. But once he started talking to parents in the support group, it didn't take him long to start to figure things out. He knew Bioflux made tuberculin, and that we had a contract with the Colorado prisons. He also knew we made vaccines for the military. There was nothing secret about either of those things. And I'd told him I was working with recombinant mycoplasma, just not in what capacity." Dora put the cigarette in her mouth and lit it. Her hands were shaking slightly, and the match trembled in her fingers.

"He called me the night before he came up, wanting to know how much I knew about the mycoplasma project. He said he'd been out to his brother-in-law's and seen some article on infectious mycoplasma and Gulf War Illness and neural tube defects."

Dora stopped talking. She took a long drag off the cigarette and then another, as if fortifying herself against what she was about to say. "I loved Carl," she said, rubbing one eye with the palm of her hand. "I want you to know that. I didn't mean for any of this to happen."

"The last day," Lucy prompted her.

"He was waiting for me in my office. I'd warned him not to come, but he was there anyway. He'd come straight from the airport. He said he was going public with everything. I told him to let it go, that no one would believe him. But he said he had proof."

"The files," Kevin said.

Dora nodded. "I didn't know it, but he'd gone through my files before I got there and taken out everything on the early mycoplasma trials, the preliminary results from the Pioneer tests, and the stuff on the military personnel. He had his briefcase with him. He must have put them in there. It wasn't until the next day that we realized they were gone."

"Where did he go from your office?" Lucy asked.

"I don't know," Dora said, flicking the ash from her cigarette. "Before he left I asked him to meet me out at my grandmother's cabin. I just wanted a chance to explain."

"And he agreed?" Lucy asked.

"Yes. He said he'd be on the seven o'clock ferry." Dora fumbled, then went on. "You have to understand. I didn't know what would happen. Carl was crazy. He was so angry, I was afraid of what he might do. I called Philip Sumner and told him what was going on: that Carl was coming out to the cabin and that I thought I could talk him out of whatever he had planned."

Lucy dropped her cigarette and ground it out with the heel of her shoe. "You set him up," she said.

"I didn't know," Dora protested. "It wasn't just the myco-plasma project that was at stake, it was the future of Bioflux, of all the projects."

"What did you *think* would happen?" Lucy stood, taking her cigarettes from the middle of the table, easing the crumpled pack into her back pocket. "You even told them what ferry he'd be on, didn't you?"

Dora shrugged. "I warned Carl. I told him to let it go, but he wouldn't. Don't you see? This is bigger than me, bigger than Carl. It doesn't matter what he knew or what you know. None of it can ever see the light of day. Try to understand."

Lucy looked down at the other woman. "Three people I loved are dead," she said. "Try to understand that."

They left Alice at the ferry terminal and headed north on Alaskan Way and then up onto the arterial tangle of the freeway. Lucy was driving, her eyes hard on the road before her, her hands strong and purposeful on the wheel. Darcy was tired of her two traveling companions, weary of their upper-middle-class morality, whatever truth they felt they had to find. She had come this far with them, but in the end it was Angie who mattered.

As they headed east across Lake Washington, Darcy peered out at the suburban promontories, the sprawling dot-com mansions that ringed the shore. She was starting to think there would be no happy ending. The only person who could help her now was Carl Greene, and he was dead.

Lucy put her foot down on the accelerator and felt the car surge forward onto the I-90 bridge. In front of them, Mercer Island rose, green and rich, each house trying to outdo its neighbor, yachts waiting patiently in their private slips.

That last day, she thought, dodging a silver Lexus, the twenty-something driver giving her the finger. Carl flew into the airport and went straight to Bioflux. And then what? According to Dora, he'd come by in the morning, and they hadn't planned to meet until that night. Dora didn't know where he'd gone when he left her office. But Lucy knew. He'd gone to the Hilton. They'd called her, hadn't they? What word had the woman used? *Personal items*. He'd left some of his personal items behind. Lucy smacked the steering wheel with the palm of her hand.

Darcy looked up from the backseat. "What's going on?"

"Dora's files," Lucy said. "I know where they are."

Chapter Eighteen

Darcy had a good chunk of Washington and the northeastern corner of Oregon to think about what, exactly, she was going to do. If Lucy was right, if nothing went wrong, they'd have the files in the morning. Here was the chance Darcy had been waiting for, and she couldn't afford to screw it up.

That evening, when they pulled into a gas station outside of Boise and both Lucy and Kevin disappeared into the bathrooms, Darcy took the opportunity to make a quick phone call.

"Roy, honey. It's for you." Carol Ann Billings stood in the doorway to the living room, holding the cordless phone in one bloated hand. She was wearing a

T-shirt that read WHAT WOULD JESUS DO? and yellow checkered pedal pushers. The short pants made her legs look stubbier and more swinelike than usual. Her neck was bright pink, creased with white where the skin folded over on itself.

Roy Billings leaned back in his recliner and regarded his wife, keeping his attention fixed on the television. "It's my wrestling show," he snapped, motioning to the screen with his remote.

"Sorry, Roy. It's some woman, says it's important, says her name's Darcy."

Billings leapt up like a hungry crocodile springing for an unattended toddler. "Jesus H. Christ!" he said, snatching the phone from his wife. "Why didn't you say so?"

It had been four days since he'd seen Darcy at Rawhide Bob's, and Billings was starting to get worried. He'd called her apartment several times, and each time he got no answer. When he tried the truck stop in Castle Rock, they told her she hadn't shown up for work since Monday.

That morning he'd even tried to call Philip Sumner. After all, it was Sumner who'd first warned him about Carl Greene, saying the files had disappeared from Bioflux and Greene was AWOL as well. But Billings couldn't get past Sumner's assistant, and he was starting to think they'd cut him loose and he was about to take a long hard fall for all of them.

Wasn't that the way it had always been? Billings thought, his face reddening as he remembered Raleigh, how he'd ingratiated himself with them. Roy Billings, the pimple-faced twenty-year-old supply sergeant with a knack for getting just about anything onto the base. Willing Roy, they'd called him, a name he hadn't found funny, yet he'd laughed nonetheless. They paid him well, double what he put out for the stockings and gin he brought back from Raleigh on his days off. But it was more than the money. Joe Auburn had a way of slapping him on the back, of hooking his arm over Roy's shoulder, so that for a moment Roy felt like he'd entered their graceful, easy, gin-drinking, jazz-listening, Viviane-screwing world.

It was Auburn who'd gotten him to agree to the tests. It hadn't been the money that had convinced him in the end, though Roy had happily taken all he'd been offered. No, it was the dinner with Auburn at the Brown Palace in Denver, porterhouse steaks and expensive wine and, later, cigars and port in the dark wood-paneled bar. Auburn had done everything perfectly, right down to the willowy and accommodating brunette who mysteriously joined them at the end of the evening and who later accompanied Roy to his suite.

They'd suckered him, as usual. Like the brunette, Roy thought. The nice clothes and expensive haircut were unable to hide the fact that she was just a hooker.

"Where the hell have you been?" Billings asked now, pressing the phone to his ear. Then, to his wife, "Go get me a beer and some of those cheese puffs, honey." He watched her waddle off toward the kitchen.

"I want you to listen carefully, Roy. I've got everything you asked for."

"You'd better have it," Billings said. "You keep jerking me around like this, and your sister's—"

"Shut up, Roy. Here's what I want you to do. Tomorrow you go to the bank and withdraw twenty thousand dollars. Cash, small bills, nothing above a hundred." She'd thought carefully before settling on this number, an amount small enough she was fairly sure Billings could handle it. It wasn't a lot, but it would get her and Angie started.

Billings snickered. "Fuck you, bitch. You hand over the files, and your speed-freak sister might finish her sentence in one piece."

"I've got everything right here in front of me," Darcy said, praying he wouldn't call her bluff. "It looks like you knew what was going on every step of the way. How much did Bioflux pay you to let them spike the prison tuberculin?"

Billings reached for his remote, muting the TV. The wrestlers fell silent, and the crowd with them.

"Just get the money. I'll call you back tomorrow. And Roy, you tell anyone about this, I swear to God I'll go straight to the evening news."

The line went dead and Billings slammed the phone down. "Goddamn it, Carol Ann!" he bellowed. "Where's my beer?"

. . .

Kevin drove the night shift, the last loneliest leg of the trip, across Wyoming and south toward Pryor. Lucy slept in the seat beside him, hands tucked under her head like a pillow. Darcy was quiet in the backseat.

Headlights blinked into view far up ahead, a lone car traveling in the opposite direction. Out here, you couldn't hold your breath for the time it took two cars to meet. Even cruising along at eighty, eighty-five, it took several minutes for the pinprick of light to roar past Kevin, flashing its taillights like two red embers.

A conspiracy to cover up the testing of biological weapons on our own soldiers, Kevin thought, a sickness that spread to the families of those soldiers, even to their unborn children. And the vice president and a former secretary of state were directly involved. Carl Greene had been right: This was important. A story hot enough to pull a half-drowned career out of the toilet and bring it sputtering back to life, and Kevin would be the one to bring it home. Even if what Sylvia Graham had said on the phone was right, he still wanted the chance to be denied.

Somewhere west of Rawlins, the sky started to lighten and the sun began to rise, revealing the monolith of the Rocky Mountains behind them, the tangled terrain they'd spent all night crossing silhouetted now like a child's paper cutout. Lucy stirred, turning her face toward him. Her mouth was slightly open and he could see the tips of her front teeth, the enamel white as pearls. No, he thought, watching her, what she'd said on the ferry had been wrong. Sometimes you get more than just one chance.

They came into Pryor from the east, along the old two-lane highway, past the dairy and the turnoff to Magpie Road. Lucy turned her head slightly to watch her own house and the others in the development pass by, dark shapes hunkered down in the corn, half hidden, like animals bedded in tall grass or like ships taking on water. There were so many reasons why she couldn't go back to that house, but still she had to fight the urge to return.

Kevin could drop her off, she thought, and she could take the familiar walk along Magpie Road, across the clipped green lawn, and up the front steps. Just a few hundred yards away the architecture of her habits was waiting for her: sundresses ranged in well-ordered closets, folded linens stacked neatly as bones in a charnel house, the hushed rooms where she'd convinced herself of some deep and implacable culpability.

"You okay?" Kevin asked.

Lucy nodded. "Just keep going."

Though it was still early, the fields were dotted with migrants, little girls in cotton dresses, men in sweat-stained baseball caps. They passed a truck piled to near overflowing with sugar beets, the roots knobby and gnarled, like giant teeth newly extracted from the earth. Kevin slowed at the bridge and crossed into town, turning at the high school, heading down Main Street. The piercing heat of afternoon had yet to set in and deep shadows pooled beneath elms and buckeyes, the night's cool as dark as freshly spilled ink.

As they neared the post office, Lucy looked at her watch. "Pull in here," she told Kevin, indicating the parking lot of the grocery store, and Pryor's one pay phone.

Kevin stopped the car and Lucy got out. Thumbing through the plastic-jacketed phone book, she found the number for the Pryor post office. It was before business hours, but Lucy knew there'd be someone in the mailroom. From where she stood she could see the front of the post office, four cars in the lot.

She dialed and let the phone ring.

"Pryor PO," a male voice answered.

"Donna Lundgren, please," Lucy said. A reformed wild child with the tattoos to prove it, Donna had been in Chick's class all through school. She and Lucy's brother had dated off and on. If there was anyone she could trust in Pryor, Lucy figured, it was Donna.

From the other end of the line, Lucy heard the muffled sounds of machinery and rock music and a man's voice calling, "Donna, it's for you." There was a rustling against Lucy's ear; then, "Lundgren here."

"Donna, it's Lucy Greene."

"Shit, girl. Where are you?"

"Across the street."

"Hold on." A door slammed, silencing the noise of the mailroom. "Are you crazy?" Donna whispered. "You know every cop in Colorado's looking for you, right?"

"I know," Lucy said. "I think you've got a package for me. It would have come in the last few days, from Seattle."

Donna didn't say anything. Lucy heard her strike a match, and the windy crackle of a cigarette igniting.

"Listen," Lucy said. "Whatever they're saying about me, you've got to know I never would have hurt Chick."

A moment passed in silence. Lucy peered across the street and saw a figure move behind the still dark windows of the post office.

"I'll meet you around back," Donna said finally.

Lucy climbed back in the car and nodded for Kevin to drive. "She's going to meet us in the alley," she told him.

Kevin looped around, pulled out of the lot, drove the half block to the back of the squat brick post office, and cut the engine.

Due west down the alley, two streets away, Lucy could just make out the back of their old garage and the truncated cross that held one end of the clothesline. What had happened to the old Fairlane? she wondered. Chick's baby. He had driven it out to her house the night he was killed. And then what? What happened to these things that no one claimed? Her brother's clothes, and hers, all the most intimate items, lipstick and underwear, old gloves and hairbrushes, half-empty bottles of hand cream.

A windowless door marked EMPLOYEES ONLY opened, and Donna Lundgren's head appeared. She stood for a moment looking out, her body hidden below the neck; then she stepped into the alley, a large brown package in her arms.

Lucy got out of the car and went to her.

"No questions asked," Donna said, handing the package over.

"Thanks." Lucy smiled.

Donna smiled back. "Now get the hell out of here."

. . .

Lucy and Darcy waited in the car while Kevin got them a room at the Buena Vista, a migrant motel off Highway 85 in Gilchrest. Still too little for field work, a handful of young kids played a makeshift game of soccer in the parking lot. An ancient woman, presumably their caretaker, sat in a metal chair smoking a pipe, a nearby boom box blasting Tejano pop music. There was a nomadic air to the one-story structure, a feeling of encampment. Temporary clotheslines had been strung along the breezeway, tired bras and dirt-stained jeans hanging off them like prayer flags. Vans and trucks sat in various stages of repair. Someone had picked sunflowers from the fringes of a cornfield and set them in a coffee can just inside one of the windows.

From the front seat, Lucy rested her chin on the cardboard box and watched Kevin through the window of the motel's office. There had been a familiar awkwardness to the way he'd kissed her on the ferry. Like the first time, leaning across the front seat of his grandfather's car, his hands shaking so hard she'd been afraid for them both.

Perhaps because of all that had happened, or perhaps simply because she was older, Lucy had never felt the same desperation for Carl that she'd felt for Kevin. There was a coolness to her husband, a competency that made her own sloppy desires seem somehow embarrassing. How long had it been, she wondered, since she and Carl had had sex? Six months? Seven? And even then it had been a kind of capitulation for both of them, something surrendered to out of exhaustion, neither one able to hold the other at bay any longer.

Kevin nodded to the man behind the counter, turned, and headed back out to the parking lot. Even now Lucy could remember the specifics of their novice lovemaking, the shape of Kevin's back when he bent to undress, his fingers on her stomach, and the pale pattern of stars and moons on his bedroom ceiling.

Lucy watched Kevin walk toward her, the key dangling from his hand. There was so little about him that resembled that boy at Miller's, arms and neck stained dark from the sun, fingers creased with dirt, and yet there was so much.

"Room one-forty-three," he said, opening the door and sliding in behind the wheel. "It's around back."

They made a U-turn in the parking lot and drove behind the front row of rooms to a second and even more time-worn building.

Kevin got out of the car and opened the door to the room, the two women following behind. The accomodations were just as Lucy had expected, bad shag carpet and two double beds, a TV and some mismatched furniture. All she really wanted was a door that closed behind her, a quiet place where she could sort through whatever it was that Carl had left, a place to get her mind in order. She dropped the box down on one of the beds, and a cloud of dust rose from the faded spread.

It was hot in the room, the air-conditioning advertised on the motel sign evidently a defunct luxury. Lucy stripped down to her tank top, pulled the Glock from its new home at the back of her jeans, and laid it on top of the TV. There was a crescent of sweat where the gun had nestled, and it felt good to let the skin there breathe.

Stepping closer to the bed, Lucy contemplated the box, as if it were a puzzle or a bomb that needed defusing. The package was nondescript, brown with heavy black writing, the return address on a neat white label with the Hilton logo.

"Here," Darcy said. She reached into her pocket, pulled out a small penknife, and handed it to Lucy.

Lucy ran the blade along the taped seams and carefully opened the flaps. The contents had been packed neatly. Carl's jacket lay on top, folded by unknown hands. Lucy pulled it out and laid it on the bed. Beneath the jacket was Carl's overnight bag, holding a pair of clean underpants, a white T-shirt, some socks, and a shaving kit. Everything smelled vaguely of their house, of Bounce and Ivory soap and Carl.

Under the overnight bag, wedged at a slant to fit into the box, was the worn leather briefcase Lucy had given Carl the first Christmas they were married. It had been an extravagance then, but one she knew he would appreciate. Lucy pulled it out and set it on the bed next to Carl's jacket and the bag.

The briefcase was heavy, the flap that held it closed locked. Lucy had to carve through the soft leather with Darcy's pocket knife. Inside, the case was crammed with documents, papers packed tightly together. Lucy pulled one out at random: RESULTS OF VARIANT U MYCOPLASMA TESTING—LH SUBJECTS. In the upper right-hand corner was the date: December 14, 1988.

Darcy craned her neck to see over Lucy's shoulder. "Any idea what an LH subject is?"

Lucy scanned the report. Carl and his colleagues spoke in initials all the time, mostly when they were talking about things that might have made them uncomfortable to name. An LP subject, she knew, was a monkey, a live primate. LCs were live canines, and LRs were rodents. LH, she thought: live human—the idea so foul she couldn't speak it. Ignoring the question, she put the report aside, pulled another one from the briefcase, and scanned it.

The files were dry and scientific, the text mostly incomprehensible to Lucy, but as she pored through the papers the larger meaning became obvious, just how much had been known, how many of the consequences of the mycoplasma testing had been ignored. One report detailed "indirect interfamilial contagion" and "the possibility of fetal defects among asymptomatic genitors."

Genitor, Lucy thought, parent, and suddenly she felt the peril of all she and Chick had shared. Plates and glasses, his toothbrush in the bathroom next to hers, a Coke can passed between them. Somehow, during that time he'd lived with them, his sickness had entered her. She hadn't known it, hadn't become sick herself, but still she had carried it, deep and secret, like an old shame.

Darcy lay on the musty bedspread and watched Lucy put the last of the papers aside, watched Kevin pick them up and thumb through them himself. He finished reading and rubbed his eyes, then got up and stretched, wincing slightly as he brought his arm up over his head.

"How's your shoulder?" Lucy asked.

"It hurts." He unbuttoned his shirt and pulled the collar down to reveal a neat line of stitches. The skin around the wound was pink and swollen.

"It looks infected," Darcy observed.

Lucy stood and went to him. She put her fingers gently on his shoulder and he grimaced. "It feels hot," she said. "Why don't you take a shower and get cleaned up a little. I'll run out and get you something to put on it. There's a store just down the road. I'll get us something to eat, too."

"Do you think that's a good idea?" Kevin asked, slipping out of his shirt. "Maybe she should go." He nodded toward Darcy.

"Maybe." Lucy shrugged. She wanted more than anything to get out of the room, to walk off the stiffness of the long car ride, to have just five minutes alone.

Kevin hesitated a moment, seeming unsure of whether to leave them.

"I'll go," Darcy reassured him.

He glanced at Lucy again, crossed reluctantly to the bathroom, and stepped inside, closing the door behind him.

Darcy sat up and looked at the papers strewn across the other bed.

"I'll be right back," Lucy said, slipping on a pair of cheap sunglasses she'd picked up on the road. "You need anything?"

Darcy shook her head. "I said I'd go."

"I'll be fine," Lucy told her, her gaze dropping to the papers as well, lingering there in a way that made Darcy think she knew just what would happen once she walked out the door.

"Be careful," Darcy said.

"You too." Lucy nodded. She shuffled from one foot to another, as if waiting for something. Then she turned, opened the door, and stepped out onto the breezeway.

As far as Kevin could tell, the Buena Vista's entire housekeeping staff had been on vacation for some time. Fungus bloomed in a dark and intricate pattern on the shower curtain. A desiccated cricket lay curled in the sink. An unconvincing paper band on the filthy toilet seat read SANITIZED FOR YOUR PROTECTION. Kevin turned the taps on, let the water heat up, and reluctantly inserted himself into the mold-speckled stall.

The hot water stung his already tender shoulder, and it was all he could do to wash himself and shampoo. He rinsed off as quickly as he could, got out of the shower, and wrapped a towel around his waist. His clothes were ripe from several days of wear, the armpits ringed with salt stains. He balled them up and tucked them under his arm. Thinking he'd grab a less rank set from the bag he'd left in the trunk of the car, he stepped out of the bathroom still in his towel.

As soon as his bare feet hit the mildewed carpet he knew something was very wrong. Lucy was gone, though her gun lay where she'd left it, a blunt black shape on the gray blanket of dust that covered the television. Darcy stood with her back to him, poised halfway between the beds and the door, Carl Greene's briefcase in her left hand. She'd taken everything, all the files, and the case was bulging, the top flap hanging open.

Kevin took a step forward, calculating the distance between himself and the freshly loaded Glock, the movement that was required to keep the woman and the files there in the room. "Put the case down," he said, dropping the clothes, reaching for the gun. He snapped the safety off, but Darcy's fingers stayed resolutely curled around the leather grip.

What did she know that he didn't? Kevin wondered. That he was a coward? A fool? That he was kind at heart? Or did she just not care? "People deserve to know the truth," he heard himself say.

Darcy turned toward him. She held the little Colt in her right hand, the barrel staring straight at him like one dark eye. "What do you think's going to happen?" she asked. "You think you can just take these files to the folks at CNN or NBC and suddenly you're a hero?" She shook her head and took a step backward toward the door.

Kevin tensed his hand around the Glock. He shifted slightly and caught a glimpse of himself in the mirror, his face shadowed with stubble, his paunch hanging out over the white folds of the towel, his shoulder bruised and swollen. When had he become such a wreck? He straightened up involuntarily and pulled his shoulders back. No, he thought, there would be no story. In the end, his was not a business of truth but of conceit, what we wish ourselves to be.

"I'm sorry," Darcy said. She slid the briefcase onto her wrist and put her hand on the doorknob. Then she turned her back on Kevin and stepped outside, her dark silhouette dissolving into a bright rectangle of sunlight.

Lucy hooked her arm around the brown paper bag and walked through the automatic doors of the little grocery store into the dry noontime heat. An old rusted Chevy pulled into the parking lot, and half a dozen dusty men climbed down off the bed and ambled into the store. It was lunchtime. Across the street, two sheriff's cruisers sat parked outside the Dairy Queen.

Kevin had been right, she thought, she should have stayed in the room. Her recklessness suddenly eroded, and for the first time since they'd called to tell her about Carl she was truly afraid. Putting her head down, shielding herself as best she could with the bag, she walked the two long blocks back to the Buena Vista.

She hadn't expected Darcy to be there when she got back, and she was relieved to see the rental car gone. She was glad Darcy had taken the chance and run.

"She's gone," Kevin said, when Lucy stepped into the room.

Nodding, Lucy set the bag down and pulled out a bottle of peroxide and some cotton balls.

"She took the files," Kevin explained. He was sitting on the edge of one of the beds, the Glock lying next to him.

Lucy moved the gun aside and sat down, eyeing his bare shoulder, the reddening welt. "It's okay," she told him, uncapping the peroxide. She wet one of the balls and touched it to the stitched skin. "How are you feeling?"

"Not so good." He flinched, jerking his shoulder away. Lucy watched a lacy froth of bubbles appear along the wound, then swabbed the skin once again.

"What are you going to do?" Kevin asked.

"I don't know." She set the peroxide aside and blotted the stitches dry. "Disappear for a while, I guess." The thought terrified her, the prospect of losing herself in the world.

"I've got a friend," Kevin said, "in Nogales. He can help you."

"Yes," Lucy said. "Maybe." She put a bandage on his shoulder and pressed the edges down till they clung fast to his skin.

He leaned across her, picked up a pen and pad of paper that sat on the bedside table, and scribbled the name *Leon* and a phone number on the yellowed stationery.

Lucy reached up and put her hand against his face. He was both familiar and foreign at the same time, changed and unchanged. "I'm scared," she said.

Nodding, he bent down till his lips were just over hers. "It'll be okay," he told her. Then he put his hand on her neck and kissed her.

She closed her eyes and pulled him toward her, her own hands trembling now, her heart lurching like an old car on a cold morning. Here's the secret, she thought: not to live without fear but to live with it.

Chapter nineteen

Darcy opened her refrigerator and surveyed the moldy contents: a greening block of cheese, a cluster of grapes covered in the delicate black fuzz of fungal five o'clock shadow. The only nonlethal foodstuffs were a bottle of ketchup and a jar of pickled okra, and even those seemed suspect. The freezer offered slightly better prospects, a rock-hard enchilada dinner and some frost-rimed hot dogs. They would have to do, Darcy told herself, tossing the enchiladas in the microwave, putting a saucepan of water on to boil.

She hadn't planned on going back to Castle Rock, but when she left the motel in Gilchrest, it had seemed the most obvious option. She wouldn't

meet Billings until morning, and she needed somewhere to wait
out the night. She didn't think anyone would come looking for
her at the apartment, but she had the little Colt, just in case.

Setting the timer on the microwave, she cracked open a can
of Diet Coke and made her way into the living room. It was six
o'clock, well past banker's hours. By now, she figured, Billings
would either have the money or not. And if he didn't? Pushing
the prospect from her mind, Darcy picked up the phone and
dialed the warden's number.

It was Billings himself who answered this time.

"You do what I told you?" she asked.

"I got it," Billings mumbled.

"All right, Roy, now listen up. Tomorrow at noon you come to
Rawhide Bob's. You bring my sister and the money, and I'll hand
over the files."

Billings didn't say anything.

"You hear me?" Darcy asked.

"Yeah."

"Noon," Darcy repeated, "at the saloon. I want Angie in street
clothes. Now, what did I say?"

"Noon. At Rawhide Bob's," Billings grumbled.

"Shit, Roy, it'll be just like old times."

Roy Billings sat for a moment, digesting what the woman had
said; then he picked the phone back up and dialed Philip Sumner's number. A man answered, Sumner's whiny assistant, Jeff.
Billings had always found his wheedling effeminate voice particularly annoying.

"Let me talk to Sumner," Billings demanded.

"Billings? Is that you?"

"Yeah. I need to talk to Phil."

"Mr. Sumner's in the middle of something."

"Goddamn it, you little prick. You get him on the phone right
now, or I'm going public with everything."

The man laughed. "I don't think you'll do that."

"Then tell him I've got his goddamn files."

Without a word, he was switched to the limbo of hold. Sumner was too classy for Muzac. Classical music blared into Billings's ear.

"Roy?" Sumner cut in.

"I've got the Bioflux files."

"Nice work. Joe always said you could find anything. I'll send someone out there right away."

"I figure it's worth at least a million," Billings said.

Sumner didn't miss a beat. "Now, Roy," he crooned, his voice smooth as good single malt, "that's a lot of money. Don't get greedy. We've taken good care of you in the past, and we're not going to forget this favor, believe me. I tell you what. You name any facility in the country and it's yours. How about a nice women's prison in California? Somewhere close to the ocean. The wife'd like that, I bet."

"Cut the crap, Phil," Billings muttered, thinking, Cheap bastard, just like at Raleigh, the rich kids nickel and diming him over the price of cocktail olives.

"No, *you* cut the crap. What do you think we're talking about here, a box of Cuban cigars? A couple of *Playboy*s?" There was an icy clarity to Sumner's tone. "You don't threaten us, Roy. You understand? You don't threaten."

"You've got a week to get the money together," Billings told him.

Lucy sat on the edge of the bed closest to the door and watched Kevin sleeping. The white glare of a streetlight filtered through the curtains so she could just make out the contours of his face, one arm flung across the pillow above his head, the tips of his feet sticking out from beneath the sheet. She had forgotten so many things about him, like the tiny scar on the inside of his thigh, the skin healed into a pale starburst that she'd liked to run her tongue across. Or how the sheer pleasure of his body stayed with her, like the lingering flush of a sunburn.

Voices sounded from the parking lot, the bright chatter of sleepy people trying to trick themselves into wakefulness. An engine started up. A door opened and closed. Kevin turned away from her, his hand grappling groggily with the sheet. She would like to have slept forever, or at least for the rest of the morning, her back pressed into his stomach, his chin just touching her shoulder. Instead, she slipped into Carl's jacket, tucked the Glock in the back of her jeans, and silently let herself out the door.

There was a crowd gathered in front of the motel, pickers waiting for their rides to the fields, others hoping to find day labor. Lucy lit a cigarette and made her way among the dark faces, asking in her halting high school Spanish if anyone was heading out toward Pryor. Finally, a girl pointed to the far edge of the parking lot.

"There," she said, indicating an old Ford, the bed of which was fast filling with young men.

Lucy thanked her and started toward the truck. Suddenly fearful that she might know the driver, that it could be one of the Nordgren kids or Miller's grandson-in-law, she peered into the cab. But the man behind the wheel was Mexican, his face weather-stained beneath the frayed brim of his straw cowboy hat.

"Pryor?" she asked, giving up on her Spanish.

The man nodded.

"Can I get a ride?"

Grinning, he stuck his thumb out and motioned toward the back of the truck.

"Thanks." She ground her cigarette out and stepped up onto the bumper.

The men looked at her and smiled, eyes and teeth startlingly white. One of them said something in Spanish that she couldn't understand, and the others laughed, not unkindly, the way you might laugh at a friend's bad joke or at a younger sibling who's just done something foolish, expecting the person to laugh back.

The truck started and they rolled out onto the highway. The sun was just coming up, the darkness thinning out, revealing the scrub hummocks of eastern Weld County, a lone oil rig toiling away on a far hill. Lucy rested her back against the wheel well and took a deep breath. The air smelled of everything familiar: cattle and corn, the pungency of fertilizer and pesticides, and the faint sour stench of the hog farm several towns over.

There was something elemental about riding in the back of the truck, the world stripped down to basics: her fragile body and this thing that carried it perilously forward. Stripped down, Lucy thought, like the person she had been once, a girl who'd hitched all the way to Las Vegas, over the Rockies and down through the scarred Utah desert, just to stand on the Strip and watch the lights shimmer and roll like some giant jeweled fan. She wanted it back, that person who had existed before Kevin or Carl, the kernel of herself.

One of the men tapped her on the shoulder, offering her a cigarette. She smiled and took it, hunkering down over someone else's tightly cupped hands to get it lit.

"Beets?" she asked, and the man shook his head. "Onions?"

"No." He grinned. "Melons today."

They drove south, then west through Pryor, and out along the two-lane highway. When they neared the turnoff to Magpie Road, Lucy knocked on the back window of the cab. The driver glanced over his shoulder, nodded, and pulled the truck to the shoulder of the road.

"Here?" the man who'd given her the cigarette asked, looking around dubiously at the dark cornfields.

"My house," Lucy said, "*mi casa,*" and the man shrugged, as if this explanation was too ridiculous to deny.

She watched them pull away and started along Magpie Road through the corn, the husks whispering like a Greek chorus, the crickets answering back.

There was crime tape on the house, strung across the front door and along the perimeter of the yard, yellow and festive as party streamers. And in the driveway, right where she'd been hoping it would be, was Chick's Fairlane. Lucy bent down on the dew-wet gravel by the car's rear bumper and groped blindly along the undercarriage, her fingers finding the small magnetized box that held the Fairlane's spare key. Prying the box free, she slipped the key into the pocket of Carl's jacket and headed up the driveway, up the front steps. She ducked under the crime tape and let herself inside.

Her steps resonated across the marble foyer, the room hollow and mournful as a mausoleum. What had they been thinking when they agreed on the design of this house? For all its pretensions, the terra-cotta tiles and the Berber carpets, the double sinks in the master bathroom, it still echoed like a tomb.

Lucy climbed the stairs to the second floor and made her way along the upstairs hallway, to the master bedroom and Carl's closet. Pushing aside jackets and shirts, she opened the wall safe Carl had had installed when the house was built.

Just a few things, she'd told herself earlier, whatever she could sell to get her by. A necklace Carl had given her two years earlier for their anniversary. An emerald bracelet Lucy had bought on a trip to the Florida Keys. The gaudy diamond and sapphire ring they'd picked out to replace the tiny solitaire he'd asked her to marry him with, the little diamond all he could afford at the time. And a few thousand dollars in cash that Carl in his infinite practicality had set aside. For a rainy day, he'd told her. You never know.

She stuffed the jewels and the cash into an old backpack, grabbed a couple of changes of clothes from her dresser, and headed back out through the house. Earlier, lying awake in bed at the motel with Kevin asleep beside her, she'd been afraid to come back here, worried she might not be able to leave. And yet, as she passed through the foyer and out onto the porch, there was no part of her that wanted to stay.

Sliding in behind the wheel of the Fairlane, Lucy groped in Carl's jacket pocket for the key. Her fingers found it, and they found something else as well. She pulled a half-folded piece of paper from the pocket and flipped the overhead light on. It was a single sheet, a page that had been torn hastily from a book, a travel book, Lucy decided on closer inspection. A little map showed part of the Yucatán and Quintana Roo. A red star marked a place labeled Tulum—somewhere, she imagined, where Carl had planned to go. But when she turned the page over, she could see it was not something her husband had left behind.

On this side of the page were three pictures: a little fishing boat floating on a perfectly blue sea, a line of neat grass huts perched along a white sand beach, and a great ruin of gray-cut stone, some kind of Mayan palace. In the upper margin, in fresh blue ink, was a handwritten note. *Thank you,* it said, and it was signed *D.*

Roy Billings was sound asleep when the phone on his bedside table rang. He'd been dreaming about the Red Lobster in Pueblo and Darcy Williams. There'd been nothing pleasant about their meeting, and Billings was grateful to be interrupted by the waiter's hand, jostling him to get his attention. The man had come to take their dessert order, but when Billings rolled over to tell him he'd decided on the mud pie, there was no waiter, just the sleep-creased face of his wife.

"Roy!" She blinked, pawing him through the down comforter. "It's the phone."

Billings rolled over and groped for the receiver. "Yes," he said groggily, pressing it to his ear.

"Roy, it's Phil Sumner. How are you doing?" The voice was chipper, jovial, the voice of someone sipping gin and tonics on a warm summer evening.

Billings blinked his eyes clear. His alarm clock said 6:45 A.M.

"Listen," Sumner went on. "I'm sorry about last night. I didn't mean to sound ungrateful."

"Um . . . that's okay," Billings said, though he had the distinct impression everything was not okay. Sumner never called himself, and he was never this cordial.

"Who is it?" Billings's wife groaned.

"It's just the prison," he told her nervously. "Go back to sleep."

"We do want to show our appreciation," Sumner crooned. "And we want to do it sooner rather than later."

Billings sat up and stared wide-eyed into the semidarkness. This didn't seem right. No, it didn't seem right at all. Stupid, he told himself. It was stupid to have asked for all that money.

"We have what you requested," the sugared voice went on, "and we'd like to send someone your way tomorrow. Would that be all right, Roy?"

"No hurry," Billings stammered. "I mean—I hope I didn't give you the wrong impression. I just—you know, I thought some compensation was only fair."

"Of course."

"And, you know, the money's not altogether necessary. Like you said, I can take that job in California."

"Oh, no, Roy. We insist. I'll be in touch. Okay?"

Sumner didn't wait for a response. The line clicked dead and Billings put the phone down. It's okay, he told himself, listening to the airy groan of his wife's breathing. It's okay. But he didn't believe it for a second. He looked across the room toward the drawn curtains, the dull rectangle of morning shining behind them, and thought, That's it. They're going to kill me.

Chapter twenty

The day was perfect as a southern Colorado August day could be. By midmorning the mercury had hit 80 degrees and was on the rise. The sky was blue and unblemished as a robin's egg. Darcy was feeling good, refreshed and clearheaded on eight hours of sleep and a real breakfast. She'd taken a shower at the apartment and packed some spare clothes. By ten she was on her way to Ophir.

She pulled into the parking lot of Rawhide Bob's just before eleven-thirty and sat in the car with the air-conditioning going, trying to convince herself that everything would be all right. It had to be. At a quarter to twelve she paid the adult admission fee and walked through the turnstile into the dusty Old

West town, the Bioflux files slung over her shoulder in a blue backpack.

It was Saturday afternoon, the tail end of summer vacation, and Bob's was packed. Bands of kids in phony Indian head-dresses whooped down Main Street, dust gummed to their candy-sticky faces. The Gunslinger's latte stand was cranking out iced mochas and blended cappuccinos faster than a six-shooter could crank out bullets.

The performers looked hot and cross in their crinolines and buckskin. A group of frontier women had hiked their heavy skirts up above their knees and were sitting in the shade of the gallows drinking Cokes. It was ten minutes till the noon shoot-out, and people were starting to gather for the big show. A camera crew from one of the Denver news stations had set up in front of the Mercantile. The reporter, a young fake blonde in a lilac-colored pantsuit, looked bored and surly, the rookie out on the obligatory local-interest piece.

As much as Darcy hated the gunfight, she figured it was the best time to meet Billings. There'd be enough people around that he couldn't try anything funny, yet most everyone's attention would be focused on the show. Darcy walked slowly toward the saloon, scanning the flood of faces for Angie and the warden.

Roy Billings had been drinking all morning, not a lot, just enough to keep himself on task. He'd come to a difficult decision, and he was worried that too much clarity might cause him to lose his nerve. It was a delicate balance to maintain, a moderate degree of sedation coupled with competence, and Billings felt like he was walking a tightrope. He took a small flask of gin from his glove compartment and slid it into the back pocket of his Bermuda shorts.

The girl cringed when he reached across the front seat, flattening herself against the door. Billings looked at her with disgust. She was nothing but a junkie, sickly and pale. Not Billings's type at all.

"You got nothing to worry about, sweetheart," he told her, the same thing he'd said when he'd had her called in from the exercise yard that morning. She hadn't looked like she believed him then, either.

Billings got out of the car and perused the parking lot, relieved to see the Channel 11 news van parked near the entrance to Frontier Town. He hadn't given any details when he'd called them earlier that morning, just explained who he was and said it would be worth their while to be at Rawhide Bob's at noon with a satellite van. He'd been fairly certain they would show. He'd used the word *exclusive* and the producer he'd spoken with had seemed eager as a bitch in heat, but still, you never knew.

"We're here," he said, walking around the front of the car and opening the passenger door. "Get out."

Angie glanced up at him, then took in the sun-baked parking lot, the faux-rustic sign: RAWHIDE BOB'S FRONTIER TOWN. "What's going on?"

Billings held his hand out. "You'll see."

Darcy found a table near the back of the bar and ordered a lemonade. Except for the piano player, the bartender, and a couple of floozies, the saloon was empty. Darcy looked at her watch. Seven minutes till noon. She couldn't even bring herself to imagine the possibility of being stood up. She set the backpack on the floor at her feet, keeping one hand hooked on the straps.

Through the swinging doors she could see a growing commotion, people massing on the boardwalk and in the sun-bright street. Six minutes to twelve. Four. A head appeared in the doorway and the door swung open. The warden stepped inside, his tiny eyes blinking to adjust to the darkness.

She's not with him, Darcy thought, as Billings lumbered forward, still near blind, scanning the shadows. In his left hand was a small duffel bag that read OPHIR WARRIORS. Why isn't she with him? Darcy wondered, starting to panic; then the door creaked open again and her sister stepped into the saloon.

Angie stopped just inside the doorway. She was wearing the

standard prison charity outfit, the civilian clothes they passed out to new parolees, the same kind of clothes Darcy had always been given for her dates with the warden: Goodwill skirt and blouse, scuffed sandals.

Darcy stood up. "Angie!"

"Darcy?" Angie looked puzzled, then her face brightened with recognition and relief. She darted forward past Billings. "What are you doing here?"

"I'll tell you in a sec," Darcy said, throwing her left arm around her sister's frail frame. "Did anyone follow you guys out here?"

Angie shook her head, pulling back to give Darcy a sideways look. "I don't think so. What's going on?"

"Nothing."

Billings set the duffel bag on the table in front of Darcy. "The files," he wheezed.

Darcy leaned forward, unzipped the bag, and fingered one of the neat bundles of cash.

"It's all there," the warden said.

Nodding in agreement, Darcy lifted the backpack up, set it on the table, and grabbed the handles of the duffel bag. "Let's get out of here," she told her sister.

There was a collective gasp from the crowd outside the saloon. "Make your peace with God or the Devil!" a voice bellowed.

Darcy grabbed Angie's hand and headed for the door.

Billings slid the flask from his back pocket and guzzled a generous shot. Then he slung the backpack over his shoulder and turned, navigating the saloon's tables like a pinball on its way down the hole. He had a moment of hesitation before he pushed through the swinging doors and out into the hot slap of the afternoon sun. He stopped, turning to take one last look at himself in the long mirror above the old oak bar. His face was sallow, his chin bloated, his body flaccid from years of abuse. He thought briefly of the girl cringing as he reached across her in the car.

Then the gin surged through him and he felt suddenly power-ful, exultant even. Yes, he thought, this was the only way, the only chance he'd get to take Sumner and Auburn down with him. He barreled through the doors, down the wooden stairs, and into the dusty street, straight into the spectacle of the gun-fight, the crossfire from which Sheriff Dooley emerged victori-ous every noon.

Vanquished, Billings thought, vanquished. He spun around wildly, searching the crowd for the Channel 11 reporter. There she was, nose up like a predator sniffing the wind, perfect ass stuffed into the seat of her pale purple pants, hand on her micro-phone. Reaching into the long front pocket of his shorts, Billings pulled out the loaded Smith & Wesson he'd taken from the prison and slammed the barrel to his temple.

"Don't look back," Darcy told her sister as they hustled down Main Street toward the gaping entrance of Frontier Town. There was some kind of disturbance in the street behind them, some-thing more than the shrieks and laughter that normally accom-panied the gunfight.

They passed through the gate and walked quickly across the parking lot. "We're getting out of here," was all Darcy said as they slid into the rental car. She jammed the key into the igni-tion and pulled out of the lot, heading west, past the prison com-plex and the Ophir Ravine, toward Shiprock and the Four Corners, toward the northern edge of the Navaho Reservation, Arizona, and the border.

Kirsten Sloan was having a personal crisis of faith, something that had recently become a common experience for the twenty-four-year-old former Tri-Delt. The senior-year marriage proposal she'd refused was coming back to haunt her. She wasn't sure she wouldn't have been better off married to Kirk Jorgenson after all. Last she heard he had a thriving dental practice in Fort Collins.

What, she wondered, could possibly be so offensive about a nice house in the foothills, a new SUV, a gym membership, and a couple of kids? It had to be better than working for Channel 11, shuttling around the plains with a case of Aqua Net, covering pickle festivals and pioneer days, fending off her cameraman's advances.

Maybe she'd take a trip to Fort Collins on her next day off, she thought, fluffing her shellacked curls, fixing her smile for the camera. She could take Kirk to lunch, maybe an extended lunch.

"Ready on three," Andre, her cameraman, told her.

She nodded, ran her lips over her teeth, and smoothed the front of her jacket. She was sweating like a pig under her suit and could only hope her makeup wouldn't melt before they finished the taping.

"I'm here at Rawhide Bob's Frontier Town in Ophir to learn a little something about how the West was won," she said, thinking, Nice, too good for this crap. She'd written the copy on the way down from Denver in the van, and she was proud of it. Her producer had grabbed her off another story just a few hours earlier, saying something about a tip from a guy claiming to be a warden from one of the prisons down in Ophir.

"Might just be a kook," her producer had acknowledged, "though it didn't sound like it to me. Run it like a regular little local-interest piece, but keep your eyes open."

Careful to keep her face to the camera, Kirsten turned her body slightly and motioned to the street behind her. "Every day at noon," she said with a flourish, "on this dusty street, a piece of history comes to life."

She watched Andre pan out, catching the scene behind her. The crowd around her shifted, necks craning to see.

"Sheriff Dooley!" a man's voice called out. "Make your peace with God or the Devil!"

A hush went through the crowd. There was a jangling of spurs and someone coughed. The first shot rang out, and at the same moment a man burst through the doors of the saloon. He was fat and pink-faced, his hair stiff with sweat. He was wearing baggy

Bermuda shorts and a tentlike Hawaiian shirt. In his left hand was a large backpack.

Definitely not part of the show, Kirsten thought. She turned to Andre, her smile dissolving like Kool-Aid in hot water. "Hook us into live feed," she snapped. "Now, goddamn it!"

The man lumbered down off the steps and into the street, stopped directly between the fake sheriff and the phony outlaw, reached into his shorts, and drew out a large and very real revolver.

"Back off!" he yelled, pressing the gun to the side of his head. "Everyone back except for Channel 11."

Kirsten stepped down off the boardwalk and into the street.

"Do you know who I am?" the man called out, looking straight at her.

She shook her head.

"Are you live with that thing?" he asked.

Kirsten looked at Andre, and he nodded in affirmation.

"Well, then, I'm the man who's about to make your career."

Kevin slid a five-dollar bill across the bar, brought the beer bottle to his lips, and took a sip. He had a good hour to kill before his flight to New York, and he planned on spending the whole thing in the airport lounge. The tail end of a Mariners game was on, the bartender was amiable and attractive, and the proximity of liquid anesthetic was a good thing for his still tender shoulder, his still sore heart.

"You got a menu?" he asked.

The bartender handed him a laminated card.

"I'll have the Mile-high Burger," he told her, salivating at the thought of hot food.

The game was close. Seattle was down by one run going into the ninth inning, and the crowd was hopeful, cheering wildly when Edgar Martinez stepped to the plate. That was the great thing about baseball, Kevin thought. There was always the possibility the losing team could pull themselves out. One perfect swing, just that one motion, would be enough to turn things around. But not tonight. Edgar faltered, knocking a couple of foul balls into the stands behind the plate before striking out.

His food arrived. Kevin wolfed down a handful of french fries and tucked into the burger. God, it was good: the mayo slightly warm from the hot bun, real bacon and cheddar cheese and thick slices of tomato.

"You mind if I change the channel?" the bartender asked. The game was over. Some kind of strong-man competition had taken its place.

"Go ahead," Kevin told her.

The woman picked the remote up and switched over to another station. "Unbelievable," she remarked. "You been following this?"

Kevin glanced at the television and shook his head.

"Prison warden," the bartender explained, "down in Ophir. He's taken some reporter hostage. You know, that blonde from Channel 11, Kirsten Sloan."

The footage was live. A man with a gun and a woman with a microphone huddled together under the glare of arc lights. A blue backpack lay between them, papers spilling out into the dirt at their feet.

"How long's this been on?" Kevin asked.

"All afternoon."

The camera zoomed in on the reporter: pretty face, nice hair, good teeth, the ideal messenger. Her eyebrows were knitted together, her lips pursed. Her serious face, Kevin thought, the one she practiced in front of the mirror in her dressing room.

"Do me a favor," Kevin told the bartender. "Do you mind switching over to MSNBC? I want to see if the national networks are carrying this."

"Last I knew they were," the woman said. She hit the remote and the screen went blank for a second; then the blond reporter's face appeared again, the MSNBC banner visible along the bottom of the screen.

"An incredible situation has developed," the reporter said.

"I'm here with Roy Billings, warden of Canyon Women's Correctional Facility in Ophir, Colorado."

She was good, Kevin would give her that much. This was her big break and she knew it; she was milking it for all it was worth. Kevin glanced at his own reflection in the bar's mirror, then back at the woman, at the perfection of her dishevelment, the hair loose around her face from the day's crisis.

She picked up the backpack and held it in front of her. "In this pack," she said dramatically, "is evidence to support executive knowledge of a decades-old government-sponsored biological weapons program—and the testing of those weapons on our own troops in the Persian Gulf."

Roy Billings looked out at the sea of faces, at the rows of police cars, emergency vehicles, and news cameras. He'd stayed close to the reporter all afternoon and evening, knowing she was the only thing keeping him alive. They'd been standing there for some eight hours and Billings was exhausted. His gin buzz was gone, replaced by a bone-deep sadness. He'd done all he could, and he wanted the long day over with. He let go of the woman's arm and stepped away, slowly, as if falling toward some unknown depth.

Chapter twenty-one

It was after dark when Darcy and her sister rolled down off the Mogollon Plateau toward the sprawling lights of Phoenix, the menace of the American Dream shining before them like some earthbound Milky Way in the flat-bottomed bowl of the Sonora Desert. They skirted the city and drove east, past Scottsdale and Mesa, following the handwritten directions Shappa had given Darcy to her friends' place in Apache Junction. They headed through the main part of the little town, past old one-story stucco motor courts, and out into the desert, into the silent, stoic army of saguaros. Ten miles out toward Tortilla Flat, a green road sign loomed into their headlights and Darcy turned the car down a dirt track.

Angie had crashed some five hundred miles earlier, finally plummeting from that last prison high. She'd slept most of the way across Arizona, her face propped up against the passenger door, a balled-up sweater supporting her head. From Darcy's point of view it had seemed a dreamless sleep, recklessly deep and unguarded. She was still asleep when they pulled up in front of the ramshackle ranch house that was their destination.

Darcy cut the engine, nudged her sister awake, and stepped out of the car. Late as it was, there was still a palpable feeling of heat, of scorched air radiating off every surface, every rock and bush. The Superstitions loomed above them, their crags just visible in the pale light of a rising moon.

A few lights were on in the house, and more blinked on at the sound of their arrival. A face appeared in the tiny window next to the front door, two anxious eyes peering out at them.

"We're friends of Shappa's," Darcy yelled, opening Angie's door for her, helping her up. "You gotta wake up for me," she whispered to her sister. "Just for a little while, okay?"

Angie nodded. Forcing her eyelids open, she stumbled out of the car.

The front door opened and a figure stepped onto the porch, the slim silhouette of a rifle dangling at its side.

"It's all right," Darcy called again. "Shappa sent us."

As the figure waved them on across the yard, Darcy could see that it was a man, about her own age, clean-cut and brutally normal-looking. "I'm Jake," he said, leading them up the steps. "We've been expecting you."

The house seemed perfectly ordinary inside. Shag carpet, faux rock fireplace, 1960s light fixtures. Jake led them through the living room and kitchen, down into the basement, and across a sprawling rec room. On one side of the room was a row of built-in bookshelves. Jake pressed one of the shelves, and the case slid aside, revealing a metal door that opened onto a narrow subterranean hallway.

"We were lucky to get this place," he said. "This old bomb shelter was here when we bought it."

Whoever had designed the place had had a long nuclear winter in mind. The shelter was spacious, the walls still stacked with freeze-dried meals and barrels of drinking water. Its present owners had turned the space into a kind of command center. There was a large map of the Phoenix metropolitan area on one wall, push pins sunk into various places around the city.

Jake followed Darcy's gaze. "I don't know what Shappa told you," he said, not unkindly, opening the door to a smaller room, "but the less you know about us, the better."

The room they entered was cramped and low-ceilinged, packed with electronics and photographic equipment, scanners and digital cameras. A skinny kid with long stringy hair and a patchy goatee sat behind a computer screen.

"This is Taj," Jake said. "He'll take your pictures."

Darcy propped Angie up against a blue photo background. "Wake up," she said again, smiling at her sister. Taj handed her a comb, and she ran it through her sister's brittle hair. "Smile, okay?"

Angie smiled, forcing her eyes open. Then the camera clicked and her head sagged forward into her chest.

"She's tired," Darcy explained.

"There's a little motel called the Topaz, right on the main drag in Apache Junction," Jake said, when Taj had finished with both of them. "Someone will bring everything out to you in the morning." He handed her a key, the blue plastic tag stamped with the number 109. "We've already got you a room."

Exhausted as she was, Darcy barely slept that night. After she put Angie to bed, she went to the gas station across the street and bought a map of Mexico. Back in the room, she traced the route she thought they would take, south from Sonora, through the fishtail body of the country to Quintana Roo. The place Shappa had told her about was right on the ocean, the black dot that marked it as a town about as far as you could go before the land gave way to the Caribbean.

Darcy tried to imagine the course of their life to come. Twenty thousand dollars would go a long way in Mexico. They could get a boat, nothing fancy, just enough for day trips, and maybe even start a little charter business. They'd have an apartment on the beach, with a patio and a hammock in the shade. That, Darcy thought, refolding the map, climbing into bed, was what Angie needed, somewhere with a view and the quiet hush of waves collapsing onto the beach.

Just after six there was a rustling sound on the breezeway and a manila envelope slid under the door. Darcy rolled out of bed and picked the packet up. She parted the curtains and saw the back bumper of an old GMC pickup turning out of the parking lot. Inside the pouch, two shiny new passports, Angie's face as it had been caught the night before, childish, happy even, and her own face scowling up at her, serious as always, creased with concern.

They left the car in the parking lot of the bus station in Tucson and bought two tickets to Hermosillo and a map of Mexico.

It was early afternoon when they crossed the border at Nogales, Darcy praying silently that they wouldn't make her open the duffel bag. There would be questions if they did, for two bedraggled women with that much cash. But the customs agent waved them right through, too busy to do much more than glance at their passports.

"Purpose of your trip?" he asked.

Darcy was surprised to hear her answer. "Pleasure."

As they rolled forward into their new country, toward Imuris and Magdalena de Kino, she thought of their little boat and Angie, barefoot on the prow, the sea spray glistening against her brown ankles. They'd have to think of a good name for their craft, something lucky. The patron saint of fishermen, maybe, though surely that name would be taken.

Darcy looked over at her sister, her eyes closed again, the lids so pale they were almost translucent. Was there a patron saint of new beginnings? she wondered.

Chapter twenty-two

Kevin shook the snow from his overcoat and wiped his feet on the doormat. His landlady, Mrs. Moscatelli, three-quarters deaf, had fallen asleep again watching her Italian soap operas. The television blared through her door and out into the hall, an impassioned female voice, this unseen actress Kevin had lately found himself dreaming about, though from what he could glean, she herself was madly in love with a baritone named Fredo.

The phone was ringing inside Kevin's apartment as he slipped the key into his lock, taking his time. A wrong number, most likely. It was Christmas Eve, almost midnight, and he couldn't think of a single soul it might be. Three rings and he was inside, pulling his gloves off, unwrapping his scarf. On the fourth ring the machine picked up, the timbre of his recorded voice as strange to him as always.

There was a long pause after the beep, the hollow, almost ghostly resonation of a bad connection, the way long distance used to sound.

"Kevin?" a voice said. "I guess I missed you—"

He sprinted for the phone. "Lucy?"

"Kevin! I thought you might be there."

"Where are you?" he stammered, greedily. "Are you all right?"

"I'm fine," she told him. "Did you get my note?"

"Yes." About a month after he'd gotten back from Colorado he'd found a postcard in his mailbox, a picture of a little white-washed church flanked by a pair of royal palms, the word MICHOACÁN in rainbow letters. And on the back side, in a hasty scrawl, *Love, L.* "Haven't you heard about Billings?" he asked.

There was a lag in the connection that made their exchange awkward, like a film played at the wrong speed, the actors jumping from one frame to the next.

"I don't get much news down here," Lucy said, though she had, in fact, heard about Billings. She'd watched the whole drama unfold from a lunch counter in Nogales the day before she crossed the border.

"He went public with everything. He saved us, Luce. You can come home."

Lucy didn't say anything. The phone hummed and whispered, millions of voices crossing and meeting along fiber-optic lines.

"There will be questions, of course, but it's over with Sumner and Auburn. Bioflux has been shut down. You could come here," he offered. "I've got plenty of room. I'm living out in Brooklyn, teaching a couple of writing classes at the New School and working on my own stuff."

"That's good," Lucy said. "You sound good."

"So do you." Kevin paused, searching for something else to tell her, something to keep her on the line, something to make her come to him.

"I should go now," she said, finally.

"Yes."

"Merry Christmas," she offered.

"Merry Christmas," Kevin repeated, looking out the window. The snow was coming down fast, the flakes thick and wet. From beyond the wall came the actress's voice, husky and sensual. In his dreams she was dark-haired and seductive, with hips like Sophia Loren's. "Take care of yourself."

"I will," she told him, finally. She turned from the pay phone where she was standing and looked across the town's main square toward the fountain, the little café strung with Christmas lights, and the old stucco church. The town was dark, but the streets were bordered with luminarias, the flames trembling nervously inside their fragile paper sheaths. Home, she told herself, starting toward the beach.

Kevin laid the receiver in its cradle and shrugged out of his wet coat. In the neighboring apartment, there was silence and then the woman's voice again, breathless, swooning. *Caro, caro.*

Acknowledgments

Thanks as always to Nat Sobel, Judith Weber, and the fabulous staff at Sobel Weber for their tremendous help and support. No manuscript becomes a book on its own, and mine could never have undergone its transformation without Jack Macrae, Katy Hope, Tracy Locke, Janet Baker, Maggie Richards, and all the usual suspects at Henry Holt who, as always, made me look like a far better writer than I am. My gratitude also to Jane Wood at Orion. And to my dear friend and French connection, Olivier Tane, for his wisdom and wit. A special and very belated thank you to Meegan Kriley, whose fabulous Montana stories I have stolen and borrowed countless times.

Of course I couldn't have written a word without the love and support of my family and friends. Love and thanks to you all: Keith, Frank, Mom, Mike, Ben, Dad, Lynn, and Grandma Pat.

About the Author

Jenny Siler grew up in Missoula, Montana, and was educated at Andover and Columbia. Before becoming a full-time writer, she worked as, among other things, a forklift driver, a furniture mover, a grape picker, a salmon grader, a waitress, a sketch model, and a bartender. She lives in Missoula with her husband and their cat, Frank.